P9-EMG-982

DISCARD

TOO MUCH MONEY

ALSO BY DOMINICK DUNNE

FICTION

Another City, Not My Own
A Season in Purgatory
An Inconvenient Woman
People Like Us
The Two Mrs. Grenvilles
The Winners

NONFICTION

Justice
The Way We Lived Then
The Mansions of Limbo
Fatal Charms

TOO MUCH MONEY

A NOVEL

DOMINICK DUNNE

CROWN PUBLISHERS

NEW YORK

This is a work of fiction. Names, characters, places, and incidents either are the product of the author's imagination or are used fictitiously. Any resemblance to actual persons, living or dead, events, or locales is entirely coincidental.

Copyright © 2009 by Dominick Dunne

All rights reserved.

Published in the United States by Crown Publishers, an imprint of the Crown Publishing Group, a division of Random House, Inc., New York.

www.crownpublishing.com

CROWN is a trademark and the Crown colophon is a registered trademark of Random House, Inc.

Grateful acknowledgment is made to Alfred Music Publishing Co., Inc., for permission to reprint lyrics from "The Extra Man" by Cole Porter, copyright © 1977 by Chappell & Co. (ASCAP). All rights reserved. Reprinted by permission of Alfred Music Publishing Co., Inc.

Library of Congress Cataloging-in-Publication Data

Dunne, Dominick.
Too much money : a novel / Dominick Dunne. — 1st ed.
1. Authors—Fiction. 2. Older men—Fiction. 3. Rich people—Fiction.
4. Socialites—Fiction. 5. New York (N.Y.)—Social life and customs—
Fiction. I. Title.
PS3554.U492T66 2009
813'.54—dc22   2009039443

ISBN 978-0-609-60387-1

Printed in the United States of America

Design by *Lauren Dong*

10 9 8 7 6 5 4 3

TOO MUCH MONEY

A FEW YEARS AGO THERE WAS A RUMOR that I had been murdered at my house in Prud'homme, Connecticut, by a cross-country serial killer of rich older men. Of course, it wasn't true, although it was a rumor that lingered for a while: Gus Bailey was dead. There was indeed a serial killer at the time, who was very much in the news. He had just killed a couturier in Miami who was so famous that Princess Diana and Elton John and his future husband attended the funeral in Milan. I confess now to having been the person who started the rumor. I couldn't figure out how to finish a novel I was writing at the time, and I wanted desperately to leave the next day for the Cannes Film Festival with Stokes Bishop, my editor at *Park Avenue* magazine, who assured me in advance that I was to be seated between the French film star Catherine Deneuve and Princess Olga of Greece at the magazine's party at the Hôtel du Cap in Antibes. I didn't want to miss that so I just grabbed the headline news of the murder in Miami and added Gus Bailey to the killer's list, thus ending the novel, and I flew to France. Do I regret having done that? Yes.

My name is Augustus Bailey, but I am called Gus Bailey by everyone who knows me. It happens that I am often recognized by strangers on the street, or in public places, and even those people call me Gus. I only use Augustus Bailey on my passport, my driver's license, the covers of the books I write, my monthly diaries for *Park Avenue* magazine, and the weekly introductions on my cable television series, *Augustus Bailey Presents,* which I host. I thought it best to tell you a bit about myself before I get into the story that I am about to tell. It should be pointed out that it is a regular feature of my life that people whisper things in my ear, very private things, about themselves, or about others. I have always understood the art of listening.

The characters in all my novels are based on real people, or combinations of real people, and they are often recognizable to the readers. Many of the ones who recognized themselves in the books became livid with me. If you could have heard the way Marty Lesky, the Hollywood mogul, who has since died, yelled at me over the telephone. There was a time when I would have been paralyzed with fear at such a call from Marty Lesky, but that time has passed. It made him more furious that I was not writhing with apologies, but the dynamic between us had changed over the years and I no longer feared him, as I used to fear male authority figures, going all the way back to the terror my father inspired in me as a child, but that's another story. I've lost several friends over my books. One I missed. One I didn't.

Losing the occasional friend along the way goes with the writer's territory, especially if the writer travels in the same rarefied circles he writes about, as I do. In time, some people come back. Pauline Mendelson did. She was a very good sport about the whole thing. Mona Berg did, sort of. Cecilia Lesky did. Maisie Verdurin adored being a character in one of my books and bought fifty copies to give as Christmas presents. Others didn't, of course. Justine Altemus, my great friend Lil Altemus's daughter, never spoke to me again. Only recently, Justine and I were seated side by side at a dinner dance at the Colony Club, celebrating Sandy Winslow's ninetieth birthday, and we never so much as looked in each other's direction for the hour and a half we were table companions.

Not too long ago I had intended to give myself a party on the occasion of my upcoming birthday, a milestone birthday, which I must confess I never thought I would reach, especially in the last two years of stress and high anxiety. This was all caused by a monstrously unpleasant experience involving some monstrously unpleasant people, who had no place in my life and took up far too much time in it, particularly when the years left to me are dwindling down to a precious few, as Walter Huston used to sing.

But it is a fact that the fault was mine. I fell hook, line, and sinker for a fake story from an unreliable source. I thought I had the scoop of my career, and I made the fatal mistake of repeating it on a radio show of no importance, and the consequences were dire. If you must know, I accused a congressman, former congressman Kyle Cramden, of knowing more than he was admitting about the case of the famous missing intern, Diandra Lomax. I made a mess, I tell you.

I tried to distract myself from my troubles by focusing on party planning. When my birthday party guest list grew to over three hundred, and I was only at the P's, I realized I would have to rethink things. I know entirely too many people. Although I have several very serious enemies in important positions, I hope not to appear immodest when I say that I am a popular fellow, who gets asked to the best parties in New York, Los Angeles, London, and Paris, and goes to most of them.

I decided to limit my party to eighty-five people, which is the age that I will soon be. It was so difficult to hone my friends to eighty-five. It doesn't even scratch the surface. Eighty-five, in fact, really means forty-something, with wives, husbands, lovers, and partners making up the other forty or so. There would be hurt feelings, to be sure. That's why I don't like to give parties. I go about a great deal in social life, but I never reciprocate. The spacious terrace of my penthouse in the Turtle Bay section of New York City, where I have lived for twenty-five years, has a view of the East River, and could easily hold a hundred people or more without much of a squeeze, but I have never once entertained there.

I felt, however, as if I deserved a party. But it was not to be, as you will find. Things happen. Everything changes.

I've noticed that concurrent with the growth of my public popularity, there is a small but powerful group of people who are beginning, or have already begun, to despise me. Elias Renthal, still in federal prison in Las Vegas as this story begins, is one of my despisers. Countess Stamirsky, Zita Stamirsky to her very few friends, is another who despises me after I refused to not write about her son's suicide from a heroin overdose while he was wearing women's clothes at the family castle in Antwerp.

And, of course, there is Perla Zacharias, allegedly the third richest woman in the world, who had me followed by investigators trained by the Mossad in Israel who collected information that she later threatened to use against me. That's the kind of person Perla Zacharias is.

I have written about all these powerful people in *Park Avenue,* or in a novel, and earned their eternal enmity. *Their time would come,* I always thought. Elias Renthal knew what he was screaming about when he said, "They're going to get you," his face all red and ugly, as he pointed his finger in my face, only moments before he collapsed on the floor of the men's room of the Butterfield Club.

CHAPTER 1

IT WAS EASTER SUNDAY. LIL ALTEMUS, THE OLD guard New York society figure, was having her annual Easter luncheon party at her vast Fifth Avenue apartment overlooking Central Park. In times to come, during her financial difficulties, Lil spoke of her Easter lunch as her Farewell to Fifth Avenue party. All her Van Degan relatives, several of whom she didn't like, and some of her closest friends, like Matilda Clarke and Rosalie Paget and Kay Kay Somerset, whom she'd known all her life, were present. "We all went to Farmington, and we all came out the same year at the Junior Assembly, and we were all bridesmaids in each other's first weddings," Lil said about them every year in her toast.

The star guest at the Easter luncheon was "that perfect darling," as Lil always called Adele Harcourt, who was almost a hundred and five and was still going about in social life. "Adele was such a close friend of Mummy's," said Lil, who was herself seventy-five, whenever she spoke about the revered Adele Harcourt. "We think of her as practically family." Adele was celebrated for having given two hundred million dollars to the city of New York. She made appearances in slums to watch the improvements her donations made possible. She always wore pearls and furs on these excursions to building sites. "That's how they want me to dress," she said to Lil on occasion. She was used to being cheered by the crowd and enjoyed her celebrity enormously.

There was also a small group of what Lil called her strays. Gus Bailey, a writer for *Park Avenue* magazine, used to argue that he was more than a stray. They had a curious friendship.

Lil and Gus had met years earlier at the Kurt von Rautbord attempted-murder trial in Newport, Rhode Island, which Gus had covered for *Park Avenue* magazine. Lil, as the best friend of the comatose heiress, Antonia von Rautbord, ever since they were roommates at Farmington, was a witness for the prosecution. Gus was impressed at how unafraid Lil was on the stand when she was cross-examined by a ruthless defense attorney of national reputation.

During a break, he introduced himself to her in the hallway outside the courtroom in Newport, after she had strongly disputed the allegations made by Kurt von Rautbord's lawyer about Antonia's alcoholism.

"You were gutsy up there on the stand," said Gus. "Some people get so terrified, they cry."

"Wasn't he awful, that lawyer? So rude. Just who does he think he is, please? I certainly wasn't going to allow Kurt von Rautbord to say all those dreadful and deceitful things about poor sweet Antonia after he lived off her money all those years," answered Lil. "Antonia even paid his club dues at the Butterfield, forgodssake."

It was Lil who introduced Gus to Marina and Fritz, Antonia's grown children from her first marriage to a Hungarian prince, with whom he became friends. It was also Lil who arranged for Gus to spend the night in the Newport mansion where the attempted murder had taken place.

Gus often said that if Lil Altemus hadn't been born so rich and married so rich, she could have been a very good detective.

Lil was always thrilled when Gus said that about her in front of others. She sometimes bragged that he discussed all the murder cases he covered around the world with her. In fact, there were those who said that Lil Altemus was Gus Bailey's source for one of his most successful books, about the shooting of banking heir Billy Grenville at the hands of his wife, Ann.

On this Easter Sunday, however, Lil's thoughts were concerned with her lunch party.

"We're twenty-four in all. I've put you next to Adele Harcourt, Gus," said Lil, walking around her beautifully set table, checking place cards with the expertise of a great hostess. Gus had used Lil as a character in one of his society novels, *Our Own Kind,* and, unlike others in New York society, she had not taken offense, nor had she stopped speaking to him, as so many had. However, she did have one quibble with her character, as Gus wrote her. She insisted every time it came up that she was very definitely *not* the one who had said, "Better dead than Mrs. Fayed" the day after Princess Diana was killed in the automobile accident with her lover, the very rich Dodi Fayed, in the Alma Tunnel in Paris, as Gus had quoted her as saying. She had, of course, said it.

"Adele *adores* meeting writers. Now, you must remember to speak up when you talk to her. She doesn't hear well, and she hates wearing the hearing aid. She's inclined to repeat herself a bit, but she's divine, simply divine. You know, she was my mother's best friend. They even worked at *Vogue* together back in the thirties. She's going to be a hundred and five on her next birthday, bless her heart, and she still goes out nearly every night of the week, all dressed up and covered with jewels."

"I've heard through the grapevine that it's your birthday too, Lil," said Gus, teasing his old friend a bit. Lil also needed a hearing aid, but Gus wasn't about to go that far with her, as she might get upset.

"Yes, but we won't speak about that, please." She mouthed

but did not speak the word *seventy,* at the same time rolling her eyes at the ancientness of the decade she was entering.

"You'd never know it," said Gus, although he knew for a fact she was seventy-five, the same age as Antonia von Rautbord, who was still in a coma.

"You're so sweet, Gus," said Lil. "How are things coming along on that ridiculous lawsuit of yours?"

"Don't minimize it to me," said Gus. "It's not ridiculous at all. I'm living it. It is time-consuming, expensive, and extremely nerve-racking, and I hate to talk about it."

"I can't imagine that awful man suing you," said Lil.

"The terrible thing is that it's my own fault. I fell hook, line, and sinker for a fake story. I honestly thought I had the scoop of my career, and I made the fatal mistake of repeating it on a radio show of no importance, and the consequences have been dire. But let's not speak about Kyle Cramden, or his terrifying lawyer. Even the mention of his name puts me into a despairing mood."

"Poor darling Gus," said Lil.

"I went to communion at Easter Mass this morning, a rare event for me, and prayed that something catastrophic, like a fatal auto accident, would happen to him."

"You didn't!" said Lil, screeching with laughter.

"No, I didn't, but I thought of it. I don't see a place card for Justine," said Gus.

He had listened while Lil spoke, but at the same time he was discreetly taking in the seating arrangement at the table. It was this kind of attention to the finer points that allowed him to write the articles that everyone talked about for *Park Avenue.* He couldn't turn it off. He was always searching for more details to round out a story—or, even better, the kinds of details that might start a new one.

"She's not coming," said Lil. "Justine doesn't like you, Gus."

"I know. I don't like her either," said Gus.

"She thinks she was a character in one of your books."

"She was."

"She thinks you went to Bernie Slatkin for information after the divorce, and he told you things."

"She's wrong. I never discussed anything with Justine's ex-husband. I wouldn't put Bernie Slatkin in that position. He's a friend of mine."

"She thinks you did."

"That's her problem," said Gus, shrugging. "Surely I'm not the reason she's not coming today."

"No, of course not. She moved to Paris with her brand-new husband number three, Henri de Courcy, who paints fashionable ladies. Actually, he's quite good. He wanted to paint me, but I said no, thank you very much, I'm much too old to be painted, and besides, Cecil Beaton painted me years and years ago, and so did Vidal-Quadras one winter in Palm Beach, and what was his name who was so divine looking who did that wonderful painting of Babe Paley?"

"René Bouché?" said Gus.

"Oh, yes. René Bouché. He was such a flirt. I can barely remember anyone's name anymore, but René painted me too, and that's quite enough paintings for this old lady."

Gus studied his friend as she moved nervously around the room, tweaking and straightening, trying to ensure perfection. Lil Altemus was tall and aristocratic. Most of her friends described her as handsome but not beautiful. Gus could see why a painter would be inclined to want her as his subject. There was something almost royal about her. She dressed in the manner of grand ladies of a certain age who once shopped from Miss Hughes at Bergdorf's. Her clothes were both conservative and expensive, mostly in blue and black shades. As Gus looked more closely, he noticed a degree of melancholy in her expression.

"Isn't this supposed to be your last party in this apartment?" he asked.

"Yes; that's why it's so sad Justine's not here. She and Hubie literally grew up in this apartment. I've lived here almost forty-five years. Hubie's dead, and Justine lives in Paris. I said to Justine on the phone last week, 'Why don't you fly over for a couple of days? It's the last party in the apartment, and you grew up here.'

"I told her everyone would love to see my granddaughter, Cordelia, and I even suggested they could drive up to Farmington and register Cordelia for two years from now. After all, my mother went to Farmington; I went to Farmington; Justine went to Farmington; and now Cordelia's going to go to Farmington. I tell you, that granddaughter of mine is simply divine. I can't wait for her to move back to New York, where she belongs. Of course, it seems there's no changing Justine's mind. She says she doesn't want to be away from Henri, but I say it's not as if she can't afford a quick trip over and back. After all, she got all of the Altemus money when her father died last year."

Lil Altemus stopped fiddling with the table, rested her hands on the back of one of the twenty-four Chippendale chairs, and sighed, looking around the room, her eyes welling up with nostalgia.

"Gus, I have such lovely memories here. Justine had her coming-out dance in this apartment. Oh, it was so pretty. The *magic* that Mark Hampton wrought. Peonies everywhere. Two orchestras. He tented in the terrace for the disco and lined the tent with blue and white toile. The oldies all danced in the hall, and Peter Duchin's orchestra was on the stairs. So many violins. It was heavenly. Peter was so good-looking in those days. Dolores De Longpre wrote in whatever paper she was writing for back then that it was the prettiest party she'd ever been to."

"I used to read about people like you in Dolores De Long-pre's column," said Gus.

"And now you write about people like us, and not always kindly my friends say, and your name is in the papers more than any of ours." Not to be diverted from her reverie, Lil continued.

"Oh, Gus—if you knew how much I miss Hubie. He was always such a comfort in family situations." Although Gus knew that not to be true, he said nothing. "If Hubie were alive, he'd have gotten Justine here for Easter lunch today. They were the closest brother and sister I ever saw. Damn that Epstein-Barr. I so wish they'd find a cure for it. They've asked me to be on the committee for the Epstein-Barr dinner dance benefit at the St. Regis Roof this year. I haven't decided."

She reached out and halfheartedly picked up a place card from the table. Still lost in her own thoughts and grief for the past, she let it dangle from her fingers, a task forgotten.

"Lil," said Gus, "the place cards are fine. The table's beautiful, and the white lilies centerpiece is a work of art. I bet Queen Elizabeth's Easter lunch table at Windsor Castle is not as pretty as yours. Now, listen to me for a minute. Your son, Hubie Altemus, died of *AIDS*. He did *not* die of Epstein-Barr, no matter how many times you say he did. Someday you have to face up to that fact."

Lil looked squarely at Gus. "It's Easter Sunday. It's also my birthday. And it's my last party in this apartment before I move to that God's Waiting Room, as everyone calls it, over on East Sixty-sixth Street that my nephew insisted I buy. I so miss my brother managing my money. Young Laurance Van Degan always makes me feel like I'm going to end up in the poorhouse. He has too much control and is making me do things I don't want to. Forgodssake, you know how much I simply can't stand my stepmother, Dodo, and I didn't want to invite her today to the family lunch, but young Laurance said I had to. As you well know, she's twenty-five years younger than I am. I don't know what my father was thinking when he married her."

Gus pulled one of the twenty-four Chippendale dining chairs away from Lil's Easter table and sat down and crossed his legs, as if settling in for a long stay. He had heard Lil's rant about her wicked stepmother getting all the family money so many times, he could repeat it word for word. He hoped the first guest would ring the bell.

Lil went on.

"Dodo was a poor distant Van Degan relation that *I* was responsible for bringing into the household after her father jumped off the *Queen Elizabeth* in the mid-Atlantic following a mortifying episode with a deckhand in the engine room that I'd be too embarrassed to go into details about. Her own mother was too drunk to take care of her, in and out of Silver Hill, she practically kept them in business. My poor father paid for all of her stays at great expense. As we all know, no good deed goes unpunished.

"After Daddy's stroke, Dodo pushed him around in the wheelchair, and when he became incontinent she didn't mind cleaning up, and he married her without telling any of us. And then, he left her *everything,* including the Van Degan trust, which, by all rights, should have come to me. She only got the money for life, thank the good lord, but I'll be long gone by the time the awful Dodo dies, and Justine will inherit everything that I should have inherited, and Justine has already inherited all the Altemus money. I'm the only one left out in the cold without anything. So, Gus Bailey, today is *not* the day to talk about the cause of Hubie's death."

"You've put me in my place," said Gus. "But, tell me, aren't there other reasons for you moving from this fabulous apartment, Lil?"

"I can't walk up that beautiful stairway since the hip replacement, so I have to go out in the hall and ring the elevator man to take me up to the next floor so I can get to my bedroom. And it takes five or six in help to take care of an apartment this size. It's gotten out of hand. But those are just excuses. I would hold on to this place regardless, but my nephew tells me I'm running out of money. If you had any idea of how those words terrify me, Gus."

Lil caught herself before she got too emotional and smoothed down the front of her skirt. "I'm going to miss this place, but I'm certainly not going to miss living in the same building as Perla Zacharias, thank you very much, with all her guards in the lobby, and her limousines blocking the parking space in front of the building, so that my driver has to double-park on Fifth Avenue, and I have to walk sideways between her Rolls-Royces, which are taking up all the room. It's such a nuisance, especially when it rains. Really, the nerve of that wo-man. I cut her dead in the elevator, and she still tries to speak to me."

Gus leaned in.

"Do you want to hear an Easter Sunday secret that nobody knows?"

"Of course I do," said Lil.

"Not for repetition."

"You can count on me not to repeat it to a single soul," replied Lil.

"I just made a deal to write a novel based on Perla's life and the tragedy in Biarritz . . . for lots of bucks," said Gus.

"Oh, my dear. Brave you. Perla's not going to be happy with you. Don't you ever worry about how people will respond?"

Gus smiled.

"All the time."

"Someday, when we have lunch, just the two of us, you *must* tell me about the fire at the villa in Biarritz. I've heard you tell it at dinner parties several times, but I think you're holding back. There's something fishy about that story, don't you think? I mean, the Zachariases had all those guards, and there wasn't a single one on duty the night of the murder. Pul-eeze. And didn't I read in your diary in *Park Avenue* that the poor male nurse who's in the Biarritz jail signed the confession in French, a language he doesn't speak? Pul-eeze again." As Lil paused to ponder this, across the apartment she saw her butler, Dudley, hasten to open the door to her first guests. "Oh, look, Gus, here comes Adele Harcourt. Doesn't she look divine, bless her heart? Look at those high heels. Don't you love it? Doesn't she limp well for someone her age? She doesn't look a hundred and four, does she?"

Lil kept speaking as she moved to receive her honored guest, "that perfect darling," Adele Harcourt.

"Oh, I didn't know she was going to bring Addison Kent. That's her walker. He takes her to the movies in the afternoon. Adele loves the movies. The *on-dit* on Addison Kent is that he used to be Winkie Williams's boyfriend, and probably still is for all I know. By the way, Winkie has cancer. Riddled, poor sweet Winkie. He called and canceled lunch today about an hour ago. Gus, be a darling and tell Gert in the kitchen to write a place card for Addison. You'd better spell it for her.

"Oh, Adele, your hat is so marvelous. Perfect for Easter. Wasn't the music heavenly at St. James' this morning? Oh, hello, Addison. It's so nice to see you. Happy Easter!"

ADDISON KENT was one of those pretty society boys on whom fashionable women doted. He had only been in New York for five years, but Winkie Williams, who had been everyone's favorite extra man for the past forty years, had more or less sponsored him, taken him about in the beginning to meet people when he first arrived in town from Grosse Pointe, Michigan, after having graduated from Brown University, which were considered good credentials. What only Winkie Williams knew, and not another soul, was that Addison's family was from South Detroit, Michigan, that Addison had attended Brown Junior College in Willis, Michigan, for two terms, and that he'd been working as a waiter in a Red Lobster restaurant in Pensacola, Florida, when they'd met six years earlier. The Red Lobster was an unlikely place for such an elegant fellow as Winkie Williams to stop for lunch.

Later, Addison told certain of his friends that fate had brought them together. Actually, Winkie had prostate cancer at the time and had to urinate a great deal. He had no intention of eating at Red Lobster after his emergency bathroom visit, but Addison, who had an eye for spotting class, put down the tray of lobster dinners he was carrying and followed Winkie into the men's room. That's where the whole thing started.

Addison brought with him great looks and a natural aptitude for assessing beautiful things. It was Winkie Williams who helped him get the job under Prince Simeon of Slovakia, the head of the jewelry department of Boothby's auction house on the Upper East Side, after Addison recognized a tiara worn by Perla Zacharias on the opening night of the opera as having originally been designed for Empress Eugénie of France. It was the sort of surprising thing Addison knew.

The cachet of working at Boothby's had proved to be an ideal stepping-stone into the right dining rooms of New York, where extra men who understood the art of conversation were always in demand. Lil Altemus, who knew a climber when she saw one, could read the excitement in Addison's eyes at being in her house on such an intimate occasion as her family Easter Sunday lunch.

"He has a bad case of Astoritis," said Lil to Gus about Addison. "He is simply dazzled by New York social life."

That Addison Kent had become such a close friend of Adele

Harcourt's had to do initially with Adele's famous emerald necklace, which had once belonged to a czarina of Russia. Even at her ripe old age, Adele had not decided whether to leave the necklace to the Metropolitan Museum of Art or to the Museum of the City of New York. And so one day, a few years back, she had her social secretary, Emma, call Boothby's to say she wanted to have the necklace appraised again, as if that might help her make the decision. As Prince Simeon was away from New York, attending a private jewelry sale of the Krupp diamond in Monte Carlo, young Addison Kent was sent along to Adele Harcourt's Park Avenue apartment. Her butler, George—famous George her friends called him, who wrote out her invitations, menus, and place cards far better than any calligrapher ever could—led Addison to her library, where Adele was sitting on a chintz sofa reading *Park Avenue*.

"I love *Park Avenue*," said Addison.

"Do you mean the street or the magazine?" asked Adele, playfully.

"The magazine," replied Addison, grinning.

"Such fun, isn't it? Sometimes I write for it. I bet you didn't know that. Stokes Bishop talked me into writing about my hundredth birthday party that poor old Laurance Van Degan gave for me before his terrible stroke."

Right from the beginning they got along. The hundred-year-old grande dame, who still enjoyed a good laugh, was simply enchanted with the twenty-four-year-old Addison Kent, who, it turned out, told her he knew her first husband's step-grandson from Harbor Springs, Michigan, where his family had "a summer place." Addison always established a social connection, however remote, with any new person of consequence he was meeting. He didn't tell Adele he had known her first husband's step-grandson only for a seven-minute quickie in a cabana of the Harbor Springs Yacht Club during a dance, and that they had never spoken again once the zipper flies of their white linen trousers had been re-zipped and they had left the cabana separately to return to the dance, where their dates in summer evening dresses had been waiting to foxtrot.

Addison was simply overwhelmed by the beauty of Adele's jewels, especially her famous emerald necklace. Adele loved being complimented on her emeralds and enjoyed telling the many stories of its previous owners. "Barbara Hutton owned this necklace at one time. You're too young to know who Barbara Hutton was, but she was quite something in her day. It was stolen from her in Tangier, where she had a house in the casbah," she said. "I want to leave something to Lil Altemus, and something to darling Loelia, and to Rosalie Paget. Something substantial, like a ring or a bracelet. You must help me decide, Mr. Kent."

"Call me Addison, Mrs. Harcourt."

"POINT ME to where I'm sitting," said Adele, taking Lil's arm after Addison excused himself to use the lavatory and Gus stepped out of the room to make a phone call. "I don't see as well as I used to."

"I've put you next to Gus Bailey, Adele," said Lil. "I know how you love talking to writers. Don't say anything to him that you don't want to read later in one of his books or in his diary in *Park Avenue*."

"Who's he writing about now?" asked Adele. "So many of my friends were unhappy with him after he wrote *Our Own Kind*. Do you remember when Dolores De Longpre walked out of the Temple of Dendur benefit at the museum because Mr. Bailey was seated at her table? It was the talk of the party."

"That sort of thing happens to him," said Lil. "Listen, don't mention this to him—it's a big publishing secret—but he just signed a deal for a great amount of money to write a novel about Perla Zacharias."

"Oh, dear!"

"Did you read his pieces in *Park Avenue* on the Zacharias trial in Biarritz? Believe me, there's something fishy in that story. Ask him why there were no guards on duty that night at the villa."

"That Mrs. Zacharias sent me the most enormous orchid plant for Easter. Too big, really. Addison said it must have cost at least a thousand dollars. Why would she send me flowers? I don't even know the woman."

"But she wants to know you, Adele," replied Lil. "You are who she wants to be in New York. You're going to have to send her a thank-you note for her thousand-dollar orchid plant. Next thing she'll invite you to dinner and make an enormous contribution to the Manhattan Public Library, which will in turn get her invited to your house, Adele. Ask Gus Bailey about her. He knows everything about Perla Zacharias, going all the way back to her Johannesburg past and her first two husbands. Gus is the one who made her famous, some say infamous, writing about her month after month in *Park Avenue* magazine, after the murder in Biarritz. I tell you, a novel about Perla Zacharias, with all the things Gus knows, will be the talk of the town."

"You have me simply riveted, Lil darling," said Adele. "Mr. Bailey seems to be everywhere. Now the big news is that he's being sued for slander by that ex-congressman nobody ever heard of before all the controversy, Kyle Cramden. Gus said something about the disappearance of that girl, whatever her name is, that Cramden is supposed to have been involved with, that she was dropped at sea, or something like that," said Lil.

"Diandra Lomax," said the butler.

"What?" asked Lil.

"The missing girl's name is Diandra Lomax," said the butler.

"Yes, yes, thank you, Dudley, Diandra Lomax, who went missing, but Gus doesn't want to talk about the lawsuit. He practically bit my head off when I mentioned it earlier," said Lil. "He's frantic about it."

"Yes, I read about that in the paper," said Adele. "Quite a lot of money, isn't it?"

"Eleven million," whispered Lil into Adele Harcourt's deaf ear, although she heard it.

"Dear God," said Adele. "He doesn't have that kind of money, does he?"

"Of course not," said Lil. "Oh, look, here comes Dodo, my dreaded stepmother."

"Happy Easter, Lil," said Dodo, smiling and friendly, fully aware that she was disliked by her stepdaughter. Dodo Van Degan was not pretty. Nor was she ugly. She was pleasant look-ing. The help always liked her. She remembered their names. Even when she began to buy expensive clothes, she never looked stylish. She used to say she needed someone to put her together. "I bought this new suit just for your Easter lunch, Lil."

"Oh, green. Difficult color, green," said Lil, waving to Janet Van Degan, her sister-in-law, whom she loved, who had just walked in the front door.

"You always lift my spirits, Lil," replied Dodo. The two women looked at each other with dislike. "Happy seventy-fifth," she said in a loud voice. "I can't wait to see you blow out all those candles."

A HALF hour later, after glasses of champagne and trays of caviar hors d'oeuvres had been passed around by Dudley, Lil's guests were seated at her dining table.

"Isn't Lil's table just perfect?" said Adele Harcourt, ad-dressing her remarks to Gus, whom she didn't know, while look-ing down the length of the table. "So pretty. So Easter, the whole thing. Lil's always had the prettiest table in New York. Look at those wonderful flowers. That's Brucie's signature, those tangerine roses. Brucie is the florist we all use, from the Rhinelander Hotel, but you probably knew that. Oh, and look at these dear little chocolate Easter bunnies. So sweet. I always give these party favors to my maid, Blondell. She has so many children.

"I understand you don't want to talk about your lawsuit, Mr. Bailey. It must be simply horrid, being sued and being in the scandal pages of the papers all the time."

"That's right, Mrs. Harcourt. I hope you don't mind," said Gus. "Lawyer's orders. I tend to talk too much, and people quote me later, and it gets me in trouble, which isn't good with this eleven-million-dollar slander suit in the offing."

"Good heavens, Mr. Bailey, I'd never want to get you in trouble, so let's go on to another topic entirely," said Adele. "I am absolutely riveted by your pieces in *Park Avenue* about the Konstantin Zacharias case in Biarritz. Mrs. Zacharias just sent me a thousand-dollar orchid plant for Easter, and I don't even know her."

Gus laughed. "People say she wants to be you."

Adele Harcourt wrinkled her nose dismissively and changed the subject. "You probably don't remember, but I was at the table at the Temple of Dendur at the Metropolitan Museum on the night Dolores De Longpre walked out when you sat down."

Gus laughed again. "Stomped out would be more like it. Of course I remember. How could I forget? Dolores was one angry lady that night. She thought she was a character in my book *Our Own Kind* . . . and, well, she was right."

Gus was having such a wonderful time with Adele Harcourt that he decided he would share his recent news with her. It was just too good to keep to himself. With a mischievous expression on his face, he leaned in and in a lowered voice said, "Would you like to hear a secret I've been itching to tell someone?"

"Of course I would," replied Adele. "I'm mad about secrets."

"I just signed a deal with a publisher to write a novel based
on a notorious woman."

Adele grinned knowingly.

"Yes, I heard. This woman certainly won't be happy with
that bit of news. No thousand-dollar orchid plant for you, Mr.
Bailey."

CHAPTER 2

ON EASTER SUNDAY, WHILE LIL ALTEMUS WAS giving her farewell lunch at her twenty-eight-room apartment on Fifth Avenue, Ruby Renthal was the sole passenger, except for her manicurist, in her husband's G550, which the international interior designer Nicky Haslam had recently redecorated as part of Ruby's plans for her husband's reentry into New York society after his release from prison. What she had learned during the several years she and Elias had been on top in New York was that there was nothing the old rich enjoyed more than getting free rides in a billionaire's plane, and those European titles couldn't get enough, either. Ruby's manicurist, Frieda, had come along at the last minute when Mrs. Renthal, who was used to getting what she wanted, made her a financial offer Frieda simply couldn't refuse, with her teenage son in all that trouble with the law and the lawyers' fees mounting, even if it meant infuriating Lil Altemus, Rosalie Paget, and Matilda Clarke, who had their regular appointments on Sunday morning, when Frieda went to their apartments. Frieda could always use extra money, and Ruby Renthal was very generous when she went after someone or something she needed. Frieda's life was overwhelmed by her son's transgressions. She feared that prison might be in his future.

"It's a four-and-a-half-hour flight to Las Vegas. I'll be at the, ah, the facility for several hours, and then we'll fly right back to New York," said Ruby, after the financial arrangements had been worked out. Ruby always used the word *facility* rather than *prison* when she spoke of the circumstances of her husband's life. "There'll be a second car waiting at the airport to take you home when we get in. Where do you live? Queens, isn't it? The driver will take you there, and Michael, Michael's the steward on the plane, he'll take you out to lunch in Las Vegas, and drive you around. You'll find it's very amusing, the Strip and all that sort of thing. I fly out to visit my husband every other weekend, and we've all gotten to know Las Vegas, haven't we, Michael? Marvelous paintings at the Bellagio, like a private museum, if that sort of thing interests you. Mr. Wynn, who owned the place, had the last picture Van Gogh painted before he committed suicide, or cut off his ear, or whatever he did."

They sat at the backgammon table for the manicure.

"Who was Lil Altemus having for lunch today?" asked Ruby.

"Mrs. Altemus doesn't really talk to me when I do her nails," said Frieda, "but I heard from Gert that old Adele Harcourt is coming. But it's mostly family, I think. And what she calls her strays, those people who have nowhere to go. She's having that writer Augustus Bailey."

"I used to like Gus Bailey, but now I just can't stand him," said Ruby, looking at the color of the fingernail polish on her left hand. "He came to our apartment for lunch and dinner on several occasions, and then he wrote in *Park Avenue* that my husband was guilty. He agreed with the jury's verdict. My husband will never forgive him for that, and I have to go along with my husband on things like this, but I sort of miss Gus at the same time. Don't tell anyone, but I have a strong bond with him that neither of us ever mentions. Years ago, in another lifetime, I used to go out with the same guy who murdered Gus's daughter. He beat me up a few times, and I ended up in the hospital. I was supposed to be a witness at the trial, but the judge wouldn't let me testify in front of the jury. Keep that one to yourself. Even my husband doesn't know. I love that color, Frieda. What's it called?"

"Jungle Red," replied Frieda.

"From now on, we're going to rename it Ruby Renthal Red."

Frieda, who rarely smiled, smiled.

"So Adele Harcourt's going to be a hundred and five, huh? I hear she's gaga. She wears those straw hats all the time so the wig doesn't come off."

"I wouldn't know about that," said Frieda.

"Who's Gert?" asked Ruby.

"Mrs. Altemus's cook."

"Oh, *Gert*. Of fig mousse fame, I suppose," said Ruby. "They say that Lil used to bring her into the dining room after her dinner parties, and the guests would all clap for her."

"I wouldn't know about that. Can I ask you something, Mrs. Renthal?" asked Frieda.

"I suppose so. What?" asked Ruby.

"It's none of my business, really."

"What?"

"When you and Mr. Renthal talk at the prison, do you have to talk over telephones through glass partitions, like they do on *Law & Order*?"

"Mr. Renthal is in a facility."

"Oh, I thought he was in prison," said Frieda in an apologetic voice.

"Facility," repeated Ruby. She assumed the look on her face that she always assumed when people asked her about Elias in prison. It was not a subject she enjoyed sharing with others, but she knew that poor Frieda was probably worrying what it would be like if her son was sent to prison for dealing drugs (which he eventually was). "We did talk over phones through a glass partition in the beginning, when he first went in, but they've eased up a bit, and now I meet him in one of those little rooms where lawyers meet with their clients," said Ruby. "I can't stand being with those other prisoners' wives. I never know what to say to them, and they all hate me. 'Oh, how's your private plane, Mrs. Renthal?' one of them said to me right before she made her way to the Greyhound bus terminal."

"I was just wondering," said Frieda.

Ruby Renthal had changed over the years. Her basic sweetness had hardened since her husband, Elias Renthal, had gone to prison for financial malfeasance. People who used to be her friends no longer invited her to dinner. She was greatly criticized for divorcing Elias when he was in prison. She was also greatly criticized when she remarried Elias at the federal prison in Las Vegas, Nevada, several years later, after her divorcée status had not worked out as she had hoped.

What people said about her was that she had tried to get Loelia Manchester Minardos's former husband, Ned Manchester, but in the long run, she had come to realize that Ned had never really gotten over Loelia. Then there was Baron de Liagra in Paris, who never had any intention of leaving his wife for her, although he greatly enjoyed the afternoon pleasures they shared at a charming apartment on the Rue du Bac that he kept for such purposes. She felt cheap and used when she discovered that his intentions to make her his baroness were nonexistent.

The trashy Ruby that she used to be before the first of her two marriages to Elias Renthal, the Cleveland billionaire, resurfaced. She threw the ruby bracelet the baron had just given her as a kiss-off present at him, hitting him in the face with it before it fell on the marble floor by the fireplace. She told him he was a lousy fuck, that his dick was too little and that it tilted sideways, and that he came too quickly. Then she put on her sable coat and stormed out of the flat on the Rue du Bac, slamming the gold and white door behind her. The next morning at the Hôtel Ritz, in the Coco Chanel suite overlooking the Place Vendôme, Ruby Renthal drank cup after cup of black coffee and deeply regretted her behavior of the night before. She was back to her ladylike self, and she wrote the baron a charming note, apologizing for her appalling behavior and asking him if he would please— "please, please, please"—return the ruby bracelet to her, as a keepsake of a love affair she would always remember as a high point of her life. The baron never replied. The fact was, on her own she was just another ex–trophy wife who had lost her social footing in New York. A year later, she remarried Elias in the warden's office at the federal prison in Las Vegas, Nevada, with the warden and his wife as witnesses.

"Every time you come out to visit Elias, you must come and see us, Mrs. Renthal. There are some wonderful restaurants in Vegas. We even have a Le Cirque here. I bet you didn't know that," said the warden's wife, Estelle Gelson, who remembered reading about Ruby back in the 1980s when she and Elias were conquering New York. "Oh, I'd love to," replied Ruby. She never did, of course. She had no intention of becoming friends with Estelle Gelson, the warden's wife, thank you very much. She flew out to Las Vegas on Elias's plane and she flew right back after the visit. She never spent an extra minute in Las Vegas.

Soon Elias would be out of prison, and Ruby had already started to plan their new life.

"I can't tell you how much I hate that orange jumpsuit they make you wear, Elias. I can't see *why* on visitors' day they can't let you wear the blue jumpsuit instead of the orange one. Or khaki; they should have khaki uniforms. You look thinner in the blue, unless you're putting on weight again, with all that junk food you eat from the vending machines. You just ate two whole bags of Fritos in about eight minutes." She opened her Hermès Birkin bag and brought out the new magazines and paperbacks. "That mean guard with the shaved head was on duty, and he took away all the magazines and paperbacks I brought you, but the nice guard, the one I like, Spike I think his name is, the one I gave the Gucci wallet to last Christmas with the hundred-dollar bill in it, he gave them back to me."

Elias smiled. "Kiss me," he said.

"You've got elephant breath," she said after obliging him.

Elias shook his head slowly as he stared at her. "Were you always such a bitch, Ruby? Or did love make me blind way back then, when I picked you up on American Airlines?"

"Oh, let's not go all the way back to American Airlines again, please. You know you picked me up on a private jet. And anyway, didn't we have enough of that 'Mrs.-Elias-Renthal-the-former-stewardess' talk when we were riding high?" said Ruby. She turned away, gathering her things as if to leave.

"You may as well put down your twelve-thousand-dollar Hermès Birkin bag and sit down. There are no early exits during visiting hours, and no doors to slam," said Elias. "You're stuck here in this room with me for the next two and a half hours. So, what are we going to talk about?"

Elias, to everyone's surprise, was a good prisoner, liked by both the guards and the other inmates. He played bridge regularly with the former president of a rock-and-roll record company, who was doing time for shortchanging his stars on their royalties; a big-time Ponzi schemer, who'd ripped off a lot of very rich people, some of whom were friends of Elias's; and a forger who signed a film star's name to a bogus check and cashed it. Although none of his fellow card players was poor, exactly, none could quite match the vastness of the Renthal fortune, or even come close. Elias rarely talked to them of his former exalted station in life, but they all knew of it, as did every prisoner and guard in the facility. Elias was hurt when he heard that his thirty-nine-room apartment, where the famous Renthal ball had taken place, had been sold, even though Ruby had told him she didn't want to live there anymore. The Park Avenue apartment represented everything he had ever strived for in his life. He had enjoyed the astonished looks on the faces of even the most established and wealthy visitors when he showed them through it. "I bought that Tintoretto at Waring Hopkins's gallery in Paris" was the sort of thing he used to say in better times.

"Look, Elias, I fly out here every other weekend, and I think you could show me a little more courtesy when I make all this effort." She started handing him the magazines. "I've brought you *Time, Newsweek,* Friday's *Wall Street Journal, Barron's, Financial Times,* and *Park Avenue.* Did you read Gus Bailey's piece on Perla Zacharias in the issue of *Park Avenue* that I gave you last month?"

"Let me tell you something about Gus Bailey. Gus Bailey is all wet on Perla Zacharias," said Elias. "Perla isn't hiding anything, for Christ's sake. I knew Konstantin. I did business with Konstantin. Konstantin was no choirboy, but he was the best financier in the world."

Ruby was glad they had a subject they could hold a conversation about. She liked talking about the Zacharias murder in Biarritz. "It was odd, though, Elias, even you have to admit it, that there were no guards on duty on the night of the fire, the murder, or whatever you call it, when he had hired twenty-five guards trained by the Mossad and housed them in the barracks he built for them on the outskirts of Biarritz. I wouldn't go so far as to accuse Perla of murder—there is no evidence of that—but I think there is more to the story than what's being reported."

"The guards drove Perla crazy. She couldn't stand having them underfoot all the time. She hated it when they farted on duty. She said she didn't have any privacy," said Elias.

"How do you know so much about the guards' farts driving Perla crazy?" asked Ruby.

"I called her collect from here after Konstantin's funeral," said Elias.

"How about the famous surveillance system not working that night?" persisted Ruby. "It was supposed to be the latest, the best in the world, or so Konstantin told me the last time I sat next to him at dinner before the fire. Do you know what was in the surveillance cameras on the night of the murder? Old footage of guests arriving at a dinner party Perla gave the week before Konstantin died for the Baron Alexis de Rede, who was visiting her from Paris."

"Look," said Elias, in his voice of authority, wanting to end the conversation. "There's been an arrest. There's been a trial. The nurse signed a full confession."

"In a language he didn't speak," replied Ruby, topping him.

They looked at each other angrily.

"Is it true that Perla's the richest woman in the world?" asked Ruby, changing the subject slightly.

"No, of course not. Maybe the third richest. She's got more money than the Queen of England. That's all I know about the matter."

"Did I ever tell you about her diamond and sapphire salt and pepper shakers? She's got twelve pair of them. And her dining room table seats forty."

"You've told me that several times."

"She knows how to spend money, that's for sure," said Ruby. "I hear she spends a hundred thousand a year on caviar."

"You don't do so bad yourself in the spending department, Max Luby tells me."

"Oh, fuck what Max Luby tells you about me," said Ruby.

Max Luby was one of Elias's oldest friends dating back to his Cleveland days, before he and Ruby moved to Manhattan. He now handled Elias's money. There was a time when Max Luby liked Ruby, but since her husband was incarcerated he had disapproved of both her conduct and her spending habits.

"Perla does nothing but good for people, with all that money she gives to charity," said Elias. "She's going to be one of the great philanthropists of our time. You wait."

"Yeah, but she gives all that money for the wrong reasons. She doesn't give to the Manhattan Public Library because she loves books. Her kind of philanthropy is to get her name in the papers so she gets invited to all the swell houses for dinner. I read that in one of Gus Bailey's articles."

"How's that different than any of the rest of us? Perla's going to get even with Gus Bailey. You wait and see. Perla's the type who always gets even. She's patient. She waits. She knows the right time to strike. That's what I like about her."

"Speaking of Gus Bailey, he's being sued for slander by former congressman Kyle Cramden for something he said about Cramden on a radio show. Eleven million bucks worth of slander," said Ruby.

"That's the first good thing I've ever heard about Kyle Cramden," said Elias, relishing the news with a shit-eating grin.

"Kyle Cramden was supposedly involved with that girl who disappeared, Diandra Lomax."

"Kyle Cramden would fuck an umbrella," said Elias dismissively. "So he's suing Gus Bailey, huh? Good. Gus Bailey thought *I* was guilty, and he wrote it in *Park Avenue,* and I thought the guy was a friend. He came to our house for dinner, for Christ's sake, if you remember."

"And lunch," Ruby reminded him, although she always felt guilty when she talked about Gus.

"Right. And lunch. You wait, that guy's going to get it someday. Perla Zacharias hates him. Gerald Bradley Junior hates him. We're talking powerful people here. Somebody's going to get him one of these days." Elias clenched his fists in delight, barely able to contain his enthusiasm over the inevitable demise of that prick Gus Bailey.

By now Ruby had lost interest in talking about Gus Bailey, or Perla Zacharias or Gerald Bradley Junior. She had something on her mind that she had wanted to say for a long time. "You *were* guilty, Elias," she said quietly, simply.

"I was *not* guilty!" Elias said angrily. "I can't fucking believe you said that to me."

"Oh, bullshit, you didn't do it. I'm sick of that act. 'Oh, Elias *never* could have done anything like that.' I can't tell you how many times I've had to say that over the years, and those people all nod like they believe me, and none of them does. I can see the way they look at each other. They *all* think you're guilty. Even the juror who sold tokens in the subway booth thought you were guilty. Just remember, I'm the one who picked up the phone that awful day when that poor Byron Macumber, with the two little daughters and the pretty wife, who jumped off the roof the following week, called you at the apartment. I heard the whole conversation. Now let's change the subject."

Elias started to breathe heavily. He hated to be reminded of Byron Macumber's suicide. He didn't bring up the fact that he had provided for Macumber's widow and set up a trust fund for the education of his two little daughters.

"If there's one thing I've discovered in my nearly seven years in prison, it's that you're not at the top of everyone's popularity list. I don't know what the hell happened to you, Ruby, but you lost yourself along the way," said Elias.

"So did you, Elias. That's why you're doing seven years in the federal penitentiary, oh I mean facility, in Las Vegas, Nevada," said Ruby.

"I never expected to be on my hands and knees on the bathroom floor cleaning the inside of a toilet bowl that forty-five prisoners have shit in," said Elias.

"They didn't make you do that?" replied Ruby, shocked. "You never told me that, Elias."

"They all got a big kick out of watching the fat rich guy with the six houses and the G Five Fifty on his knees cleaning toilets. I provided a lot of laughs for them."

"Oh, Elias, I had no idea," said Ruby. "I'm shocked."

"That's when I came up with the idea of buying out the vending machines each month and letting all the prisoners get their candies, Fritos, Doritos, and ice cream bars free from the machines instead of having to save up quarters. After that, everyone got nicer."

"You were always a great deal maker, Elias," said Ruby.

"Listen, I have something to tell you," she added. "Just hear me through before you go off on a rant. I've decided to go to St. Moritz for Christmas. Bunny and Chiquita Chatfield asked me to stay at their chalet." Bunny and Chiquita Chatfield were the Duke and Duchess of Chatfield, and two of the only people who still spoke to the Renthals after Elias's trouble began. Ruby felt it was necessary to maintain these relationships and use them when she and Elias were ready to climb back to the top after Elias was released. Besides that, she hated spending the holidays at the facility.

Elias, surprised, replied, "I was rather hoping you'd fly out here."

"I've spent so many Christmases here, Elias, and I'm simply not going to go through it again. Singing Christmas carols with all those prisoners and their wives and all those crying children, and the warden and his pushy wife who wants to be my best friend. Not to mention that awful turkey dinner with the cold mashed potatoes and the thick gravy. No, thank you very much.

I can't, Elias. I just can't do that again. I hate it when the prisoners' wives all call me Ruby. 'Got any room in your private plane to fly me and the kids back to Newark, Ruby?' I could die when they do that."

"Ruby, you're no different from any of those prisoners' wives out there, except that you have a private plane and a husband with a billion dollars. You're a prisoner's wife. Max Luby tells me people in New York refer to you as The Convict's Wife."

"I can always count on Max Luby to come through with the definitive statement on just about anything in my life," said Ruby bitterly.

"I heard they turned you down for membership at the Corviglia Club in St. Moritz," said Elias.

"Who told you that?" she snapped.

"A little birdie."

"It's all because of you," she hissed. "They told Chiquita Chatfield, who was one of my sponsors, that they couldn't have a member whose husband was in *prison*."

"Let me tell you something, Ruby. Say, just say, it was Loelia Manchester Minardos who was in the same predicament you were in, with a husband in the clink. *She'd* have gotten in. We may have the money, but she has the class. In those circles, that's what counts."

Ruby looked at Elias. She knew he was right.

"I learned a little about society during the nine years we were in it," said Elias. "Imagine what an asshole I was to have paid a million dollars to put a new roof on Chiquita and Bunny Chatfield's castle, just so they'd have to start inviting us to the shoots, and now she can't even pull her Duchess of Chatfield weight to get you into the Corviglia Club." He shook his head. He remembered himself in his shooting tweeds, made to order by Huntsman in London, with his Lobb boots laced up in front.

He had been on top of the world then, shooting at Deeds Castle with Bunny Chatfield and his weekend party. He knew he'd never wear those clothes again after he got out of prison, even if the Chatfields asked them out of courtesy. He knew he'd lost the panache to carry off that kind of dressing anymore. The light within him that had made him such a favorite with the aristocrats had gone out, and he knew it.

"You still haven't gotten those people straight, Ruby. You still want to be one of them. It'll never be the same for either one of us. I know about the baron in Paris, who went back to his dyke wife rather than marry you. She may like to rub her face in hair pie, but she has lineage, like a title, and a family château and all that stuff. You don't. You're tarnished goods, Ruby. They used to call you The Billionaire's Wife; now they call you The Convict's Wife. I know why you remarried me. You had no place else to go, and I still had a billion dollars, even after all the fines, and a plane at your full-time disposal. I was the best that you could do."

Ruby started to cry. "Prison's changed you, Elias," she said. She looked at him. She realized that he didn't love her anymore. "You always said we were a wonderful partnership. We could still be that, you know."

CHAPTER 3

"KYLE CRAMDEN, THE CALIFORNIA CONGRESSMAN, is suing you personally, Gus. He is not suing *Park Avenue*. It's not libel, you see. It's slander," said Mitch Weill, the lead lawyer for the publishing empire, Forward, that owned *Park Avenue*. They were sitting in the office of the editor, Stokes Bishop, along with the associate editor, Lenore Cummings, and Gus's personal editor, Lance Wilson, who had edited every story Gus had written for the magazine for the last twenty-odd years. He feared he was going to be fired, even though he was long past retirement age.

Outside, the city, as seen from the twenty-second-floor office, had never been more beautiful. People had finally adjusted to the missing twin towers of the World Trade Center that had so drastically changed the skyline. "That's where they used to be," Stokes always said to people who were in his office for the first time.

Inside Stokes Bishop's office, everyone was uncomfortable. They had all worked together for years and were friends, except for the lawyer, Mitch Weill, whom Gus had never met before. Gus was miserable and ashamed to be in the position that he was in.

He was being sued for slander for something he said on Patience Longstreet's under-watted radio show. It was broadcast only in limited locations. The audience for Patience's show was minimal. The following day, Patience, in an effort to publicize her show and increase her audience, telephoned Gus's amazing story in to Toby Tilden, the gossip columnist of the *New York Post*. It was that column that quoted Gus as having said that Diandra Lomax had been kidnapped by five Middle Eastern men who drugged her and put her onto a commercial-size private jet heading for Saudi Arabia and that Kyle Cramden knew all about it. It was the fake story, brilliantly told, that Gus had fallen for hook, line, and sinker. In months to come, Toby Tilden's gossip column turned out to be the main reason that former congressman Kyle Cramden sued Gus Bailey for slander, and that's where his troubles had begun.

Gus knew he had more in him to write, despite the enormous embarrassment of having fallen for a false story of national importance and having told it on a radio interview. As he sat in a very modern steel and black leather chair, his posture was that of defeat, a posture he had not experienced for twenty years.

"Yes, I understand that," he said in reply to Mitch Weill's statement. It was he who was being sued, not the magazine, and he would therefore be responsible for legal fees and restitution. What he was thinking at that moment was that there would be nothing left to leave Grafton and Sandro, his sons, when he died, or Sarah, his granddaughter, whom he had promised to educate in the best schools in the land. Feelings of failure overwhelmed him. Failure was a state he had experienced before, until late-life success had defeated it, or so he thought. *Failure* was a word that he feared.

Mitch Weill stood up to leave, his mission accomplished. "I'm going to call Flora Dickens. She's with the Los Angeles firm of Erskine, Sondheim, and Hollerith, but she's in the Washington office, and she's the best in this field. I'll have her call you."

"You mean she's not here in New York?" asked Gus.

"No," replied Mitch.

"Won't that be difficult, having a lawyer who lives in a different city?" asked Gus.

"Oh, no, not at all. We do it all the time."

"With this sort of case?" asked Gus.

"Flora Dickens is the best there is," replied Mitch, in a bragging tone. "She was number one in her class at law school. Editor of the *Law Review*."

"Thank you," said Gus. He shook hands and said good-bye to Mitch. He didn't like him. He also bid farewell to Lance and Lenore, who filed out behind Mitch, leaving him alone with Stokes Bishop.

"I talked to Hy Vietor in Vienna this morning," said Stokes, lowering his voice, although they were now the only two in the room. Hy Vietor owned the vast publishing empire of which *Park Avenue* was an entity. "The magazine is going to stand behind you. You've been our most popular writer for over twenty years. You helped make this magazine."

"Thanks," said Gus. "I was beginning to think everyone had forgotten that." The fear of being poor again terrified him. He had had the experience once. He didn't want to have it again.

"But you've got to keep that under your lid. That can't get out," said Stokes, continuing in his low cautionary voice. "We can't pay your legal bills because we haven't been sued, but you will be given a bonus when this is over to cover all of them."

"Oh, God. Thanks," said Gus.

Stokes leaned back in his chair and studied Gus. "You're like a zombie," said Stokes, louder now that business had been taken care of. Editor and writer they were, with Gus in the subservient position, as Stokes was the one who renewed his contract year after year. They liked each other. Gus always said about Stokes Bishop, when people who didn't know him asked about him, "Stokes is a great editor. He's made *Park Avenue* the most successful magazine in the country, maybe the world." And Stokes often said about Gus, when he was being interviewed, "Wherever I go, people ask me about him." They were part of a team.

"I feel like a zombie," replied Gus.

"Are you going out? Are you seeing people?" asked Stokes.

"No. I've canceled out of every speech, every lecture, and most parties. I was supposed to have lunch at the Four Seasons tomorrow with Beatrice Parsons about the new novel, but I moved lunch to the coffee shop at the Waldorf," said Gus.

"No! That's exactly what you shouldn't do. Call Beatrice and change your lunch back to the Four Seasons, or Michael's. See people. Go out. Go to the parties. Don't hide," said Stokes.

Gus looked at him searchingly. "Do you think my career's ruined? I can't believe I fell for that bogus story. I wish I'd taped the call, Stokes. He was calling from a horse farm in Dubai, where he was training the polo ponies of an emir. That's what he does for a living, all over the Middle East. All those sheikhs and sultans have polo ponies or race horses. First he told me his father had been a friend of John Steinbeck's. Then he said that Elia Kazan, whom he called Gadge, which only Kazan's closest friends called him, had asked him to teach James (he called him Jimmy) Dean to be a Salinas boy. This was how he caught my interest, which was his intent. Then he started telling me about the kidnapping of Diandra Lomax, which was the point of the call. I still can't understand why he picked me to call and spin his tale to."

"Gus, you're not ruined. You're news," said Stokes. "Just imagine Kyle Cramden on the witness stand here in New York. Look at the kind of life the guy leads. It's in all the tabloids now.

This trial's going to be sensational. Christine Saunders, everyone will be covering it."

"I wish those words brought joy to me, but they don't," said Gus. "I don't want to be in the papers, or on the television news."

THAT NIGHT Gus read about himself again in Toby Tilden's column in the *New York Post,* which was mean-spirited on every occasion when he was mentioned in connection with his slander suit. BAILEY'S BOGUS SOURCE ID'D was the headline that day. "What a shit he is," said Gus about Toby Tilden. A reporter friend of Gus's had told him that Win Burch, Kyle Cramden's lawyer, had a close relationship with a junior member of Toby Tilden's staff.

"That explains a lot," said Gus, resigned. He then reminded himself that Stokes was in his corner and his legal fees would be paid for. *I could hug Stokes,* he thought before drifting off into the most restful sleep he'd had in some time.

CHAPTER 4

WHEN IT CAME TO NEW YORK RESIDENTIAL real estate at a very high level, there was no one wiser that Maisie Verdurin. Fifteen years earlier she had been a respected art dealer and gallery owner who became fascinated by the real estate business and the riches that could be made from it. Her switch from one high-powered career to another was highly publicized and rated a cover story in the Sunday *New York Times Magazine*.

It was Maisie who arranged the secret meeting with Ruby Renthal in the tearoom of the Neue Galerie on Eighty-sixth Street and Fifth Avenue, which at one time was the New York residence of Mrs. Cornelius Vanderbilt, who was for three decades the most notable figure in New York society. Maisie and Ruby pretended to run into each other at the Christian Schad exhibit. "Hello. How are you? How lovely to see you. Don't you adore that picture of the chic dyke with the monocle standing at the bar in Berlin? Elias would be simply mad about that picture. Let's have a cup of tea." They sat in the far corner of the nearly empty tearoom.

"It just occurred to me that the very first major painting Elias and I ever bought back in the old days was from you," said Ruby.

"I remember it well," said Maisie. "A Monet of water lilies. That was when you first came to New York."

"I loved that picture," said Ruby, taking a sip of her tea. "We had Cora Mandell paint the walls of the living room where it hung over the fireplace the same color pink as the inside of the lilies."

"What ever happened to it?"

"Storage, I suppose," Ruby answered with a sigh.

Maisie smiled, lifting her teacup to her lips. Then she looked at Ruby squarely.

"Not for long. We're here to talk about where you and Elias are going to hang that Monet, and I think I've got just the place. You know the old Tavistock mansion on East Seventy-eighth, between Fifth and Madison?"

"It's a bit run-down, don't you think?"

A broken-down mansion was not at all what Ruby had in mind for the new life she envisioned for herself and her husband, who was still a billionaire several times over, despite the enormity of his fines. Ruby very definitely knew the ten buildings in New York where she wanted to live—four on Fifth Avenue, three on Park Avenue, one on Gracie Square, one on Sutton Place, and one at Fifty-second Street and the East River.

"You've got to be practical, Ruby," said Maisie. "You're in quite a different position in New York now than you were before Elias went to prison for seven years. The buildings you want to live in don't want someone with a prison record to blacken their exclusivity. I don't care who you know on the board, the boards on those buildings are not going to accept you, and it'll be all over town that you got turned down and then it'll be in Toby Tilden's column in the *Post* that you've been blackballed by the ten best buildings on the Upper East Side. That's not going to be a good start for your return to New York."

Ruby turned red. It embarrassed her to hear this, but she knew that it was true.

Maisie knew what she was talking about. Several months earlier she had taken it upon herself to meet with Lil Altemus, who was still the president of the board of her Fifth Avenue apartment house. She had only to speak the name Renthal to get a negative reaction.

"*Never!*" said Lil Altemus firmly. "Never, never, never. That man has been in prison."

"But isn't it true that you are leaving the building, Lil?" Maisie asked.

"If you must know, yes," replied Lil, rolling her eyes. "I am being downsized by my nephew, who handles my money now that my brother, Laurance, is incapacitated by his stroke. But be that as it may, I am still the president of the board and will be so until I leave. Further, I can assure you that my successor and friend Binkie Bosworth will give you the same answer."

"What if Elias Renthal were willing to buy your own apartment for five million more than what you are asking?" suggested Maisie.

"I wouldn't sell it to him in the first place, and I really do need the money," said Lil. Maisie liked her honesty. Not many people in Lil's kind of life would admit that they were broke, she thought.

"And in the second place, Elias Renthal would be turned down by Binkie Bosworth and the whole board."

Maisie treaded lightly.

"Elias Renthal has served his time," she stated gently. "From what I gather, he was a model prisoner, admired by both the guards and the prisoners."

"Good for him. Hurrah! Hurrah! Applause, applause," said Lil, clapping her hands in fake praise. "I will *never* forget that my father died in the Renthals' house on the night of their ridiculous butterfly ball, and he laid my father, Laurance Van Degan, one of the most important and distinguished men in the city of New York, on the pool table and locked the door so that it wouldn't ruin his two-million-dollar party. Let's talk about something else, Maisie."

Maisie, who was known to be expert in selling problematic rich people to buildings with difficult boards, knew when she was beaten.

"LISTEN, RUBY, it's better that you hear this from me, an old friend of yours and Elias's, rather than from some hoity-toity society lady who's dabbling in real estate and will tell the girls at lunch at Swifty's that you turned red when you heard you wouldn't be found acceptable in any of the buildings you wanted to live in. I heard it directly from Lil Altemus, who was the head of her board."

"Lil Altemus!" cried Ruby, with contempt in her voice. "Who cares what her opinion is anymore? I saw her standing in line for the Madison Avenue *bus* the other day."

"Lil's a terrible snob, I know, but she's old school and she once mattered a great deal in New York. She's going through bad times," said Maisie. "I've always been fond of Lil."

"Hmm," replied Ruby. She couldn't wait to get even with that broke bitch for blackballing her and Elias.

"Who's the new head of the board now that Lil can't afford to live there anymore?"

"Binkie Bosworth, and she thinks the same way that Lil does," said Maisie.

"It's not prison-prison, you know, where Elias is in Las Vegas. There are no bars on the windows. He has a little room, not a cell, and he has his own television, and all the latest DVDs, and he gets the *New York Times,* and the *Wall Street Journal,* and the *New York Post* every day, and he never misses reading Kit Jones's and Dolores De Longpre's columns. I mean, there are no killers or rapists there, or anyone like that," said Ruby.

"It's still prison, Ruby," said Maisie in a matter-of-fact manner. "Elias will have done seven years by the time he gets out. Having been in prison for seven years is going to be the first line of his obituary when he dies no matter what amount of good works he intends to do when he is released. Prison is part of your life now, for the rest of your life. He'll never be in a room where someone's not going to ask him about it, or, worse, whisper about it to other people while he's there. No one's going to forget it, so deal with it, make it work for you."

"So what are you suggesting?" asked Ruby.

"The kind of building on Fifth or Park that *will* take you is not the kind of building you want to live in," said Maisie. "Am I right?"

Ruby nodded agreement without vocalizing it. She was still beautiful, Maisie thought, watching her. More mature. She had learned about style from Ezzie Fenwick in the years when she and Elias had been in society. Ezzie had taught her how to dress, and she always had been a quick study. She had never actually been a manicurist in Cleveland, as the article in *W* said about her when she was riding high. She had been a stewardess on American Airlines and later on private jets, which was where she had met Elias. Maisie looked to see if there had been any "work" done on her face during the years she had dropped out of sight in New York when Elias was in prison, but she couldn't spot any. Her red hair was smartly cut.

"I love your haircut," said Maisie. "That's either Kenneth or Frédéric."

"No, it's Bernardo. He's so sweet, Bernardo. He takes me at seven in the morning, before the salon opens, so I don't have to worry about running into any of the people I used to know."

"I see you're still partial to Chanel," said Maisie, looking at Ruby's understated suit.

"That prick Ezzie Fenwick turned me on to Chanel," said Ruby. "Ezzie was fine when we were riding high and we let him borrow the Rolls and driver, or let him use the apartment in London when we weren't there, but after all the troubles came, I never heard from him again, and he said some terrible things about us that were repeated back to us. I realize now, after Gus Bailey's lawsuit for slander, that I could have sued Ezzie for slander."

"Ezzie died," said Maisie.

"I was happy to hear there was only a small turnout at his funeral," said Ruby. "That's the kind of bitch I've turned into. Even Pauline Mendelson didn't go, I heard. Nor the former first lady."

Maisie laughed. "The one you have to get to know when you start going about again is Addison Kent. He's much nicer than Ezzie ever was, and a better dancer, a better bridge player, and he's just under thirty."

"Hold on there, Maisie. I have to get used to living with my husband again before I start thinking about a walker taking me to charity balls," said Ruby.

"Let's get back to the Tavistock mansion," said Maisie.

"Are you really talking about that filthy dump with the boarded-up windows?" asked Ruby, clearly disappointed.

"That filthy dump with the boarded-up windows happens to be one of the most beautiful houses in New York underneath the grime. It also happens to be the widest private house in the East Seventies. It's the width of three brownstones," said Maisie. "You could turn the ballroom into a projection room and show movies on Sunday nights after people come in from the country. Between your plane and your projection room, you'll be back in no time."

Maisie never pushed too hard when she was selling. She wanted the client to think the idea had been hers. "How about if you and I go through the house together? There's an old caretaker living there. I'll make the arrangements with him. We'll go through the service door on the side, and no one will see us."

"Didn't somebody's cook jump out the window of that house?" asked Ruby.

"That cook was nuts, absolutely nuts," said Maisie. "Ask Gus Bailey about that cook who jumped out the window. He mentioned her in one of his columns in *Park Avenue*. She was nuts."

"We don't speak to Gus Bailey," said Ruby, shaking her head.

"Who's we?" asked Maisie.

"Elias and I. Not that Elias has any chance of not speaking to him from the federal facility in Las Vegas, but he wouldn't speak to him if he did have the chance. We hear Gus Bailey is doing 'The Elias Renthal Story' on his television series about crime among the rich."

"Gus is a friend of mine," said Maisie. "I go way back with Gus. I knew Gus when he first married Peach."

"Gus Bailey said that he thought Elias was guilty when he wrote about the case in *Park Avenue,* after he came to lunch and dinner at our house," replied Ruby.

Maisie looked away. She also thought Elias had been guilty. So did everyone in New York. Ruby knew in her heart that Elias had been guilty, too, but she had gone along with Elias's insistence for the last seven years that he had been innocent of the financial malfeasance with which he had been charged.

"When shall we look at that house?" asked Ruby.

CHAPTER 5

GUS BAILEY WAS OFTEN STOPPED IN THE STREET or in restaurants by people who recognized him from his appearances on the *Harry Sovereign Show,* or as host of his own television show, *Augustus Bailey Presents.* Mostly they were interested in hearing if there was anything new on the Konstantin Zacharias case. He told his friends and his editors that he felt like a magnet for people with some sort of information on that story. Several times men said things like, "I was a friend of Konstantin Zacharias's. Konstantin wanted to tell me something, but Perla wouldn't let me be alone with him." Gus wrote notes in his green leather notebook from Smythson of Bond Street in London; Stokes Bishop gave him one for Christmas every year.

After all the distress he felt over Kyle Cramden and his expensive lawsuit, the only thing that distracted Gus was his novel. He had been feeling so tired lately and so weighed down by anxiety, but when he was writing, the creative energy made him feel renewed. It was a refuge for him. He found himself thinking about it most of the time.

Gus stopped on Madison Avenue and Eighty-first Street in front of the Grant P. Trumbull Funeral Home, the most prestigious mortuary in New York City, to make a note about Perla

Zacharias's having been seated next to the secretary of state the previous night at a Washington dinner in honor of a former first lady. He wrote that he was astounded that such a universally disliked person had been seated so importantly.

Looking up for a moment, Gus noticed that a green Nissan Sentra, the same one he'd seen parked there earlier, had a driver in it who seemed to be staring at him. But before he could react, out of the corner of his eye, he saw Winkie Williams, the popular society walker, slowly exiting the funeral home, looking left, then right, before turning left in the direction of his apartment.

Winkie Williams had been an extra man on the New York social scene for decades. Every hostess in New York wanted Winkie Williams at her table. "Winkie Williams told me the *most* hilarious story last night about the Duchess of Windsor being a hermaphrodite," said Ormolu Webb after one of her dinners. He was a particular favorite of Lil Altemus, who doted on him and never gave a party without him, before her lifestyle had become so reduced. "He adds so much to the table," Lil said to a reporter from *Quest,* who was writing an article on Winkie's lunch parties. "He's such fun, such a good dancer, such a good bridge player, he gives charming lunches in that tiny apartment of his. Everybody loves Winkie. You'd never know he was ninety in a million years. Ninety's the new sixty, he always says."

"Winkie," called out Gus, quickly scribbling something down before closing his notebook and tucking it into the inside pocket of his jacket. He noticed that Winkie, who was *over* ninety, had suddenly begun to look very old, after having frequently been described as sprightly and full of fun for the past few decades. Winkie seemed nervous at meeting Gus.

"What scandalous thing are you writing in that famous green leather notebook of yours on the corner of Madison and Eightyfirst Street?" asked Winkie, who was adept at social conversation, so as to forestall any questioning.

"Actually, I was just jotting down the license number of that green Nissan Sentra, with the big guy in dark glasses staring at me. Do you see him? I think the guy is following me or trying to freak me out. The doorman in my apartment building told me yesterday he thought I was being followed by a tall man in a green Nissan Sentra, and here he is."

"Oh, heavens! You don't suppose Perla Zacharias is behind the whole thing, do you? You're not her favorite writer," said Winkie, his eyes twinkling as he teased Gus flirtatiously.

Gus laughed. Winkie took a gold cigarette case out of his suit pocket. He offered a cigarette to Gus, who declined it.

"Haven't smoked for years," said Gus. "But I sure do like that gold cigarette case. I haven't seen a gold cigarette case since people stopped smoking."

"Cole Porter gave it to me," said Winkie. "It has the lyrics of 'The Extra Man' engraved inside. I'm leaving it to the Costume Institute at the Met."

"That's a treasure. By the way, who died?" Gus said, pointing his head toward the door of the funeral home.

"What do you mean?" asked Winkie.

"I can't imagine anyone going into Grant P. Trumbull unless he was visiting a corpse."

"Oh, I just had a sudden urge to pee," he said quickly. Then, changing the subject, he said "Gus, I can't get enough of the Zacharias story, and now I hear a hush-hush rumor that you're working on a novel about it. How exciting! I visited several times at their villa in Biarritz that used to belong to Empress Eugénie of France. I've never seen such luxury. I don't believe word has reached Perla yet, but I don't envy you when it does. She thinks that what you have written about her in *Park Avenue* is what's really keeping her from making it in New York society. She'd love to be the next Adele Harcourt, you know. And speaking of society, I thought you'd be at Lil Altemus's first dinner party in her new apartment last night."

"Well, the book deal is just about to be announced, so I

guess I have something to look forward to," said Gus. "I couldn't go to Lil's last night. You probably heard, or read, that I'm being sued for slander. I stayed home to watch Kyle Cramden's lawyer, Win Burch, on the *Harry Sovereign Show*. Mr. Burch is one slick customer, with a lot of fake charm. I'd never seen him before, but I've certainly heard a lot about him."

"How's your lawsuit coming?" asked Winkie.

"Slowly. Expensively. I'm scared shitless of this Win Burch. He's said to be terrifying when you're on the stand. People say that he scares people for a living. They call him The Pit Bull."

"Everyone's rooting for you, Gus," said Winkie.

Gus shook away the thought of Win Burch. "How was Lil's new apartment?" he asked.

"A bit charmless. Low ceilings. Poor Lil. She hates it, but she's being brave about it. She can't stand her nephew for having her move out of her Fifth Avenue apartment after she lived there for so many years, and she never lets up on poor Dodo for inheriting all the family money. Thank God she has Gert."

"Yes, yes, good old Gert," said Gus.

WINKIE WENT off to meet Addison Kent for an early dinner at Swifty's. Winkie had lied to Gus when he said he had gone into the Grant P. Trumbull Funeral Home to use the men's room. He had gone to make the arrangements with an assistant funeral director named Francis Xavior Branigan for a cremation in three days.

"For whom?" asked the assistant funeral director, eyeing Winkie somewhat suspiciously.

"For me," replied Winkie. He was an elegant-looking fellow, even in his advanced years, and the assistant funeral director noticed how beautifully he was dressed, although his recent weight loss made his gray pinstripe suit appear to be too large for him. Though dazzled by this glamorous figure, Xavior was made uncomfortable by his request.

"A cremation for you, Mr. Williams? Tell me, how exactly do you know the precise date you will be ready for cremation?"

Winkie just held his gaze, silently communicating to the assistant funeral director that he knew what he was doing and that he would not be deterred. "This is a very delicate matter, Mr. Branigan. You won't breathe a word, will you?"

"You're putting me in a very awkward position, Mr. Williams."

"Oh, don't be silly," Winkie replied airily.

Xavior changed the subject.

"I feel like I know you. I recognized you right away. I've been reading your name in Kit Jones's and Dolores De Longpre's columns for years, and I see your pictures in *Park Avenue* at the grandest parties. You're the most famous extra man in New York. Is it true that Cole Porter wrote 'The Extra Man' about you? It's one of my favorite songs of his."

"Cole always said it was about me, yes," said Winkie, who loved his social celebrity. "Of course, I was awfully young then, and I was the best dancer in New York; at least that's what Dolores De Longpre always wrote about me."

"Is it true what I read that you never go out on the anniversary of Marie Antoinette's death?" asked Xavior.

"No, no, no. I don't know who started that ridiculous story," said Winkie, shaking his head.

Francis Xavior Branigan was bursting with excitement that he was engaged in such a glamorous conversation and was completely charmed by the handsome Mr. Williams. He hated to turn back to the boring business of practicalities, but he felt it his duty to get to the bottom of the request.

"What brings you to this very sad act that you are contemplating? Is it all right if I call you Winkie?"

Winkie laughed. "Of course. I would like you to call me Winkie. All the waiters at Swifty's call me Winkie. I love it."

"But you haven't answered my question," said Xavior.

"I'm riddled with cancer. Absolutely riddled. I don't have a chance. I'm not in pain, thank God, or thanks to Lil Altemus, rather. She's on the board of the hospital. She took her brother's place after Laurance had that terrible stroke. The pain clinic is at my command, so I'm a little high at all times. I have gone to my last party, and seen everybody one last time, and kissed a lot of ladies on the cheek, and discussed Tina and Freddie Tudor's divorce, and asked Lil for one last dance. Now I am ready to do it. I don't want to be a burden to anyone. I have prepared the announcement for the *New York Times* obituaries."

Xavior stared at Winkie for a moment, his mouth slightly agape.

"Oh, dear. I find this so sad," he finally answered, shaking his head. "I believe I have a legal responsibility to inform someone of your plans."

"No you don't," Winkie stated pointedly. "Who will ever know we had this conversation?"

Xavior looked away for a moment.

"Don't they call you a social gadfly in the columns?" Xavior asked, deciding at least to humor Winkie.

"This is my reputation, yes," said Winkie.

"You seem deeper."

"I am deeper. But, you see, I have wasted my opportunities," said Winkie. "It's not good to inherit a few million when you are as young as I was. Especially way back when a million dollars was still considered a lot of money."

"Rich family?"

"A rich lover or two would be more accurate," replied Winkie, and they both chuckled. "It made me idle. There were things I could have done. I could have written, I'm sure. My eye was perfect. I missed nothing. I could turn a phrase better than anyone."

"But why didn't you?" asked Xavior.

On Winkie's face was a look of profound weariness that had nothing to do with being tired but had a great deal to do with having seen too much. He stared straight ahead. Xavior was aware of a moisture that appeared in Winkie's eyes, as if he were fighting tears. He shook his head slowly. "It's a terrible thing to come to the conclusion that your life has been so unimportant as mine has been."

"But you have friends. Many, many friends."

"Yes, yes, there is that," replied Winkie.

"Do you have a friend who will find you? It's awful when nobody stops by for a few days, and the cleaning woman comes a week later and she tells the television reporter for the evening news that your body had started to stink," said Xavior.

"Oh, no, we mustn't have that," said Winkie, with a gesture of horror. "I wouldn't like it a bit to be found in a state of decay. I am about to have dinner at Swifty's with a very close friend of mine who will find me the next morning. His name is Addison Kent, a charming young man. He will send the announcement to the *Times,* and he will be in touch with you about picking up the body. I'm afraid I've forgotten your name."

"Francis Xavior Branigan."

"Yes, of course, Mr. Branigan."

"Xavior," he said.

"Xavior, yes. Let's discuss price, so I can pay in advance," said Winkie. "I've brought my checkbook along."

Seduced by the profound role that the famous Winkie Williams was asking him to play in New York social history, Xavior chose to go forward with the suicide plan.

"The basic cremation price is six thousand."

Winkie's face took on a look of financial surprise. "I think that's a little pricey for a burn-up, Xavior. I hope you're not thinking about a fancy casket. I read Jessica Mitford on the American way of death, and I know about the exorbitant charges in the mortuary world. I want the cheapest wooden box there is. I wouldn't mind if it was cardboard, as a matter of fact."

"It's still six thousand," said Xavior. "Make the check out to Grant P. Trumbull Funeral Home."

Winkie took his checkbook from the inside pocket of his pin-stripe suit and wrote out the check. "Outrageous, you know," said Winkie.

Francis Xavior Branigan smiled. "I know a funeral home up on One Hundred Twelfth Street and Amsterdam Avenue where you can probably get a better deal, but that wouldn't be the right thing at all for you, Winkie."

"Here," said Winkie, handing him the check for six thousand dollars.

"Will there be a service?"

"No funeral. No memorial. It's in the announcement. It says, 'William (Winkie) Williams passed away in his sleep on such and such a night. There will be no funeral or memorial service.' "

"That's to the point. No music, I suppose."

"Maybe a little Cole Porter. I think Bart Howard made a recording of 'The Extra Man' back in the fifties," said Winkie.

"I know the lyrics," said Xavior.

Addison Kent knew what Winkie planned to do. He knew him well enough to know never to try to talk him out of it. He knew that for Winkie it was the right thing to do. He knew Winkie's cancer had spread to his bones and that it had metasta-sized. "I'm riddled," he'd said to Addison. Later, after it was all over and people discussed the late Winkie Williams, Addison al-ways said, "He was like a mentor to me when I first came to New York from Michigan."

They sat at the corner table in the back room of Swifty's. Between the two of them, they knew almost everyone in the room. They waved. "Hi, Sass. Hi, Blaine." They threw kisses. They only nodded to Yehudit Tavicoli, who was searching for a new rich husband and dining with an obscure Arabian royal. Winkie ordered martinis. No one in the room could have guessed that they were discussing what clothes Winkie should be laid out in before his cremation. He didn't want to be put into the flames in the blue silk pajamas with his monogram on the pocket that Perla Zacharias had given him, along with his own monogrammed towels, when he visited her at her villa in Biarritz, shortly before the terrible fire took place that killed Konstantin. His plan was to wear them to bed the night he took the thirty-seven pills he had been able to get from the pain clinic at the hospital. He thought the blue silk pajamas were perfect to be wearing when he would be found the next morning, but he had always been a fashion plate, so he wanted Addison to have his latest pale gray pinstripe suit from Huntsman in London taken up to Mr. Francis Xavior Branigan at the Grant P. Trumbull Funeral Home, along with his favorite blue shirt with his monogram on the pocket, and the lavender tie from Turnbull & Asser that Lil Altemus had given him for his birthday the previous week.

"I haven't worn it yet. She'll be thrilled to hear. You must tell her afterward. I've asked her to be the executrix of my will. It will keep her occupied in that new apartment she hates so much."

"Is there any porn in the apartment that I should get rid of?" asked Addison. "You wouldn't want Lil Altemus to find any of those videos I've seen in there, would you? Especially the one with you and the three black guys."

"Perish the thought," said Winkie. "The videos are in that French chest with the ormolu decoration. By the way, Lil has always said that the French chest should go to Boothby's to be auctioned. She said it could be worth quite a lot of money if it's the real thing, and Lil knows her French furniture. She said it's the ormolu that makes it so valuable. Remember, Lil gave all that eighteenth-century French furniture to the Metropolitan Museum, and they named the room after her, back when she still had so much money."

"Where did you get that chest?" asked Addison.

"There was a very rich Argentinian named Arturo Miramonte who lived in grand style in Paris back in the fifties, and he took rather a shine to me. Actually, it was more than a shine. He almost left his wife for me. Instead he left me that cabinet with all the ormolu in his will, among other things, like money, quite a lot of money, as a matter of fact. That was all years and years ago. I was quite good-looking back then. Arturo said he left it to me because I was the only one who had ever figured out there was a secret panel. I must remember to tell Lil Altemus about that."

"I always heard that it was Pauline Mendelson's late ex–brother-in-law, Donald Mendelson, who left you your money," said Addison.

"That was my second inheritance," said Winkie. "There was almost a scandal. Donald died in his apartment at the Sherry-Netherland from some bad heroin that his great friend Lady Wetmore brought with her from the South of France. Thank God for Thomas, the butler, who worshiped Donald and knew of his habits. He told the devastated and stoned Lady Wetmore to pack and fly back to France on the first plane out, went to the lobby and got her a cab, cleaned up all the evidence of needles and drugs, and then called nine-one-one, or whomever they called in those days to report a dead body. Not a word made the papers, other than a paid obituary that said he died of a heart attack. I don't know about you, Addison, but I'm going to have another martini. After all, what difference does it make?"

The day after he made his cremation arrangements with Francis Xavior Branigan at the Grant P. Trumbull Funeral Home and later had dinner at Swifty's with Addison Kent, where they decided on the clothes Winkie would be cremated in, and got a little drunk at the same time, Winkie Williams was out and about making further final decisions. He had decided to do it quickly, to get it over with. He always had an instinct for knowing the right moment to leave a party.

ORMOLU WEBB ran into Winkie on Madison Avenue, and they stopped to chat for a moment after Winkie had kissed her on both cheeks and admired her new short haircut from Bernardo. Ormolu never gave a dinner where Winkie wasn't at an honored place at her table. "Mica said she saw you at Swifty's last night," said Ormolu, laughing gaily, as she always did, covering the fact that she was shocked by his appearance. Later, Ormolu said to her husband, Percy Webb, when they were dressing to go to Rosalie Paget's dinner, "I saw Winkie Williams on Madison Avenue today on my way from Bernardo, my hairdresser's. Poor darling Winkie, he looked simply terrible. I almost didn't recognize him, but he was in such good humor, full of fun as always."

WINKIE WENT into Thierry's Wine and Liquors on Madison Avenue. He went straight to Jonsie, his old pal Jonsie, who had been selling him wine for a couple of decades for his little lunch parties in his "small and terribly chic" apartment, as *Quest* magazine had described it, just around the corner.

"I want the most expensive bottle of champagne in this overpriced shop," said Winkie to Jonsie, who was once, when they met back in the 1940s, the substitute piano accompanist for Mabel Mercer, the nightclub chanteuse beloved by unmarried men of the period. Winkie was one of the few people who ever saw Jonsie accompany Mabel Mercer when she sang "You Are Not My First Love" at Tony's on West Fifty-second Street.

"What are you celebrating? It's not your birthday?"

"Special occasion, Jonsie," said Winkie.

"I've got just the bottle of Cristal champagne, although it's six hundred dollars."

"Money is no object today, Jonsie. And I'll be paying in cash, if that's okay."

"Fine by me. Did you read Gus Bailey on Perla Zacharias?" asked Jonsie as he rang up the bottle of champagne.

Winkie nodded agreement. "Now he's writing a book about the whole situation. Perla hasn't found out yet, but she will be crazed over it. I wouldn't want to have Perla for an enemy, I'll tell you that. I saw Gus yesterday making notes on the corner of Eighty-first and Madison. Gus has got an inside source on that story, and it's driving Perla mad because it's so accurate. She can't figure out who in her employ is talking to him."

Winkie grabbed his change and reached for the bottle.

"Listen, sorry to rush, but I've got to run. So long, Jonsie."

Jonsie, hoping he'd linger just a bit more, said, "Let me give you a holiday hug."

Later, after it happened, Jonsie told people he'd hugged Winkie good-bye. "He was just skin and bones. I knew it was for the last time."

From the liquor store Winkie walked through the lobby of the Rhinelander Hotel into the florist shop at the rear of the hotel.

"Hi, Winkie."

"Hi, Brucie," said Winkie. "Oh, it looks so festive in here. Look at the color of those roses. Too beautiful."

"Tangerine, you know, my trademark," said Brucie. "From this marvelous man in Peru."

"Give me a dozen of those to take with me. Actually, make it a dozen and a half. I'm here to spend a great deal of money," said Winkie.

"Music to my ears," said Brucie, who had been an understudy in the original cast of *Company,* and had gone on one time in the two-year run, when the leading man was sick, singing and dancing to Stephen Sondheim's music. Winkie sometimes had Jonsie play the piano and Brucie sing Sondheim selections when he had a cocktail party for his society friends.

"This order is to go out in the morning two days from now. I want the best orchid plants in full bloom that you can find. Beautiful ones. Nothing skimpy. White phalaenopsis, like Lil Altemus used to have when she still lived on Fifth Avenue. I want them wrapped dramatically, in cellophane with blue and lavender ribbons. I have the addresses here on the envelopes."

"My God, Winkie, this is going to cost you a fortune," said Brucie.

"I have a check here made out to the shop and signed by me. Just fill in the amount."

"Are you going away?"asked Brucie.

Winkie sang in a camp voice from the old Negro spiritual, "To a better land I know."

Brucie joined in singing the spiritual, "I hear the gentle voices calling, Old Black Joe."

They roared with laughter. "I used to cry for poor Old Black Joe when they sang that in school when I was a little boy about a hundred years ago," said Winkie.

"I wouldn't advise singing it in public these days," said Brucie.

Brucie put green tissue paper in a white cardboard box and carefully laid a dozen and a half tangerine roses one by one inside.

"Do you want a card for this?" asked Brucie.

"No, the roses are for me, for the table next to my bed," said Winkie. "I think I'll take one of these scented candles as well."

"Are you okay, Winkie?" asked Brucie. He felt strangely disconcerted.

"I'm fine. I'm even serene, in fact." Winkie started to walk out. "So long, Brucie," he said. "I'm so glad I was in the audience the night that you went on in *Company* when Larry Kert was sick."

"It was the greatest night of my life, Winkie. I got a standing ovation." The memory still brought him happiness.

"Good-bye, Brucie," said Winkie, giving him a hug.

"Why do I feel like crying?" asked Brucie.

"Don't," said Winkie. "The orchid for Lil Altemus has to be extra special."

AFTER WINKIE had gone, Brucie, still humming "Old Black Joe," looked through the blue envelopes that Winkie had left. He recognized almost all of the ladies' names, as either they were customers of the shop or he had read about them in Dolores De Longpre's column. For Lil's plant, instead of the card, there was a letter on Winkie's engraved blue stationery from Smythson of Bond Street in London. He picked up the letter addressed to Mrs. Van Degan Altemus, East Sixty-sixth Street, walked to the back room of the shop, where the teakettle was on a hot plate plugged into the wall, and turned up the heat. When the steam came out, he held Lil Altemus's letter over it. He checked the front room for customers, and then he took the letter out of the envelope.

> *My darling Lil,*
>
> *I am gone. I have decided to end my life. I'm sorry not to have said good-bye. I'm sorry not to cry. Please do not be sad. I know that what I am doing is the right thing. I wouldn't be good as a pathetic creature being wheeled up*

Park Avenue by an illegal alien from a Third World coun-
try, and I certainly don't want to be incontinent like Wallis
Windsor. I do hope that I have not overencumbered you
with my request that you be the executrix of my will. It will
give you something to do other than complain about your
new apartment. About the ormolu chest that Arturo Mira-
monte left me in Paris years ago, I've told Addison Kent to
call Boothby's auction house. Whatever it sells for is my be-
quest to you, as spelled out in my will. Throw out those old
red damask curtains from the Fifth Avenue apartment.
They dwarf your little living room with the low ceilings.
Brighten up the place. Tangerine is the new color this sea-
son. Call Ferdy Trocadero in to paint the walls. No one can
distress walls like Ferdy Trocadero. Before Boothby's comes
to pick up the ormolu chest, you should take a look at it first
to get everything out. And one last favor—stop saying
Hubie died of Epstein-Barr.

Love, Winkie

Brucie, ashamed, put the letter back in the envelope and
sealed it. No one would have known it had been opened. He
called Jonsie over at Thierry's Wine and Liquors and said, "I
have a bad feeling about Winkie."

"I have the same feeling," said Jonsie. "He bought a six-
hundred-dollar bottle of champagne from me. He said it was for
a special occasion. What did he buy from you?"

"Like almost eleven thousand dollars' worth of orchids, to
be sent to eleven of the fanciest ladies in New York. I think he's
going to do it tonight. He bought tangerine-colored roses for
next to his bed, eighteen of them at six bucks a stem, and he
never buys himself flowers unless he's having one of those little
lunch parties he gives. He also bought a scented candle."

"Which scent?" asked Jonsie.

"He wanted the one named after C. Z. Guest, but I didn't have any in stock, so I put the one named after Perla Zacharias in the bag," said Brucie. "Did you know that Konstantin Zacharias's male nurse, who was taking care of him because of the ALS he suffered from, started the fire that killed him in Biarritz with a scented Perla Zacharias candle?"

"Yeah, I read that in Gus Bailey's diary in *Park Avenue*. Why do you think he's going to do it tonight?" asked Jonsie.

"If I tell you something, will you promise not to tell?" asked Brucie.

"I promise."

"No, swear to God on your word of honor you'll never tell."

"I swear to God on my word of honor I'll never tell," said Jonsie.

"I steamed open his suicide note to Lil Altemus," said Brucie.

"You didn't!" replied Jonsie, in a shocked voice.

They became helpless with shamed laughter.

"That's the worst thing I've ever heard," said Jonsie when he caught his breath from laughing. "What did the note say?"

WINKIE WAS in his bed. As planned, he was wearing his blue silk monogrammed pajamas that Perla Zacharias had had made for him at Charvet in Paris, when he visited her at the villa in Biarritz. His best Porthault sheets, pillowcases, and sham were on his bed. On his bedside table were his beautiful tangerine roses in a Steuben vase that Lil Altemus had given him from the house in Northeast Harbor, when she had to give it up. A Louis Vuitton bag had been packed with the clothes Addison was to take to the Grant P. Trumbull Funeral Home the next day. For a person taking his own life, Winkie was in very good spirits. He and Addison were drinking very expensive champagne from beautiful glasses. The vial of pills from the pain clinic at the Medicine Center was next to him on the bed.

"How many have you taken?" asked Addison, who was simply ecstatic at being present at such a time as this.

"I think about fourteen or sixteen," said Winkie. "I'm kind of getting hazy. I'm planning on taking thirty-seven. The thing you mustn't do is take too many. Did I ever tell you about poor Lupe Vélez? She was divine, Lupe. She was madly in love with Gary Cooper, and he went off with someone else, and she got herself all dressed up in the best nightgown she had, and her hair was done, and she was made up to within an inch of her life so she'd look beautiful when they found her in the morning, and then she took far too many pills, like sixty or something like that, and she vomited, and the maid found her the next morning with her head in the toilet bowl full of puke. Mustn't have that."

They both roared with laughter.

"Do you know something, Addison?" He took two more pills. "That was the last big laugh of my life."

"I guess so," said Addison. "I'm going to miss you, Winkie."

"Now you'll wash up the champagne glasses and then get out of here and come back in the morning and find me," said Winkie in a very weak voice.

"We've been over this fifty times," said Addison. "I'll wash up the glasses, take the dirty videos, and be out of here. I'll leave the Vuitton bag here until tomorrow when I find you. How many have you taken now?"

"About twenty-two, I think."

"Is there anything else?" asked Addison.

"Yes."

"What?"

"Tell me something about yourself that you've never told anybody in the whole world. Tell me your deepest secret," whispered Winkie.

Addison thought for a moment. "Okay," he said. He reached out and pulled over toward the bed a French bergère chair that Donald Mendelson, Winkie's second rich benefactor after the death of the rich South American in Paris, had bought for him from the Kitty Miller auction at Boothby's back in 1962. Addison loved the history of the bergère chair and hoped that it would soon be his. What he was about to say he had never told another soul, but he knew that his secret would be safe with the nearly dead Winkie, and he knew that it would help him to speak the words.

"Tell me," said Winkie.

"Do you remember the story you told me about the cook who jumped out the window at the Tavistock mansion on East Seventy-eighth Street?"

"I was there when the poor woman jumped," whispered Winkie. "So was Adele Harcourt. She landed on a terrace outside the dining room where the lunch party was going on. Plop, right there in front of us. Ruined the party."

"You're pretty alert for—what is it now—thirty pills?" said Addison.

"That's as good a memory as any to die on. What's your secret?" asked Winkie.

"The cook was my mother. Her name was Doris. I was a year old at the time, living in a maid's room on the top floor," said Addison, relieved for having finally told his deepest secret.

Winkie, dying, smiled. "You never let me down."

Addison took the glasses to the kitchen, rinsed them out, dried them, and put them in the bar. He picked up the tote bag of pornographic videos. He went over to the bed and looked down at Winkie's dead body. "Good-bye, Winkie. Thanks for picking me up at the Red Lobster in Pensacola when I was still a waiter."

On the bedside table, next to the empty prescription bottle, was Winkie's gold cigarette case from the forties. Addison knew that Winkie had promised Diana Vreeland to leave it to the Costume Institute at the Metropolitan Museum. Addison opened it and looked at the lyrics to Cole Porter's song "The Extra Man." The case was so stylish that it became irresistible to him. He told himself that Winkie would have wanted him to have it. He slipped it into his pocket and left.

CHAPTER 6

THE FOLLOWING MORNING ADDISON KENT HEADED over to the Grant P. Trumbull Funeral Home. On Winkie's instructions, Addison met Francis Xavior Branigan, the assistant funeral director, and handed him an old Louis Vuitton bag of Winkie's that Addison meant to keep after handing off its contents. Neatly packed inside were a gray pinstripe suit from Huntsman in London, a blue mono-grammed shirt from Turnbull & Asser on Jermyn Street in London, and a Turnbull & Asser lavender tie that Lil Altemus had given Winkie for his birthday.

"I didn't know about underwear, whether you put it on for a cremation or not, but I brought some undershorts anyway," said Addison to Francis Xavior Branigan as he was handing him the bag, giving him the eye at the same time. Addison Kent was a very promiscuous young man, and within five minutes of his handing over Winkie's clothes, he and Francis Xavior had a quickie in a toilet stall in the men's room, in much the same manner he had once had a quickie with Adele Harcourt's first husband's step-grandson in the bathhouse of the beach club in Harbor Springs, Michigan. Francis Xavior, mistaking the quickie for love, said that he preferred to be called just Xavior. That was okay with Addison, who never planned to see him again anyway, until Xavior asked Addison if he would like to attend the cremation itself.

"I hadn't thought of that, no," said Addison. "Do you do it here?"

"No, in New Jersey. I'm going to sing," said Xavior.

"You're going to what?" asked Addison.

"I talked it over with Winkie when he was here to make the arrangements."

"Winkie? You called him Winkie?" asked Addison, affronted by the impertinence of the assistant funeral director. "He didn't tell me this, about the singing. That doesn't sound like Winkie Williams at all. What were you planning on singing?"

"'The Extra Man,' by Cole Porter, that's what he requested."

Addison shrugged and then asked, "What time is the cremation, Xavior?"

"Eight a.m. tomorrow. Get here at seven, and you can drive out in the hearse with me."

"I'll be here," said Addison. He thought, *I'll be the hit of Lil Altemus's lunch party tomorrow.*

XAVIOR TOOK time to explain the workings of the crematorium to Addison. "And then I just push this button here, and those steel doors will open, and the casket will go straight into the flames."

"I see," said Addison.

"Would you like to see the body?" asked Xavior.

"Oh, dear," said Addison. "I don't know if I'm up to that. Isn't it best to remember him as he was the other night at Swifty's? We had such a good last time."

"But he looks so at peace," said Xavior. "Do take a quick

look, Addison. It's not Winkie, you know. It's just the shell of Winkie. Winkie's gone."

He opened the casket. There was Winkie, in his gray suit, his blue shirt, and his lavender tie. "I hope you don't mind that I put the tangerine-colored rose in his buttonhole. I took it from the vase next to his bed."

"Don't you think your cosmetic person put a little too much makeup on him? He looks like he's going onstage," said Addison.

"We don't usually put on makeup for a cremation, but I wanted to give Winkie a real send-off," said Xavior. "If I had been in total charge, I would have dressed him in white tie and tails, as if he were about to do a samba with the Duchess of Windsor. There's no extra charge for the makeup person."

"I always thought Winkie should have written a book about all those famous ladies he knew, like the duchess, and Kitty Miller, and Babe Paley. All that history going to waste," said Addison. "Did you know that the Duchess of Windsor was a hermaphrodite?"

"No!" exclaimed Xavior.

"That's what Winkie always said, and Winkie knew about things like that."

"He knew everything. I'm ready for my song now." He reached into his inside pocket and brought out the lyrics, which he had printed in large letters from his computer. "Here, I brought you a copy too."

Xavior began to sing:

> *I'm an extra man, an extra man,*
> *I've got no equal as an extra man,*
> *I'm handsome, I'm harmless, I'm helpful, I'm able,*

Addison joined in with Xavior.

> *A perfect fourth at bridge or a fourteenth at table.*
> *You'll find my name on ev'ry list,*

But when it's missing, it is never missed.
And so I'll live until that fatal day,
The press will tell you that I've passed away,
And you will feel sad as the news you scan,
For that means one less extra man.

Xavior pushed the button, and the casket went forth into the flames. Addison stared after it, tears streaming down his face. He had never heard the song sung before, and he suddenly realized it was the story of his own life too.

"I WAS wondering if you would like to have lunch, Addison," said Xavior as they entered the Grant P. Trumbull Funeral Home, where Addison stopped to use the men's room after the car ride from New Jersey. "There's a nice little French place around the corner. Liza Minnelli goes there sometimes."

"Oh, I can't, Xavior. I'm sorry. I'm going to Lil Altemus's lunch party for Adele Harcourt, and I have to change out of my funeral suit and tie before I pick up Adele," said Addison.

"Oh, right," said Xavior, who was disappointed. He had thought their quickie in the men's room the previous night might have led to something, a repeat at least, especially after having shared the experience of Winkie's cremation and having sung "The Extra Man" together. For Xavior, it had been an important life moment.

"You know Adele Harcourt's a hundred and five years old, and she still goes out to lunch and dinner. She's simply marvelous," said Addison, oblivious to the fact that Xavior's feelings were hurt. "Is it all right to smoke in here? I feel like a cigarette."

"No, no smoking in the whole building. Against the law," said Xavior bitterly.

"Good-bye, then. I have to be off. Thanks for everything. I

had never heard that song sung before. I'll call you about picking up the ashes." He knew he was rambling. The cremation had unnerved him. He walked out of the front entrance of the Grant P. Trumbull Funeral Home at Madison Avenue and Eighty-first Street. He reached in his pocket and removed a gold cigarette case. He opened it. He took out a cigarette and lit it, while looking at his reflection in the gold. He read the lyrics again. Even after he slipped it back into the inside jacket pocket of his dark blue pinstripe suit from Mr. Sills, he kept rubbing his hand over it, protecting it. He knew he could not carry it to Lil Altemus's lunch party for Adele Harcourt. Surely, she'd recognize it.

PERLA ZACHARIAS awoke in good spirits. She had been a success the previous night at a dinner party thrown by her old friends Carlotta and Maurice Zenda. Perla lived extravagantly in the twenty-seven-room apartment on two floors that she kept in New York for her occasional visits, two or three times a year, from her homes in Paris and London, where she felt more welcome than she did in New York. Apart from Carlotta Zenda, she really had no friends in New York, although she bought tickets or tables at a staggering number of the charity balls that went on every night during the season. Even the tenants in the Fifth Avenue building where she lived shunned her in the elevator. She knew that the presence of her guards in the lobby and her two Rolls-Royces, always parked in front of the building, annoyed her neighbors, but it was her notoriety that they recoiled from the most, which she blamed exclusively on Gus Bailey.

Fortunately, a recent discreet visit with Hy Vietor, the reclusive billionaire owner of *Park Avenue,* had brought that to an end. As Bailey ceased to write articles about the murder in Biarritz for *Park Avenue,* Perla felt the constant talk about her lessen, just as she had hoped.

Many of the twenty-four guests present at the previous night's dinner were often written about in Dolores De Long-pre's society column, a thing that Perla herself craved. Unlike most of the rich Middle Easterners who had moved to New York in the 1980s, the Zendas were the only couple to have been received in the top echelon of New York society. And, of course, while Perla would never admit it, she was jealous that Carlotta had been elevated to the head of the board of the Metropolitan Opera, a position of social importance that Lil Altemus's mother had long occupied.

Still, Perla felt she had been a success at the Zendas' dinner, especially in telling stories about the beautiful and tragic Empress Eugénie of France. Since buying the empress's villa in Biarritz thirteen years earlier, Perla had worked hard at acquiring Eugénie's possessions and memorabilia, when they came up for auction, or when an impoverished royal or collector had to sell. One of her greatest treasures was a Nymphenburg porcelain breakfast set sent to the empress as a thirtieth birthday gift from her great friend and relation Ludwig, the mad king of Bavaria, who would have loved her and married her if he had been inclined to love women.

Helga, Perla's maid, entered the room. Perla had brought Helga with her from Johannesburg years earlier. Always claiming to have the ability to read her mistress's mind, on this morning Helga had intuited that it would please her mistress to use King Ludwig's historic breakfast set on Perla's tray. Perla was thrilled.

"I was just talking about the empress last night at dinner!" she exclaimed cheerfully.

Helga smiled and poured the coffee, asking if her mistress had had a pleasant time at the Zendas'.

"A simply wonderful time, Helga! In fact, that reminds me that I must call Carlotta and thank her."

Perla picked up the phone and dialed Carlotta Zenda. The

instant she heard her friend's voice on the other end, Perla spoke excitedly.

"I had such a nice time at your dinner last night, Carlotta," she said, "and I was so thrilled to meet Constance Sibley."

There was a pause on the other end.

"Carlotta? Are you there?"

"Oh, Perla," Carlotta said finally, "I'm so upset for you."

Perla's expression changed to one of utter surprise.

"Upset? For me? But why?"

"Obviously you haven't read Kit Jones's column in the *Post*."

Perla, her hand over the mouthpiece, motioned to Helga to hand her the *Post*.

"Call me back when you've read it," said Carlotta.

"No, hang on," replied Perla, who then said to Helga, "Turn to Kit Jones's column. Quick."

The headline of Kit Jones's column read, PUBLISHER SIGNS AUGUSTUS BAILEY TO SEVEN-FIGURE DEAL FOR NOVEL TO BE TITLED *INFAMOUS LADY*.

Perla's jaw dropped and she let out a little shriek.

"That has to be *me* he's writing about! Why can't he let this drop? He's obsessed with me! Hold on a moment, Carlotta," she said weakly, dropping the phone onto the bed and half-burying the mouthpiece under the covers so her friend wouldn't hear what was to come.

"The *infamous lady* . . . that's how I'll be remembered!" Perla cried.

Almost immediately, her face turned red and blotchy. The veins on her neck bulged. Perla closed her eyes and let out a gut-wrenching scream. Her charming Johannesburg accent turned harsh and common.

"I hate that fucking Gus Bailey! I'm not going to let that piece of shit get away with this!"

She hurled the Nymphenburg coffee cup, still filled with

coffee, across the room. As it crashed against the persimmon-colored laquered bedroom wall, to which Ferdy Trocadero had applied seventeen coats of paint in an effort to get the effect he wanted, brown coffee splattered everywhere. Perla followed this by swinging the coffeepot at the wall too. The pot, craved by museums in New York, Vienna, and London, crashed against all those layers of paint, breaking into pieces.

"Oh no, Madame!" cried Helga, who fell to her knees and began gathering up the broken porcelain.

Perla paced the room, stepping over the broken chunks.

"I'll tie up that publishing house in slander suits until they go out of business! I tell you, Helga—I just want to know if any-one in my household is talking to him."

Perla stopped suddenly when she saw the phone peeking out from under the blankets on the bed. She walked over and slowly picked it up.

"Carlotta?"

"What was that smashing noise and that scream? Are you okay, Perla?"

"Helga dropped the breakfast tray and the coffee cup smashed. She was upset. You must be more careful, Helga," she said in a scolding voice.

Helga, who was used to such treatment, continued to pick up the smashed pieces.

"I think you should call your lawyer," said Carlotta. "Books can be stopped, you know. There was that woman in England who had a book about her life withdrawn and pulped."

"Yes, yes, I will do that," replied Perla quickly. "He's already written six articles in *Park Avenue* on my beloved Konstantin's death. You'd think that would be enough. And that's just a magazine, after all. Articles come and go. They get thrown out and people soon forget. But a book is forever," she continued with a sigh. "Books are artfully displayed in the windows of bookshops. 'Oh, that's the book about Perla Zacharias,' people will say."

"Perla, please," Carlotta interrupted.

"But it's true, isn't it? Books are placed on bedside tables in guest rooms. Books end up in libraries, like the Manhattan Public Library, where they stay forever."

Perla paused to catch her breath.

"*Forever,* Carlotta."

"You should think about making a major philanthropic gift to deflect this unpleasantness. No one can fault someone who does tremendous charitable work. Look at Adele Harcourt."

Perla rested on the edge of the bed and rolled her neck back.

"Oh, Carlotta—last night at your house I had such a nice talk after dinner with Percy and Ormolu Webb. They never mentioned the fire or the articles in *Park Avenue,* and I thought people were finally beginning to forget this business and accept me for who I am. They just loved hearing about Empress Eugénie of France, they really did." Her voice trailed off to a whimper.

Perla placed her hand on her forehead.

"And now *this!*"

After hanging up with Carlotta, and sitting quietly for a moment thinking, she motioned to Helga, who was still on her hands and knees picking up the pieces of the destroyed Nymphenburg porcelain, and said, "Helga, when you're done cleaning up that mess, please tell Willard to meet me in the study. I'll play Mr. Bailey's game. Willard has collected an entire file's worth of unsavory gossip about the *esteemed* author. Gus Bailey has been on the scene so long and made so many enemies that the stories could fill up five novels. I'm sure he won't want some of these rumors back in circulation; especially with that lawsuit of his pending. I'll just have to remind him who holds the power here. I'm sure we can come to some kind of agreement."

"Yes, Madame." Helga nodded. "You will make him sorry."

Perla resumed pacing back and forth. She knew it wasn't

enough to stop Gus from writing, although that would be fun. She needed to carefully construct a plan, one where she would come out smelling like a rose. First she would try to charm Gus. He was bound to decline but at least she could tell everyone she tried and shake her head sadly at his rejection. Then she would need to appeal to Manhattan society in a big, memorable way. She needed to get her name associated with a great institution, one that would overshadow anything that the Gus Baileys of the world could ever say about her. And Perla knew just the one that would simultaneously give her social prestige and piss-kick Gus Bailey right in his writerly balls.

"Simon, it's Perla. Listen to me. I'm going to made a donation to the Manhattan Public Library that's gonna knock everyone's socks off. And, Simon, I'll go to the library myself but I want an announcement straight from you."

Helga looked up at Perla from where she had gone back to picking up the pieces of Empress Eugénie's teapot and noticed her employer's trembling hands, her still-blotchy face. She had seen her boss like this before and she knew it was best to quietly do her job and then flee the scene as quickly as possible.

"This is only just beginning. I'll shut down his shitty little book! I'll give him infamous lady!"

CHAPTER 7

LIL ALTEMUS HAD SUCH A DIFFICULT TIME DECIDing whom to invite to her first lunch party in her new apartment, as her dining room, which had originally been a spare bedroom, only seated eight comfortably, or uncomfortably, as Lil had taken to saying after her first dinner party the previous week. In her old dining room on Fifth Avenue, she could easily seat twenty-four without giving it a second thought, not even having to bring in an extra chair or two from the massive front hall. Lil wanted everything to be particularly nice, as her guest of honor was Adele Harcourt, "that old darling," as Lil said about her when she invited the other five guests, with the ever-present Addison Kent, whom Adele asked if she could bring, making up the eight. "Addison's such fun, and he takes me to see all the movies," said Adele, who was going out less and less. When Adele arrived, beautifully dressed as always, in her black suit, white gloves, and straw hat and veil, she seemed tired as she leaned on Addison's arm. Addison had changed into a well-cut tweed jacket, with a pocket handkerchief and matching tie that Lil recognized as having belonged to Winkie Williams. He made no mention of the cremation he had attended earlier in the day, but it was apparent from Lil's expression that she had been informed of Winkie's passing.

"I miss Winkie so. Oh, Addison, I can't believe he's gone!" Lil said, grabbing his hand, swept up in her grief for her friend and forgetting for a moment the disdain she normally felt for Addison Kent. Her eyes began to well up with tears. She turned to Adele. "I got a letter from him just this morning. And look at this exquisite orchid he sent with it!"

Addison squeezed her fingers and said, "I know, I know. He didn't want a fuss made over him."

Lil continued talking.

"That's just like Winkie, not to want a fuss. When I gave those large dinners at the old apartment I always asked Winkie to do the seating. He was a genius at placement."

Lil turned to Adele and mouthed the word *suicide,* and Adele nodded, wide-eyed.

Adele, always kind, in an attempt to get her dear friend's mind off of her shocking loss, looked around at Lil's new apartment and raved about it. "It's sweet, Lil, so sweet, and I recognize those red damask curtains from the Fifth Avenue apartment," she said.

"Rosalie Paget said they overpowered the room. I think Rosalie was right, don't you?" asked Lil, "In his letter Winkie said I should get new ones, that tangerine is the color of the season."

"Perhaps if you took the valances down," said Adele.

"The rooms are small, Adele, and the ceilings are low, and the furniture all looks much too large. I suppose I'll get used to it. There are so many things to get used to these days. Thank God for Gert. I don't know what I would do without Gert. You must let me know if the Canaletto of Westminster Bridge overpowers the dining room, which is tiny, tiny, tiny."

"It looks lovely, darling," said Adele. "It's supposed to overpower a room. That's the point of owning a Canaletto."

"You are dear, Adele. My grandfather bought it from Lord Duveen when he was building the big house on Park Avenue and

Sixty-fifth Street," said Lil. "I'm so glad I grabbed it right out of my father's dining room after he died, or my stepmother, the dreaded Dodo, would have nicked it for herself."

"I have to sit down," said Adele. "Addison, will you help me over to that chair?"

"Let's go right in to lunch," said Lil. "The soufflé's ready. Adele, you're sitting next to me, with Addison on the other side. And you here, Ormolu. And Kay Kay's there. And Jamesey Crocus between. I asked Prince Simeon of Slovakia, but he had to back out at the last minute."

"Simmy flew to Monte Carlo for the sale of the Krupp diamond," said Addison, who loved to impart new information, as a way of securing his position. "Faye Converse, the movie star, is selling it in great secrecy. She wants fifty million, and there's a Saudi prince who's interested."

"Faye Converse was always my favorite actress," said Adele.

"My friend Gus Bailey, you met him at my house at Easter, produced one of Faye Converse's movies when he was in the movie business, but I never can remember the name of it. Let's sit down."

"I so enjoyed having Winkie Williams on occasions like this. I just can't believe he's gone," said Lil in Adele's ear, to deflect attention from Addison, who was telling a story about Faye Converse as if he knew her, which he didn't. "I think we should drink a toast to Winkie. I heard from Brucie when he brought over the centerpiece this morning that Addison went to the cremation. Tell us about it, Addison."

Addison, usually loquacious, chose not to offer his information on the cremation. He didn't want Lil and Adele and the other ladies and Jamesey Crocus to know that he and Francis Xavior Branigan, with whom he had had a quickie in the men's room of the Grant P. Trumbull funeral home, had sung "The Extra Man" by Cole Porter as Winkie's body turned to ashes. "It was brief, just the way Winkie wanted it," said Addison.

"I heard that Ruby Renthal wants to buy Winkie's ormolu chest before the Boothby auction," said Kay Kay Somerset. "I haven't seen Ruby in years, ever since Elias went to prison."

"Ruby sees almost no one," said Addison, who had never met her.

"Almost no one sees Ruby would be a better description of the situation," said Kay Kay Somerset.

"I have a letter from Winkie asking that the ormolu chest be auctioned off and the proceeds be given to me. But just imagine Mrs. Renthal of all people, coming to my rescue with her checkbook. Little does she know I was the one who blackballed her from getting an apartment at my old building on Fifth Avenue."

Addison, who had more news to impart, spoke up. "It looks like someone bought the Tavistock mansion on East Seventy-eighth Street and is having it done up inside to a fare-thee-well. Even an indoor swimming pool, I heard," he said.

"Didn't somebody's cook jump out the window in that house?" asked Ormolu Webb.

"It was Tootie Scott-Miller's cook," said Lil. "Tootie criticized the soufflé, rather harshly, apparently—you remember how Tootie could get at times—and the cook was so hurt she jumped from the cook's room on the sixth floor. Right in the middle of a lunch party. Plop, right outside the dining room window."

"I was there for lunch that day," said Adele Harcourt. "So was Winkie Williams. It was years ago. She still had her apron on, the poor thing. Plop she went. If you ask me, I think it's a bad-luck house."

NONE OF them knew that the cook they were talking about who had jumped out the window of the Tavistock mansion during Tootie Scott-Miller's lunch party twenty-seven years earlier was Addison Kent's mother. Addison, who was once called

Artie, could listen to such a story about his mother and not react. He had been not quite a year old when his mother, who was still suffering from postpartum depression, jumped out the sixth-floor window after being rebuked by Tootie Scott-Miller for a disappointing soufflé. An aunt, his mother's unmarried sister, who was the cook for Miss Winifred Staunton, the richest lady in Grosse Pointe, Michigan, took him in and raised him in the servants' quarters of the vast Tudor mansion where she worked. As the years passed, the rich lady, now confined to a wheelchair and lonely, began to take an interest in the handsome boy. It was she who thought Addison would be a more suitable first name than Artie. She liked to have him dine with her. By the time he was ten, Addison knew how to remove the doily and finger bowl from the dessert plate and place them ahead to the left before serving himself the ice cream in a silver bowl held by his aunt Agnes, the cook. By the time he was twelve, he could look at a diamond and tell how many carats it was. Miss Staunton, who adored him and might have left him everything, gave him a jeweler's loupe as a stocking present that Christmas. He often said, when asked about his history, "I was brought up by a Miss Winifred Staunton in Grosse Pointe, Michigan. We had a summerhouse in Harbor Springs."

What was virtually unknown in Addison Kent's history was that Miss Winifred Staunton, the richest woman in Grosse Pointe, ultimately felt betrayed by Addison Kent, whom she had championed, whom she had intended to send to Brown University in Providence, Rhode Island, until a sapphire ring, the disappearance of which had caused great consternation in the household, was discovered in a rolled-up pair of socks in his bureau drawer. There were no scenes, no police, no punishment. He was simply sent on his way to whatever life held for him. His mortified aunt Agnes offered to resign her post, but Miss Staunton did not accept her resignation. They never mentioned

Addison Kent's name again, until they read about him in the papers years later, where he was pictured in the society pages on the arm of Adele Harcourt.

Miss Staunton, who was very old by then, looked at Agnes, who was still her cook, and Agnes, holding a silver tray with Miss Staunton's morning hot water and lemon juice, looked back at Miss Staunton. "It's quite Dickensian in its own way," Miss Staunton said to Agnes as they peered down at the photograph. "Quite what, ma'am?" Agnes inquired. Miss Staunton then folded the paper, said it didn't matter anyhow, and put it aside.

AFTER THE fig mousse, which was Adele Harcourt's favorite dessert, they continued to sit in the little dining room for their demitasse.

"I think moving to the living room sort of breaks up the mood, don't you?" asked Lil.

Adele started to get up from the table.

"Where are you going, Adele?" asked Lil, leaning in. "Oh, the fig mousse. I know it's your favorite. That's why Gert insisted on serving it, although she thinks it goes better with dinner than with lunch. Shall I ring for Gert? She'd be so thrilled."

"No, I'll go in the kitchen," said Adele.

"You've always been the most thoughtful person, Adele. Mother used to say that about you. Addison, will you please help Adele into the kitchen?"

"It was delicious, divine, better than ever, Gert," said Adele.

That night Addison headed off to a dinner party. "To say Gert was ecstatic at Adele's praise would be the understatement of the year," he told the other guests. He didn't bother saying that it was during the moment that he let go of Adele's arm so that he too could shake hands with the cook that everything happened.

As Adele turned to reenter the dining room for the champagne toast to the new apartment, she tripped on the linoleum floor that had become slippery from overuse over the years by prior old tenants of the apartment and broke her hip.

"Such screams as you've never heard," continued Addison, who was the center of attention. "Adele was gallant, simply gallant. Lil, on the other hand, was crying and wringing her hands, saying she'd been meaning to have the linoleum changed ever since she moved into the apartment."

WHEN LIL returned from the hospital, after having ridden in the ambulance with Adele and Addison, whom she didn't like, Gert, who had brought her a cup of tea, said to her, "It was Mr. Kent. He let go of Mrs. Harcourt's arm to shake hands with me, copying the way Mrs. Harcourt did, and that's when she fell, when he let go of her."

"I've been meaning to change that linoleum ever since I moved into this damn apartment, ever since that Guatemalan maid slipped, do you remember, Gert? The one who recently worked for poor Winkie."

"Immaculata," said Gert.

"What?"

"Immaculata. That was the Guatemalan maid's name."

"She couldn't sue, thank God. Wasn't she an illegal alien?"

"I don't know, Missus." said Gert.

"They all are these days."

"Missus, I know this isn't a very convenient time, but there's something I have to talk to you about," said Gert.

A nervous expression passed quickly across Lil's face, as though she knew what Gert was going to ask and she dreaded the answer she knew she had to give. She was careful not to betray herself to her cook.

"And there's something I have to talk to you about, Gert. About the trip to Ireland this year to see your niece. It's just not going to work out for me. Ever since Dodo, that ghastly step-mother of mine, got all the money that was supposed to come to me, and since young Laurance is keeping me on such a tight financial leash, I think we're going to have to put the trip off until next year. From now on, make it every other year rather than every year."

CHAPTER 8

IT WASN'T UNTIL THE BOARDS WERE REMOVED FROM THE windows of the old Tavistock mansion on East Seventy-eighth Street between Fifth Avenue and Madison Avenue and the limestone was washed for the first time in sixty years that people in the neighborhood began to notice that there was magnificence in the French château that they had walked by every day for years but overlooked in its neglected state. The original owners, back in the 1920s, were the Clarence Pierpont Tavistocks, who brought so much of the exquisite paneling in the library and dining room from Kingswood Castle in Wiltshire, as arranged and brokered for them by Lord Duveen, then in the twilight years of his famous career of providing art and sculpture from the great houses of England, France, Italy, and Spain for the new great houses of New York, Boston, and Newport. The house itself had been designed by Odgen Codman, a Bostonian architect and decorator not much remembered these days other than as the collaborator with Edith Wharton, whose novels dealt with the occupants of such grand houses, on her book on the art of decorating. The Clarence Pierpont Tavistocks never lived in the beautiful mansion they had so lovingly built and decorated. On the night before they were to move in, they were killed while returning from the opera in an automobile accident caused by their chauffeur, O'Connor, who ran a red light and crashed into a telephone pole on the corner of Park Avenue and East Seventy-eighth Street. O'Connor, who was drunk, served ten years.

On East Seventy-eighth Street, people were beginning to wonder *who* was spending the fortune that it must be taking to restore the house to its former grandeur. Even very rich people who never had to worry about money and could always have anything they wanted without thinking about cost couldn't stop discussing how much money someone was spending on the extensive renovations.

"I heard whoever bought it paid in excess of forty million dollars," said Christine Saunders, the famous television news star and interviewer, at one of Maisie Verdurin's dinner parties, honoring former president Bill Clinton. Maisie Verdurin, the most prominent real estate broker in the city and a hostess of note in the media society of New York, was rumored to have brokered the deal between client and estate, but Maisie, who was notoriously tight-lipped on pending deals, chose to remain mum on the subject.

"Come on, Maisie. Tell us who is spending all that money. I've never seen such beautiful front doors in my life. The bronze work is simply ravishing. If anyone knows, you know, Maisie. It's become the most discussed house in the city."

"I don't know any more about it than you do," Maisie replied, holding up her arms in mock innocence and enjoying being the center of conversation at her own dinner party, as the former president listened in amusement.

"What do you think, Mr. President?" asked Christine Saunders, turning to Mr. Clinton, who was seated prominently next to her. Gus Bailey, who mostly listened at dinner parties these days and seldom spoke up, admired the way Christine Saunders asked a teasing question of such a world-renowned figure.

"I haven't any idea," replied the president.

"Make a guess," insisted Christine.

"Someone getting out of prison maybe," the president observed, grinning.

Everyone laughed except Maisie. It was at that very moment that Maisie rose from her seat to give her charming toast to the president, although the hired waiters had not finished passing the crème brûlée or pouring the champagne. Gus, observing the moment from his end of the table, knew exactly who would shortly be getting out of federal prison in Las Vegas, Nevada, after having served seven years and paid fines of seven hundred million dollars, but he said nothing. He had stopped telling his stories at dinner parties, ever since he had been sued for slander for something he had said on Patience Longstreet's under-watted radio show.

"THERE'S THIS man in England I've been meaning to tell you about," Ruby said over the telephone to Elias when she told him she wouldn't be out to Las Vegas that weekend as she was going to England. "His name is Simon Cabot. He's very much a background figure. You wouldn't have read about him or seen his picture in the papers, which is the whole point of him.

"His speciality is people with tarnished reputations, like ours. Whenever one of the young English royals smokes pot or gets drunk or something, they call him in, and he deals with the media in the most ingenious ways."

"Why are we talking about a man named Simon Cabot, whom I've never heard of?" said Elias.

"He will be perfect for us," said Ruby. "He'll get us back where we were. Look what he did for Perla Zacharias at the murder trial in Biarritz. To the public, Perla came out smelling like a rose. The crowds cheered. The chief rabbi of France came to Biarritz as a witness. He arrived from Paris in Perla's plane.

That was all Simon Cabot's idea. Simon wouldn't let Perla use the Rolls-Royce to go from the hotel to court. It was his idea for her to arrive in an SUV, along with her staff all crowded in, like she was just real folks instead of the third richest woman in the world. He wouldn't let her wear any jewels, even gold jewelry, nothing except her wedding ring from Konstantin. It was Simon's idea that she wear that twenty-five-year-old Yves Saint Laurent pantsuit on the opening day of the trial, and she looked divine in it. Gus Bailey had a picture of her in it in his article in *Park Avenue*. Nasty as the article was, she still looked perfectly resplendent. Simon Cabot could do the same for you, Elias, when you get out of that dump. He'll turn the whole affair into something very positive. There will be an enormous amount of publicity, and he'll think of some wonderful thing that you can do for families of people in prisons, or something. He's brilliant, absolutely brilliant."

RUBY ASKED Martin, Claridge's famed hall porter, to arrange a discreet corner table in the reading room at Claridge's, out of sight of the fashionable lobby crowd, as both she and Simon Cabot, although not famous, were each recognizable faces to certain of the guests who frequented the hotel, and their meeting would certainly be commented upon and give rise to speculation that Elias Renthal was going to use Simon Cabot to help ease the way back into society after a long prison sentence. It was the sort of situation that Martin understood perfectly, and their tea meeting went unobserved.

"Perla spoke so highly of you, after the trial of her husband's alleged murderer in Biarritz," said Ruby. "She said you gave her such marvelous advice."

"Fascinating woman," said Simon. "Like someone in a novel." Simon was not one who talked about his clients.

"Yes, yes, she is fascinating," said Ruby. "Have you seen the villa in Biarritz? I'm sure you have. Most beautiful house I ever saw. And the French furniture! My God. Better than the furniture at Versailles."

"I have been to the villa in Biarritz, yes," said Simon.

"So awful, that terrible fire in Biarritz. Poor Konstantin dying like that. He didn't actually burn to death, you know, as people say. My husband always says that Konstantin was the finest banker of his day."

"It is my understanding that Mr. Zacharias was a fine man," said Simon.

"I'd hate to die like that, wouldn't you? Gasping for air. It was the smoke that killed him, and that poor Filipina nurse who died with him. She tried to escape from the safe room, did you know that? But Konstantin was overmedicated and paranoid that he was going to be murdered, and he hit her, the poor Filipina lady who has six children in New Jersey, to keep her from opening the door. There was a settlement, I hear."

Simon, who had heard all the versions of the murder, didn't reply. He didn't want Ruby Renthal, who talked too much, to say in conversation in New York, "Simon Cabot told me . . ."

"Perla told me at the funeral in Johannesburg that he was simply covered with soot. She said his face was entirely black. When the firemen finally got there two hours later, poor Konstantin was already dead. Is it true that the police gave the order to put the head guard in handcuffs, when he finally arrived with the only key to the villa after hearing about the fire on the radio?"

"I am unfamiliar with the moment-by-moment activities of that terrible night when Mr. Zacharias was asphyxiated," said Simon.

"Oh, yes, of course," replied Ruby, hoping she hadn't gone too far. "The whole thing is so sad. Is Perla in London?"

"She's at the house in Paris, I believe. She's being honored at the British embassy for her philanthropic work. She moves about. I could have my office check her whereabouts for you," said Simon.

"No, no. I'm going right back. I came only to see you, Mr. Cabot," said Ruby. "I'm flying back to New York tomorrow and then I'm going on to Las Vegas to see my darling husband. You'll like Elias so much when you finally meet him. He used to go shooting every year at Deeds Castle with the Duke of Chatfield, and he has so many friends here in London."

"Yes, yes. I wish you had let me know in advance that you were coming, especially as you came here primarily to see me," said Simon. He was clearly uncomfortable with the position he was in. "I was surprised to receive your call yesterday when you arrived in London. You see, I don't think it's going to work out for us, Mrs. Renthal."

"For heaven's sake why?" asked Ruby, openly shocked that he did not leap at the offer she had made. "We are prepared to meet your price, whatever it is. I know what Perla pays you."

"Believe me, Mrs. Renthal, it's not the money," said Simon Cabot. "I have other clients. Very well known people of high rank. Some royals even, on occasion. I've had to discuss the possibility of representing you with them. I'm afraid I must be blunt, Mrs. Renthal. They are not pleased that I should be representing someone who is in prison in the United States."

"What my husband is in a federal facility for is not even a crime in this country," said Ruby.

"Nonetheless, he is in a federal prison and has been for some years," said Simon.

"I see," said Ruby, clearly hurt by the rejection. She wondered if Perla Zacharias, who had told her somewhat reluctantly about Simon Cabot when Ruby had run into her after leaving a hair appointment at Bernardo's and congratulated her on the photos from after the trial that had accompanied Gus Bailey's article in *Park Avenue,* had not wanted a person with a criminal background on her publicist's client list. She remembered that Perla had not returned her first two calls and suddenly realized that if Perla had not happened to have picked up the telephone herself, something she rarely did, the third time she had called her, she might not have returned that call either.

"Perhaps after your husband has been released we could talk again, if you haven't made other arrangements," said Simon. He signaled to the waiter for a check.

"No, no, put it on my room, please," said Ruby to the waiter.

RUBY FLEW back to New York, feeling that she had failed in her mission. She felt that so many people had let her down since Elias went to prison. She remembered the night that Bunny and Chiquita Chatfield, who were visiting in New York, had given a little dinner in the back room of Swifty's for a select group of people during Elias's trial. Bunny stood and tapped his knife against his wineglass and said, "Ladies and gentlemen, if I could have your attention for a minute." Lord Chatfield was an imposing figure with a deep and resonant voice, and all conversation ceased as the guests turned to look at him. His famous title, with its imposing place in English history, never failed to dazzle his rich New York friends. "We all know what a difficult time this has been for our dear friend Elias Renthal and his simply super wife, the beautiful Ruby. The newspapers have been full of such terrible rot about Elias. We all know him to be one of New York's great citizens, and I wish all of you would rise and lift your glass to Elias and join me in wishing him the greatest luck in the days ahead."

Several people in the room, but not all, cried out, "Hear! Hear!" It was the deliberate silence of those who did not that Ruby remembered most.

Gus was at his country home in Prud'homme, Connecticut, working on his novel, *Infamous Lady,* for which he was being paid a million dollars, when the unexpected call came. He almost didn't answer, thinking it would be Beatrice Parsons, his editor, making her weekly phone call to see how the novel was coming along, wanting pages faxed to her. But he did answer.

"Hello?"

"Is that Augustus Bailey?" said a woman's voice.

"May I ask who is calling?"

"Of course, Mr. Bailey. This is Perla Zacharias calling from London."

Gus was stunned. The widow who was richer than the Queen of England was calling him in Prud'homme, Connecticut, from London. Her voice was deep. She had a slight foreign accent, though she spoke English fluently. There was a tone of recent-widow bereavement in her voice, even though a few years had passed since her husband's death.

"Yes, Mrs. Zacharias," he replied. He allowed no sound of surprise to appear in his voice that he should be receiving an international telephone call from her.

"We have a mutual friend in the former first lady," said Mrs. Zacharias.

Gus recognized the ploy of using an important name to establish an immediate intimacy. He had used it himself. "Oh, Nancy, you mean."

"Yes, Nancy. Have you seen her?"

"I haven't, no. I haven't been in Los Angeles for months, and she rarely travels these days," Gus replied.

"Such a marvelous wife she was to the president," said Mrs. Zacharias.

"Yes," replied Gus. He waited, making no attempt to fill in the dead air. He knew she wasn't calling him about the former first lady.

"I am leaving shortly for Paris, where I will be living while they rebuild the top two floors of the villa in Biarritz. Actually," she added, "we've met. That darling Winkie Williams introduced us once at the opera a few years back."

"I would have remembered that, Mrs. Zacharias," said Gus.

It was time for Perla to get around to the purpose of the call.

There was silence on the other end of the line for a few moments. Gus waited, patiently. Finally she began.

"It is my understanding that you are planning to write a novel about a notorious lady, who I assume is me," she said sternly. "It would seem to me that you have sufficiently covered the story of my late husband's death in *Park Avenue*. According to my count, you have written six very long articles on the case."

"That's *infamous* lady, not notorious. There is much that is unanswered," replied Gus cautiously.

"It is my understanding that you even interviewed my dental hygienist," said Perla.

"Your dental hygienist sought me out, not the other way around. I was unaware of her, and she had a very nice story to tell about you."

"I have never been interviewed. People have wanted to interview me over the years, or photograph the villa in Biarritz, things like that, for *Vogue* and *W,* but Konstantin was a very private person, and he never wanted any publicity."

"I am aware of that," said Gus.

"I very much admire you, Mr. Bailey," she said. "I have read your books and many of your interviews, and I have decided that I will allow you to interview me for your book. It is very important that you get the facts straight."

"My plan is to go to Biarritz and look at the villa where the fire was," said Gus.

"Come to Paris afterward. I'll be living at the Plaza Athénée."

THE NEXT morning, at the very same time that Perla Zacharias had called Gus the day before, the telephone rang at his house in Prud'homme. The call was from Paris. The man calling spoke English with such a strong French accent that he was difficult to understand. He was also extremely agitated. He identified himself as Pierre La Rouche. He was Perla Zacharias's lawyer. He was infuriated that an arrangement for an interview had been made without his knowledge. Gus had seen him at the trial in Biarritz, and afterward in Johannesburg, talking outside the synagogue following Konstantin Zacharias's funeral. He had also spotted him on several other occasions when the nurse, Floyd McArthur, who had taken care of Konstantin because he suffered from a disorder of the nervous system, had been arrested and sentenced to ten years in prison for the crime.

Gus remembered Pierre as a dramatic looking fellow with a superior attitude and slicked-back gray hair who chain-smoked through a long tortoiseshell cigarette holder. Gus remembered disliking him.

"I am having a very difficult time understanding your English, Mr. La Rouche," said Gus. "Perhaps if you would eliminate the anger in your voice, it would be easier for me to understand."

"Madame Zacharias cannot have an interview. It is impossible. How dare such a thing be discussed without consulting me?"

"Calm down. You have the dynamic wrong here. Mrs. Zacharias, or *Madame* Zacharias, called me at my unlisted number in Connecticut that you are now calling. I did not call Mrs. Zacharias. I was greatly surprised to hear from the woman. It seems to me that if you're going to scream at somebody, you should scream at her. But you probably can't afford to do that because she's so rich and paying you a fortune, so you call and blow off steam to me. Get over it."

"What sort of things do you intend to ask her?" The tone of La Rouche's voice had changed considerably.

"About the fire. Where she was. How she found out the villa was burning. If she called Konstantin in the bathroom from her cell phone. Why the police kept the fire department from entering the apartment for two hours. Things like that."

"But that's exactly what she won't talk about. That was all dealt with at the trial," said La Rouche.

"Even you know that it wasn't dealt with sufficiently," replied Gus.

"There are other things to talk about. Her philanthropic works, for instance. Are you aware that the French government is presenting her with its highest civilian medal of honor for her philanthropic work for the poor children of Paris!"

"I'm not interested in writing about her philanthropic works, or her eighteenth-century French furniture or her Fabergé egg collection or her jeweled salt and pepper shakers. I repeat, she called me. I didn't call her."

"I have a solution," La Rouche replied quickly. "Why don't you e-mail me specific questions you are planning to ask Madame Zacharias. I will decide what you can and what you cannot ask, and I will be present during the interview."

"Good-bye," said Gus. He hung up.

CHAPTER 9

FOR REASONS INCOMPREHENSIBLE TO MOST OF HER friends, Lil insisted on having regularly scheduled luncheon engagements with her stepmother, Dodo Van Degan, whom she was known to loathe and about whom she spoke badly behind her back. She would tell Dodo how important it was for the family that they at least give the appearance of unity. Lil also was heeding the advice of her nephew, young Laurance, who pointed out that it would be bad for his business if there was a public rift with Dodo. After all, he noted, she was the richest one in the family.

From the beginning, the hatred these two women felt for each other hung between them as they dined at Swifty's. Every word and gesture, no matter how pleasant on the surface, was laced with contempt.

"The pea soup is simply delish," said Lil to Dodo during one of their earliest attempts at preserving the Van Degan unified front.

"I hate pea soup," said Dodo, disinterestedly. Raising her finger to get the waiter's attention, she said, "Octavio, I'll have a gin martini straight up, with an olive, and the chef's salad."

"Those are my mother's pearls you're wearing," said Lil.

"Your father, my husband, gave them to me on my last birthday before he died," replied Dodo, fingering her pearls. "He said he liked to look at them on my neck, that they were being wasted in that black velvet box."

"My father had no right to give my mother's pearls to you. If he wanted you to have pearls, he should have taken you to Mr. Platt at Tiffany's. Mr. Platt knows more about pearls than anyone in New York. Mother always wanted me to have those, and my father knew it. My father was growing senile, and you took advantage of him."

Dodo put her hands behind her neck and unscrewed the diamond clip of the pearl necklace. Before Lil could stop her, she dropped the necklace in her stepdaughter's "delish" pea soup.

"You awful woman! Look what you've done!" cried Lil in horror. "You've dropped Mother's pearls in my pea soup. I'm sure they're simply ruined."

"Don't be silly. Good for the sheen, I hear," replied Dodo, a wide grin stretched across her face.

As TIME went on, however, the two women began to grow more accustomed to each other, and the results of their luncheons became less disastrous. On their most recent date, Lil was sitting at her regular corner table in the back room of Swifty's with Dodo across from her.

"Did I tell you I had the loveliest letter from Winkie Williams?" she said, before taking a dainty spoonful of her French onion soup. After the incident with her mother's pearls, she could no longer stomach the pea soup.

She continued, "It was as if he had sent it from heaven. It came with a very expensive and beautiful orchid plant, everything written and ordered the night before he died. I'm to be the executrix of his will. He said it would take my mind off my apartment, which of course you know I'm always complaining about. Good old Winkie. He always did everything right."

After a pause and another sip of the French onion, Lil shifted in her seat. These lunches had taught Dodo enough about her stepdaughter's gestures to signal to her that whatever was coming was the topic Lil Altemus was really dying to talk about.

Lil said, in a low voice, "Everyone's acting strange lately, I don't know why. Something astrological, probably. Mercury in retrograde, whatever that means. Like Gert, you know, my cook. I don't know what's the matter with her. There was no rose on my breakfast tray again this morning. And she got huffy with me when I counted the change she brought back with her from buying the groceries at Grace's Marketplace."

"That's the same thing as accusing her of stealing, after she's put up with your crap for twenty-five years. She had every right to be huffy," said Dodo.

As always, Lil ignored what her stepmother said, especially when she used coarse language, which she knew Dodo did to rile her. "I suppose she could be upset with me because it's time for her to go on another trip to Ireland to visit that niece of hers. She's named after me, don't you love it? Miss Lillian Altemus Hoolihan of Roscommon, Ireland. I have to keep from laughing when Gert calls her that. These annual trips of hers to the old country are getting a little costly for me, so I suggested to her that she go over to Ireland every *other* year rather than every year."

"I told you to sell the pearls if you need more money," said Dodo.

"I just couldn't sell Mother's pearls. Addison Kent of Boothby's auction house looked at them and he said they were beautiful, and he could do very well with them at auction, but I just couldn't sell them. Not just so my cook can make her trips."

"No wonder she didn't put any roses on your breakfast tray," said Dodo.

"She'll get used to it," said Lil. "It's cutback time. It's as simple as that."

THE TRUTH was that Gert missed the old apartment on Fifth Avenue. The big kitchen. The maids. The butler. The dinners for twenty-four. That was what she had become accustomed to over the years. She liked having Adele Harcourt come into her kitchen to compliment her on her fig mousse. She especially liked it when Lil brought her into the dining room after a particularly delicious dinner to introduce her to the distinguished guests, who clapped for her and called her Gert. She wouldn't say such a thing to a single soul, but she knew that she had been the star society cook in New York, and she missed her importance. She was the one everyone wanted to sit next to on bingo nights at St. Ignatius Loyola church, on Park Avenue at Eighty-fourth Street, where she went to early Mass nearly every morning. "Jackie Kennedy's funeral was at St. Ignatius," she often said when she described her church to her relatives in Ireland. She was thinking about those Fifth Avenue days as she walked home from Grace's Marketplace, a fancy grocery store on Third Avenue and Seventy-first Street, carrying shopping bags of food back to the white-brick building on Sixty-sixth Street between Third and Second Avenues. She hated the building. She hated the apartment. She hated the stove in the kitchen. She was used to bigger and better. She hated the old linoleum on the kitchen floor. She particularly hated her room, which was half the size of her room on Fifth Avenue. But she would never say a word. She knew that Missus, as she called Lil Altemus, was having money troubles. She was a daily listener to Lil's diatribes against her nephew, Laurance Van Degan Jr., who had put her on a strict budget to live, and her stepmother, Dodo Van Degan, who had inherited all the money that Lil had thought she was going to inherit.

A dark green chauffeured Mercedes limousine pulled up by Gert as she was walking slowly down Third Avenue, the plastic grocery bags from Grace's Marketplace weighing her down. A darkened window slowly descended.

"Gert?" a woman's voice called out. "It is Gert, isn't it? I thought I recognized you."

"Yes, ma'am," Gert replied, trying to recognize the woman who was speaking to her.

The woman removed her dark glasses. "You don't remember me, Gert. I'm Ruby Renthal. Mrs. Elias Renthal. My husband and I used to go to Mrs. Altemus's dinners from time to time several years ago."

Exactly once, thought Gert. She had the same opinion of the Renthals that Mrs. Altemus had. She answered, "Yes, ma'am, I remember. Wasn't it in your house that Mrs. Altemus's father, Ormond Van Degan, died on the pool table during a party?"

"Oh, I wish you hadn't remembered that unhappy experience," said Ruby.

"Mrs. Altemus still talks about it from time to time," said Gert.

"You're still with Mrs. Altemus, aren't you?"

"Yes, ma'am."

"I hear she moved to that building they call God's Waiting Room on Sixty-sixth Street," said Ruby.

"It's a very nice apartment, ma'am," said Gert. "The other was getting too big for her, especially after the hip replacement. She had a hard time going up those winding stairs."

"Say, Gert. Here's my card, with all the private numbers here in the city, in the country, and at the house in St. Bart's. Actually, I'm staying at the Rhinelander Hotel until my new house is finished. You shouldn't be carrying all those heavy grocery bags at your age. In my house, the chauffeur would do that. I'd save you for the parties I'm planning when my husband is able to return to New York. Whatever you're earning at Mrs. Altemus's, I'd go half again higher for the first six months and half again higher six months later. That would be double."

"I'm very happy where I am, Mrs. Renthal," said Gert. "I've been with Mrs. Altemus for almost twenty-six years."

"Lil is *such* a marvelous woman. I so admire your kind of loyalty," said Ruby.

"Thank you, Mrs. Renthal."

"In my new house on East Seventy-eighth Street, the cook's room has its own sitting room, and, of course, you could use my husband's plane when you go back to Ireland to visit your family. Elias always has business in London, and he could just drop you in Dublin on the way."

"Oh, my god," said Gert, as she remembered something she had forgotten to do.

"What's the matter?" asked Ruby.

"Nothing really, ma'am. It's just that I forgot to stop at Clyde's pharmacy to pick up a special order for Missus from England. I have to go back uptown," said Gert.

"You'll do no such thing, Gert. You get right in this car. Jacques will drop me off at the hairdresser and then he'll take you up to Clyde's pharmacy for Lil's order, wait for you, and drive you back to Sixty-sixth Street, won't you, Jacques."

AT THE Wednesday night Sodality of Mary bingo game at St. Ignatius Loyola church, Gert Hoolihan, Lil Altemus's cook, sat next to her best friend, Rosemary Quinn, who was Kay Kay Somerset's personal maid. Gert and Rosemary had known each other since they went to Our Lady of Sorrows girls' school in

Roscommon, Ireland, when they were ten. They had come to the United States at the same time nearly thirty years earlier. Between them, they knew all the stories of all the people who came to the two houses where they were in service. Gert always took a cake or a pie or cookies she had baked to the Sodality meetings. She was considered by the ladies of the Sodality of Mary to be the luckiest bingo player of the group. She and Rosemary could play and talk at the same time.

"Do you remember a woman who used to be around New York named Ruby Renthal?" asked Gert as she put a chip on G5.

"The one whose husband went to prison?" replied Rosemary.

"Her."

"What about her?"

Gert looked around before she answered to be sure Mae Toomey, on her other side, who worked for young Laurance Van Degan, Lil Altemus's nephew, wasn't listening. "She offered me a job for when Mr. Renthal gets out of prison," she said in a low voice.

"I don't believe it," gasped Rosemary. "She was a pushy one, as I remember, or at least that was what Mrs. Somerset used to say about her."

"I was walking back to the new apartment with the groceries from Grace's Marketplace, and she pulls up in her chauffeur-driven Mercedes limousine and rolls down the window and speaks to me," said Gert.

"Is she still pretty?" asked Rosemary. "Mrs. Somerset used to say she was pretty in a cheap sort of way."

"I couldn't tell, really. She was wearing huge dark glasses, like Jackie Kennedy used to wear," said Gert. "She had one of those big silk scarves from Hermès over her head tied under her chin. She looked glamorous, I'll say that, like a movie star almost, like Faye Converse used to look, but I couldn't really see her face."

"Did she talk money?" asked Rosemary.

Gert leaned forward and talked directly into Rosemary's ear. "Double what I make with Missus. Great big kitchen again. My own bedroom and little sitting room, and several trips a year to Ireland on Mr. Renthal's private plane when he goes to London on business."

"Dear God, Gert. This is like manna from heaven. What are you going to do?" asked Rosemary.

Gert, bewildered, placed her chip on B8. "Oh, I couldn't leave Missus. I just couldn't, not after all these years. I'm the only one she can talk to about Hubie."

"The one who died of AIDS who had the Puerto Rican boy-friend?" asked Rosemary.

"She still won't admit it. So I go along with the Epstein-Barr talk."

"Still, Gert, that's an awful lot of money and an awful lot of perks The Convict's Wife is offering you," said Rosemary. "Chances like that—double the salary, private jet free to Ireland—don't come around often, probably never again. Think of it that way."

They stared at each other. "Look, you won the bingo, Gert."

"She always wins," said Mae Toomey.

CHAPTER 10

"IS *PARK AVENUE* PAYING FOR YOUR CASE?" ASKED Christine Saunders, who was often referred to in magazine articles as the first lady of television. Photographs of Princess Diana, President and Mrs. Obama, and Adele Harcourt, among others of equal rank, stood in silver frames on a side table. Christine was on intimate terms with world leaders, all the living American presidents, and several of the leading ladies in New York society, who welcomed her with open arms. She entertained frequently at elegant dinner parties with very important people and fascinating conversation in her Park Avenue apartment, which had been done up by Mario Buatta. She and Gus were New York friends. They knew a lot of the same people. They went to a lot of the same parties.

"It's a moot point," replied Gus. "Stokes said he had spoken with Hy Vietor in Vienna that morning I met with him at his office and yes they would pay, but it's never been mentioned again; even when I asked about it I was ignored, and there's nothing official. There's no record of what he said to me. If Stokes were to leave *Park Avenue* to become the head of a studio in Hollywood, as has been hinted in Toby Tilden's column, there's nothing on paper. I'm beginning to get the hint that the silence I receive when I inquire about such matters means that the idea has been dropped and they are trying to avoid an awkward situation. I'm afraid I'm on my own now. "

"That's a lot of money for you to be shelling out every month, isn't it?" She was lighting candles on her round dining room table, which was set for sixteen.

"It's dizzying. I have money nightmares."

"Do you at least like your lawyer?"

"Another moot point."

"You've got to like your lawyer, Gus," said Christine.

"It isn't that I dislike her. She's supposed to be brilliant, and I believe that. One of *Park Avenue*'s lawyers assigned me to her. I never even had a meeting with her first. She doesn't live in New York, which is a pain in the ass. I've only seen her face-to-face once."

"Oh, no, no, no, Gus," said Christine, turning from the candles to look at him. "You can't have a lawyer who lives in another city. I don't care how good she is. You need somebody who's always there for you. Look at you. You're a wreck. You have to have ready access to your lawyer."

"As I was expecting *Park Avenue* to pay for her, I didn't object sufficiently at the time," said Gus.

"I may have someone in mind," Christine continued. "His name is Peter Lombardo, he lives in New York, and he's a tough one. He's perfect to go up against Win Burch, who I hear is terrifying. I will get in touch with Peter Lombardo for you."

Gus, who trusted his friend's instincts, breathed a small sigh of relief.

LATELY, RUBY Renthal had started tipping the three telephone operators at the Rhinelander a hundred dollars a week apiece to monitor all her calls before the caller was put through to her suite. After the news appeared in the *Wall Street Journal* and the *Financial Times* that Elias was soon to be released from the Las Vegas prison, reporters had started to call. Marietta Elgin from the *Times* was particularly insistent, leaving message after message requesting an interview. Ruby had no intention of speaking to any reporter until she had Simon Cabot on board, which she believed she would eventually accomplish, but she most certainly didn't want to be caught on the phone when Marietta Elgin called. She had read Marietta Elgin's piece on Gus Bailey. She had enjoyed the article, "mean though it was," because her husband so disliked Gus, but she knew that she was as vulnerable as Gus had been when Marietta Elgin had caught him at his house in Connecticut.

Gert waited until Lil Altemus left for her lunch date with Kay Kay Somerset at Swifty's before she dialed the Rhinelander Hotel and asked to speak to Mrs. Elias Renthal. Candelaria Lopez was the telephone operator on duty. She was a great admirer of Ruby Renthal's and was very protective of her. "She tips good, she speaks to all the help, and she looks like a movie star," Candelaria said about her.

"May I have your name please?" she asked.

"Gert."

"Gert what?"

"Mrs. Renthal will know. Tell her it's Mrs. Altemus's cook, Gert."

"Lil Altemus? Who's always in Dolores De Longpre's column?"

"Her."

"Hold on just a moment." She dialed Ruby's suite.

"Yes?" answered Ruby.

"Lil Altemus's cook, Gert, is on the phone. Do you want to speak to her or shall I take a message?"

"Thank you, Candelaria. I'll speak to Gert."

"Mrs. Renthal?"

"Hello, Gert. How lovely to hear from you."

"Ma'am, I wanted to know if I could make an appointment to come and see you about what we talked about on Third Avenue that day."

"Of course, Gert."

"My day off is on Thursday. I could come on Thursday afternoon."

"Come at three, here at the hotel. Just go to the front desk and ask them to ring me."

"I just want to check one thing."

"What's that?"

"You did say I could go over to Ireland on your husband's jet, didn't you?"

WHEN GERT carried in Lil Altemus's breakfast tray, her hands were shaking and the dishes were rattling slightly as she placed the tray in front of Lil and then started arranging the morning newspapers in the order of Mrs. Altemus's preference. Lil turned immediately to the obituary page of the *New York Times,* which was the first thing she read each morning.

"No one interesting died today," she said in a disappointed voice, tossing the paper aside. "But people have been dropping like flies in my circle. Poor Sass Buffington. We'll all miss Sass, I can tell you that. And darling Pat. And Winkie, to say nothing of my dear friend Antonia von Rautbord, after twenty-seven years in a coma. I must send flowers to her children. Oh, good, Gert. You remembered the rose. It makes the breakfast tray so much prettier, and you've sometimes been forgetting it of late. And my favorite china coffee cup, the Spode. So cheery in the morning. That came from Mother's house in Northeast Harbor, as you well remember. Help me fluff up these pillows, will you?"

she said, leaning forward in her bed so that Gert could fluff up the pillows behind her. "That's perfect. Thank you, Gert. Do you have *all* the papers? Yes, of course you do. Open up to that awful Toby Tilden's column in the *Post,* which I'll read next. I saw him at Kenneth's the other day. I was having my manicure and Mr. Tilden was having his hair highlighted. Don't you love it? I can't wait to tell that to Gus Bailey. What's the matter with you this morning, Gert? You seem a bundle of nerves. Is there bad news from your niece in Ireland?"

Gert paused nervously, took a deep breath, and looked her employer in the eyes. "Missus, you don't know how hard this is for me to say, after you've been kind to me for so many years," said Gert. "But it's time for me to say good-bye. I have to move on."

"What in the world are you talking about at this hour of the morning?" asked Lil. "Look, there's a chip in this coffee cup. You must have hit the faucet when you were washing it. I can't believe what you're saying to me. Are you thinking of going back to Ireland to live? I know Ireland's doing awfully well these days economically, although that's about to change, my nephew tells me. But you'd miss New York after all these years you've lived here, Gert. You'd miss all your friends in the Sodality of Mary at St. Ignatius Loyola on bingo nights. Hand me the *Post,* will you, Gert?"

"No, ma'am. I'm not planning on moving back to Ireland," said Gert, still shaking. "I've been offered another position. It's something I just can't turn down."

"Is it because I said I could only afford the trip every other year? How silly that was of me to say that about every other year. Of course you can go to Ireland to visit your divine niece. Lillian must be quite the colleen by now. It was so sweet when your sister, bless her heart, named her after me, of all people. I only said that about every other year because my nephew has clipped my wings so, but I know how important that trip to Ireland is to you."

Gert had planned her resignation speech in front of the mirror in her little room off the kitchen, and she continued talking. "It's taken me some time to come to this decision, Missus. The only person I confided in was Rosemary, who's been my best friend all my life, who works for Mrs. Somerset, as you know. I sat with her at the Sodality of Mary bingo night last Wednesday, when you were having dinner at Swifty's with Mrs. Somerset. I told her I was going to turn the offer down. Rosemary said I should give it some thought because I may never get an offer like this again."

Lil started to cry. "But, Gert, you're the only person I can talk to about Hubie. You're the only one who doesn't correct me when I say he died of Epstein-Barr." She was sobbing. "Get me the Kleenex, please. Thank you. Gert, you're all I have left of my old life."

Gert, crying, said, "Don't make it harder on me than it already is. I'll stay with you until I break in someone new. I'd never leave you in the lurch without training a replacement. There's a young girl I met at the Sodality of Mary, Moira Shea her name is. She might be perfect. I'll try her out. I have plenty of time because I don't actually move in until the new house on East Seventy-eighth Street is finished, and I won't start cooking for her until her husband gets out of prison."

"Prison!" screamed Lil. "Her husband's in prison?"

"It's not exactly a prison-prison, Missus. They call it a facility," said Gert.

Lil's face hardened as it dawned on her who Gert would be working for. She had heard recently about the Elias Renthals' purchase of the Tavistock mansion.

"Who *are* these people who are stealing you from me?" she asked, though she knew full well.

There was a long pause before Gert answered. "Mrs. Elias Renthal, Missus," she replied.

"Ruby Renthal? You are leaving me after more than twenty-five years to go to work for Elias and Ruby Renthal? My father *died* at their butterfly ball and Elias Renthal put his body on the pool table and locked the door so it wouldn't ruin their party. So that's where you're going? GET OUT! NOW! Get out of my house. I don't want you here under my roof one more minute."

CHAPTER 11

DURING THE TIME THAT THE TAVISTOCK MAN-
sion on East Seventy-eighth Street was being restored
to Belle Époque perfection, both outside and in, with
craftsmen and artisans brought from Paris and Rome, Ruby
Renthal lived quietly in a suite at the Rhinelander Hotel. She
was not hiding, but she was not being seen out either. She had
grown very close to Maisie Verdurin, whose idea the house had
been. Mostly they talked on the telephone, but on rare occasions
they lunched together; however, they stayed away from Swifty's,
where they were likely to see people they knew.

"That was a very good idea you had of turning the old ballroom into a projection room. I told Elias the last time I visited
him, and he arranged for Max Luby, who does his investing for
him, as he's been barred for life from trading, to buy a ton of
Paramount and Disney stock. Sherry Lansing's sending me a
fantastic man who designs the best projection rooms of anyone
going. He designed Spielberg's. He designed Eisner's. He designed Tom Hanks's. It's going to have an Art Deco theme.
We're going to get all the latest pictures. We're going to be
able to see them a week before they're released to the theaters,
just like all those Hollywood moguls do. I want to start getting

to know some movie stars, to glam up the place when we have our movie nights and buffet dinners. Mix up the crowd a bit."

"I told you that in no time those same people who cut you dead after your fall are going to be banging on your new bronze doors to come to the movies and a buffet supper afterward," answered Maisie. "Old Alice Grenville was famous for her Sunday nights in the Waldorf Towers, where she moved after her son's murder. Everyone wanted to go. Claudette Colbert was a regular, just to give you an idea of the tone of the crowd, and so was Babe Paley."

"I'm going to do my version of that when Elias gets out," said Ruby. "Sunday night at the Renthals'. Dinner and a movie. I like the sound of it, don't you?"

"I can't talk you into coming to my dinner Thursday night, can I? I could use a beauty like you," asked Maisie.

"Thanks, Maisie, but I'm not going out anymore until Elias gets out of the facility," Ruby replied. She made no attempt to see old friends or meet new people. She wanted to reenter New York as the wife of Elias Renthal, and not a moment sooner. Ruby wanted to be half of a couple very much in the news. Elias would have served his time without complaint. He would be holding his head high. He would have made an enormous donation to the prison system of America. Most important, he would still be richer than most of the people he knew. Her days were occupied with meticulous preparations for the next phase of her life. "I lost my position in New York when my husband went to the facility. I don't like to be seen about. I went to that damn opening of the Costume Institute at the Met, and women I used to have lunch with at Swifty's looked at me and started whispering to each other. I'm not going to let that happen to me again."

"Please reconsider, Ruby," said Maisie. "There's a French couple I've just sold Cora Mandell's old maisonette on Fifth

Avenue to for them to use as a pied-à-terre when they're here in New York, and I'm having the dinner for them."

Ruby, laughing, was shaking her red hair in a gesture that meant, No, I'm not going out these days, when she heard Maisie say the words *Baron and Baroness de Liagra*. Ruby stopped her gesture. Her face turned bright red. She turned away.

"Oh, my god," said Maisie. "I totally forgot. Didn't you have an affair with him years ago, after you divorced Elias and before you remarried him? I never put that together."

"It was absolutely untrue that Baron de Liagra and I were having a romance. I don't know who started that story. It could have been Toby Tilden, for all I know, or Dolores De Longpre, or it could have been in *W,* or in 'Page Six,' I don't know, but it wasn't true. Poor Elias, he even heard it in the facility."

"You must have met the baron at least," said Maisie. "There was an awful lot of talk about you and him."

"Yes, I met him," conceded Ruby. "Yes, I had an affair with him that didn't end well. I never met the baroness." She didn't tell Maisie that one of the great embarrassments of her life was that she had behaved in such a trashy fashion when the baron had broken off with her. "Elias once told me he heard from Max Luby that the baroness was a dyke."

"I don't know anything about that," said Maisie. "I'm only the real estate lady. She's the chicest thing I ever saw, I'll tell you that, and those wonderful French looks. If there were ever a movie about her, Jeanne Moreau would have been perfect thirty years ago."

"I'll come," said Ruby. "Will you seat me in the back room next to someone friendly and ask Dolores De Longpre *not* to list my name in her column? It drives Elias crazy when he reads my name in the columns."

"You can have either Jamesey Crocus or Addison Kent. I have Mayor Bloomberg on one side of the baroness, and I need a camp on the other side to make her laugh, so take your choice, Jamesey Crocus or Addison."

"I'll take Jamesey. You take Addison. Jamesey never stopped being nice to me when other people did, after our public embarrassment," said Ruby.

MAISIE ALWAYS had sixty for dinner. Tables were set up in the living room, dining room, and library as the guests had cocktails. Maisie then expertly guided her guests to the right room after the tables were set up. The most famous people were seated in the living room. Christine Saunders, the television news star, and Dolores De Longpre, the society columnist, were always seated at the number one table. The dining room had the second echelon of guests. The wives or husbands who were considered less interesting than their mates were in the library. There had been a last-minute to-do when Baron de Liagra, who would have been the guest of honor, and who would have been seated to Maisie's right, with Dolores De Longpre on the other side, backed out suddenly, explaining, falsely, that he had eaten a bad oyster at lunch and had been "sick-sick-sick" for the entire afternoon, as he said over the telephone in his charming French manner. The truth was that he had heard from Frieda, his wife's manicurist, that she had to do Mrs. Elias Renthal's nails after she finished the baroness's nails, as Mrs. Renthal was making a rare New York appearance that evening at Maisie Verdurin's party. Henri de Liagra, who considered himself a dashing figure, having had a succession of beautiful mistresses, had never forgotten that the very same Mrs. Elias Renthal had once criticized the size of his penis and told him he was a lousy fuck, which were her words, not his. He feigned illness to Charlotte when she returned from the hairdresser downstairs in the Rhinelander

Hotel, where they were staying, and insisted that she go on alone to Maisie Verdurin's party.

The guests were to come eight o'clock. Forty-five minutes were allotted for cocktails, and they were asked to sit down to dinner at 8:45. Baroness de Liagra stood next to Maisie inside the entrance to the living room. She was gracious and charming to each person she met. "I simply adored your interview with President and Mrs. Obama. He is such an elegant man," she said to Christine Saunders. "You like my dress? Oh, *merci*. It's Valentino. He dresses me totally," she said to Pauline Mendelson, who was visiting from Los Angeles. "We'll probably be spending three months a year here. Henri's bank bought Konstantin Zacharias's bank after the murder and is opening a branch here in New York," she said to Percy Webb.

Ruby arrived five minutes before the guests sat down. She had heard from Frieda, the manicurist, that the baron had eaten a bad oyster and wouldn't be attending. She chose to remain a background figure. She had dressed simply. "Oh, there you are at last," said Maisie to Ruby. "I thought you were backing out on me. This is Charlotte de Liagra. Her husband *has* backed out on me."

"My poor darling husband. I'm always saying to him, 'Don't eat shellfish, Henri.' Now look what's happened. My dear Mrs. Renthal, he was green, simply green. He swallowed a bad oyster at lunch at the French consulate." The baroness looked carefully at Ruby. "What wonderful red hair you have," she said.

"Thank you," said Ruby, touched by the unexpected compliment. Having heard Baron de Liagra's wife referred to as a dyke by several people, including her own husband from his prison cell in Las Vegas, Nevada, she had imagined her to have a very different look than that of the stylish and aristocratic woman who was standing in front of her. Her clothes were perfection. Dolores De Longpre would write in her society column the next day about Maisie Verdurin's party that Baroness de Liagra, visiting from Paris, was by far the best-dressed woman at the party. In time, Ruby would hear that in society she was called Charlotte and described as the daughter of a noble family. In certain circles, she was called Uncle Charlie.

Ruby watched the baroness stare at her in the way that men often stared at her. She liked it when men gave her that look. She noticed that Baron de Liagra's wife was wearing the same ruby bracelet he had given her as a kiss-off present when he had broken off their affair and that she had thrown at him when she had called him a lousy fuck. She realized she was not offended by the baroness's stare.

"Well, finally I am meeting the fascinating Mrs. Renthal," said Charlotte.

Ruby looked at her quickly to see if she was being sarcastic. "We hear about you in Paris, the glamorous Ruby Renthal flying out to Las Vegas on her husband's G Five Fifty for weekend visits in the penitentiary."

"But it's not a penitentiary. It's a facility," said Ruby quietly.

"Penitentiary sounds better," said the baroness. "I hope you don't misunderstand me, Mrs. Renthal, but there's something terribly glamorous about that to me. People say about you, 'Her husband's in the penitentiary.' It's far more distinctive than saying, 'Her husband's at Barclays or Deutsche Bank.'"

Ruby laughed. "That's a whole new way of looking at my situation. I can't wait to tell Elias when I go out to Las Vegas again next week."

"Of all these famous people Maisie has gathered here tonight for me to meet, it was you whose acquaintance I was most interested in making."

"Good heavens," said Ruby.

"But my tastes have always been different, as you've probably heard," said the baroness, arching an eyebrow.

Ruby didn't know how to answer her and remained silent. Undeterred, the baroness went on talking. "Isn't it marvelous the way Maisie handles all these people, moving them here, moving them there, while the waiters set up the tables. She's like a general. I hope you're seated at my table."

"I'm not. I'm in this little room here, and you'll be at Maisie's table. I'm sure you're seated next to Mayor Bloomberg. I'll be sneaking out early. I rarely go to parties anymore, Baroness," said Ruby. "I just came because of Maisie, who has been such a good friend to me."

"Charlotte is my name. I'll leave when you do," she said. "After all, I have a perfect excuse. A sick husband. I have a car and driver downstairs. I'd love to show you the new apartment. It's empty. Not a stick of furniture in it yet. We've just closed the deal with Maisie."

"But your husband's ill."

"Yes, so he'll be out of the way then. We're staying at the Rhinelander."

"I'm staying at the Rhinelander too," said Ruby, surprised her former lover had been living in the same building she had.

"I'll come to you then, if it will make you more comfortable. Expect a knock on your door." Her look lingered and Ruby allowed it to linger. Then they each turned and went to their own tables.

"I ADORED the mayor. He couldn't be nicer, and he made me feel so welcome in New York, although it drove me crazy that he wouldn't let me smoke. And I thought his girlfriend was very nice and very smart. I like it that the mayor of New York City lives with a beautiful woman who is not his wife. It's so French. Everyone at my table was talking about Mrs. Zacharias, who is giving so much money to charity. I didn't say a word against the woman, although I could have. Henri, my husband, simply won't see her in Paris, although she keeps inviting us. He was a business friend of Konstantin's. He says there's something wrong with the story. But I stayed mum at the table. Just listened. Such a nice view of the park from your suite here, Mrs. Renthal," said the baroness, pouring champagne into glasses. As she handed one glass to Ruby, she leaned over and kissed her on the mouth. Ruby did not resist, nor did she participate.

"You bring out the Sapphic desires in me, as Gertrude Stein used to say to Alice B. Toklas," whispered the baroness.

"Nobody ever said that to me before," said Ruby, who couldn't help but feel a little curious and a little turned on.

"Are you telling me that a beautiful woman like you has never done it with another woman?" asked the baroness.

"Yes. I mean no. I have never done it with another woman," said Ruby.

"Not even once to have had the experience?"

"No. I've just never gone in for that dyke thing. I don't have any objections, or anything like that. It's just not my scene. I love men, it's as simple as that."

"You don't have to do a thing," said the baroness. "I'll do everything. You just lie back."

"I have to get a little drunker first. Pour me some more champagne," said Ruby. She didn't know if it was the woman or the title that she was giving in to.

"Would you like to smoke a joint, as they say here in New York? My maid, Francine, rolls the most perfect joints," said the baroness, pulling out a joint from a gold cigarette case she had fished out of her evening bag and lighting it. "I was simply terrified going through Customs, but, as you must have learned yourself by now, Mrs. Renthal, attitude is everything. And of course, it helps being with Henri. My husband gives off the appearance of being an ambassador, or some sort of diplomat, instead of just another baron visiting from Paris. This is awfully good pot. Francine gets it for me from a man she knows in Alsace-Lorraine. Oh. I already feel a buzz. Here, your turn."

"I haven't smoked a joint in years," said Ruby. "Sure, I'll smoke one. A couple of tokes and you can go to town down there."

"Music to my ears, Mrs. Renthal. I simply adore red pubic hair," said the baroness. "You almost never see it." She pulled off her ten-thousand-dollar Valentino dress and threw it on the floor. She helped Ruby take off her dress and pull down her panties. She took her position to perform the act, rubbing her face into Ruby's private hair. "Talk dirty, Ruby."

"I always heard that nobody can eat a pussy like another woman," said Ruby, getting into it. She sank into the bed, letting the marijuana flood her head and the pleasure from what the baroness was doing between her legs make her body tingle. The combination was wonderful. "That's really nice what you're doing down there, Baroness. Give me directions. Tell me what to do. . . . Sure, of course I'll sit on your face."

"THAT WAS great, but no seconds," said Ruby, lying back after they had each come to completion. "I tried it. I enjoyed it, but it's not my natural inclination, even though I came three times in twenty minutes."

The baroness roared with laughter. "I couldn't talk you into doing a three-way with my husband? He's very good-looking, and he loves watching two women making love."

"No," said Ruby, suppressing a shudder at the memory of the baron. "I know that lying here nude and stoned is not the best place to have you believe this, but I'm going to play dutiful wife when Elias gets out of prison."

"How middle class," said the baroness, joking.

"At least that's a step up from being called trashy, which is how some people in this town refer to me," replied Ruby.

"You're adorable, Ruby. Can I give you a present?"

"I love presents," said Ruby.

The baroness got up from the bed, still naked, and went to her evening bag on the dressing table. When she returned, she handed Ruby the ruby bracelet.

"Oh, I can't accept this," said Ruby, blanching a bit as she recognized it as the bracelet the baron had given her and that she had thrown back at him in his secret apartment on the Rue du Bac years earlier.

"Yes, you can, Ruby. I don't know why, but I feel it belongs to you because of your name. Think of it as a remembrance of a unique experience."

Ruby put it on and admired it on her wrist. "I've always wanted a ruby bracelet. Just rubies. Not rubies and diamonds. Just rubies. Thank you. It's beautiful."

"May I give you a kiss good-bye?" asked the baroness.

"Of course," said Ruby. As they kissed, she said, "Is that my pussy I taste on your tongue?"

The baroness screamed with laughter.

"You probably think I'm cheap," said Ruby.

"It can't get too cheap for me," replied the baroness. "Is it all right if I call you, Ruby?"

DRESSED AGAIN in her Valentino gown and ready to go back to her own suite in the Rhinelander, Charlotte de Liagra waved good-bye from the door.

"One thing before you go," called out Ruby. "I have something I have to confess to you. After what's happened between us, I would feel very shabby if you left here without knowing."

"Yes, I know. You had an affair with my husband. He always tells me after his little flings are over," said the baroness.

"You mean, you're not angry with me?"

"Darling, it's me, remember? You recognized the ruby bracelet right away, didn't you?"

"Of course, but I kind of feel like a hooker taking it from you," said Ruby, looking at the bracelet once again. She noticed that one of the rubies was chipped. She thought, *Probably from when I threw it at Henri de Liagra at his love nest on the Rue du Bac in Paris.*

"We were meant to meet," Baroness de Liagra assured her.

"You're a good-looking woman, Baroness," said Ruby from her bed.

"You're not so bad yourself," replied the baroness. "Greatest tits I ever saw."

"They used to be even bigger when I had the implants, but I had them removed. We can't have sex in the facility, but Elias feels me up. He didn't like the implants, so I got rid of them."

"Smart husband you've got, Ruby. Will you have lunch with me at Swifty's the next time I come to New York?"

"Hell, yes," said Ruby. She got up out of bed and pulled on a dressing gown. "I just got an idea. Elias is getting out of prison in the next six months. Maisie Verdurin sold me a beautiful house on East Seventy-eighth Street, which is all being redone, but it's a big secret. I'm going to need some new clothes. I can't be at the couture collections and not expect to be photographed and written up, which is not good for a woman whose husband is in prison."

"What are you about to suggest?"

"We're the same size, only I've got bigger boobs. I know you're a regular at the collections anyway. Pick me out a brand-new wardrobe," said Ruby. "I want six evening dresses, six suits, and anything else you think I shouldn't live without. I don't care what it costs. Even after all the fines he's had to pay, Elias still has a billion bucks, probably more. He has this friend named Max Luby who looks after his money when he's in prison."

The baroness laughed. "We could be friends, you know," said the baroness.

"You've got the class, I've got the brass. We'd be perfect friends," replied Ruby, laughing. "I want something extra special to wear on the day that Elias gets out of prison," said Ruby. "Something with sable on the cuffs. I'm going to fly out in our plane to Las Vegas for the last time in my life, I hope. I can't tell you how much I hate the sound of those doors clanking behind me. I get a chill every time I'm there. I'm taking our chauffeur with me to hire a limousine and pick Elias up as he leaves prison. There will be photographers there. You can count on that. I'm going to have Elias's dark blue pinstripe suit taken in at the waist since he's lost so much weight in prison. We'll pose for pictures. Then we'll go directly back to the plane."

"You know, Ruby, when this prison part of your life is all over, you should talk about what it's been like at dinner parties," said the baroness. "Talk about the prison doors clanking shut behind you. You'll be the only one at the table who can say that. Everyone will be riveted by your stories, and you'll beat them to the draw of talking about you behind your back.

"You'll be the best-dressed woman in New York when I come back from the collections. I'll e-mail you from Paris."

CHAPTER 12

"THANK GOD YOU'RE NOT IN THAT GHASTLY orange jumpsuit again this time," said Ruby, after kissing Elias. She held back and didn't say one word about his breath. "You look so much thinner in the blue one. I've had about six of your old suits sent to Huntsman on Savile Row in London to be taken in at the waist. I told that nice man, Mr. Hope-Davies, he's such fun on the telephone, how much weight you've lost and he's personally overseeing the adjustments."

Elias was inattentive that day, as if he had something on his mind. Ruby wanted Elias to show more interest in the magnificent house that was being completed for them on East Seventy-eighth Street in New York. She had brought plans and photographs and some swatches that she was thinking of for the chairs and curtains in Elias's dressing room.

"Guess what, Elias? You're going to love this one. I'm having a urinal put on the wall of your bathroom, right next to the toilet. Charlotte has suggested this color green for the bathroom walls."

"Is there anything going on between you and the baron's dyke wife?" asked Elias, who wasn't interested in the swatches for his dressing room.

"Don't call her that, Elias," said Ruby, in an angry voice.

"Oh, I beg your pardon. I meant to ask if there was anything going on between you and the daughter of Belitas," asked Elias.

"What I'm saying is, and listen carefully, don't ever refer to Charlotte de Liagra as the 'baron's dyke wife.'"

"Max Luby says she's your new best friend."

"God, I hate Max Luby. No, there's nothing going on with Charlotte de Liagra. I met her at Maisie Verdurin's. She's very chic. Very elegant. She looks like Jeanne Moreau thirty years ago. She came on to me."

"See? I told you. Max Luby says in some circles they call her Uncle Charlie."

"I let her go down on me," said Ruby.

"You what?"

"You heard me. Just once. She likes hair pie, as you would say. She said she especially liked red hair. It's not my scene, she knows that. Now I've had the experience, the curiosity's gone," said Ruby.

"I can't believe what I'm hearing," said Elias, shaking his head incredulously. "Did you enjoy it?"

"Let me put it this way. It was not altogether unpleasant. As muff divers go, Baroness de Liagra is at the top of the charts," said Ruby. "She liked me to talk dirty when she was down there doing her thing. There, you satisfied? Is that what you wanted to hear? Did it turn you on?"

Elias, who did have an erection, roared with laughter. "I always loved you the best when you were cheap and trashy, Ruby."

"Charlotte says that's what makes me unique, when I talk trash. She said it couldn't get too low for her. She said I was cheap, but she said she meant it as a compliment. Charlotte's at the collections in Paris. She's helping me with my clothes for when you get out of here."

"Does the baroness know you used to fuck her husband while your husband was in prison?" asked Elias.

"You and I were divorced at the time, Elias, so I was free to do anything I wanted to do. Charlotte does know. She mentioned it once," said Ruby, glad she had decided to leave the ruby bracelet back in the plane.

CHAPTER 13

DINNER-PARTY LIFE WENT ON IN NEW YORK, even though the economy was on the skids. Rich people talked about money—who was making it, who was losing it. What were once considered great fortunes were evaporating. "The Lelands have had to put the Southampton house up for sale," said Dinkie Winthrop to Addison Kent at Matilda Clarke's dinner for Ormolu Webb's birthday in the back room of Swifty's. Unprincipled financiers were being indicted. Others were receiving bailouts and bonuses, attracting the anger of the public.

At Maisie Verdurin's dinner for Dolores De Longpre, who was retiring from writing her society gossip column after forty years, Muffy de la Roche said, to the table at large, "Shouldn't Elias Renthal be getting out of prison any month now?"

"In my day, we didn't know people who went to prison," said Lil Altemus to Percy Webb at Kay Kay Somerset's dinner.

"Ferdy Trocadero is painting the walls of Ruby Renthal's indoor swimming pool room that she copied from the indoor pool at Hearst Castle," said Addison Kent to Petal Wilson at Teddy Vermont's dinner at the Butterfield Club.

"Has anyone heard that the small Vigée Le Brun painting of Marie Antoinette that was Adele Harcourt's favorite painting is missing from her bedroom wall, according to George, the old butler that the nephew from Wyoming fired?" asked Figgy Watson at Pauline Mendelson's small dinner in the back room of Swifty's.

"I hear Lorcan Styne lost three hundred million in that Ponzi scheme," said Percy Webb to Cricket Williams at the Epstein-Barr Ball at the St. Regis Roof. "I always got a bad feeling from that guy."

"Lorcan Styne had to give up his plane," replied Cricket.

"And the helicopter," said Percy. "His own board of directors took it away from him."

"It nearly killed him, Christine told me," said Cricket.

"Strictly between us, no repeats, I mean, let's be practical. That plane was what Lorcan had to offer. I mean, Lorcan's perfectly nice and all that, at least to people like us, although not necessarily to his employees is what they say. He once flew us back from Paris, after we ran into him at the de Ravenals' dance, which was terribly nice of him, and so much more comfortable than first class on Air France, believe me, but Lorcan's not everyone's cup of chamomile, as we all know. When you have a plane to take your friends anywhere, and Lorcan's plane was divine, the last word, Nicky Haslam did it up for him in that rich Russian look, you become very popular and you get invited to all the parties. And now he doesn't have it anymore."

GUS WAS dining with Loelia Minardos and her shoe designer husband, Mickie Minardos, at their Park Avenue apartment, a rare occurrence indeed, as Loelia and Mickie felt they had been portrayed unkindly in Gus's much-publicized novel *Our Own Kind*. A rapprochement of sorts had taken place, engineered by the television news star Christine Saunders. It developed that there was a purpose to the dinner invitation, as there often is at society dinners. Gus was seated next to Constance Sibley, a rich and rarefied figure in social New York, who was a member of the board of directors of the Metropolitan Museum of Art, one of New York society's most prestigious honors. She limited her acquaintances to a very small and select group, among them Loelia and Mickie, on whom she doted. She had suggested to Loelia that Gus be invited.

"I hear you're writing about Perla Zacharias," said Constance into Gus's ear, once the general conversation had started about the divorce of Tina and Ted Dudley, to which everyone at the table had something to contribute. The conversational buzz was loud enough so that Constance knew she would not be overheard. Normally not loquacious with people she did not know, Constance monopolized Gus's ear through the entire dinner.

"Now I know why I was invited," Gus said, laughing. "Actually, I'm writing about Konstantin's death, which I find very mysterious. The confession of the male nurse is too preposterous. I'm not specifically writing about Perla. I was to meet with her in Paris, but her lawyer called that off."

"She lives in my building when she's in New York, which is more and more. I heard that Konstantin hated the dinner parties that Perla so enjoyed throwing. He was only interested in money, not their social life. The man was also obsessed with security, and yet that night, none of the surveillance equipment was working. He built a barracks on the grounds for the twenty-five guards he had on the payroll. All that I want to know is, why were there no guards on duty on the night Konstantin was murdered?"

"That's one of the mysteries of the story," replied Gus.

"Is it true that the Biarritz police handcuffed the guard who finally arrived with the key to Konstantin's room when he still might have saved him?"

"Yes. That's exactly the kind of thing I'm writing about in the novel."

LORD CUDLIP was late for Ormolu Webb's dinner at the Rhinelander Hotel, where Ormolu and Percy Webb were living temporarily since their cook, subsequently dismissed, had accidentally set fire to the kitchen stove, causing smoke damage and blackening the walls of the dining room, "ruining, simply ruining," as Ormolu told anyone who sympathized, the seventeen coats of persimmon paint that Ferdy Trocadero had taken three weeks to apply when they bought the apartment. And, worse, Ormolu couldn't get Ferdy Trocadero back to repaint the dining room in time for the dinner party, because Ferdy Trocadero, thank you very much, was tied up for months to come by Ruby Renthal in the refurbishing of the mansion on East Seventy-eighth Street that was being readied for the homecoming of Elias Renthal from prison.

Percy Webb, who always deferred to his wife, suggested to her that perhaps they should go in to dinner in the private dining room beyond the hotel dining room, where the tables had been set with Ormolu's own dishes and glasses and candlesticks, brought over from the apartment to the hotel for the occasion.

"We shouldn't wait any longer," said Percy. "People were asked for eight, with dinner at eight forty-five, and now it's nine fifteen. They'll be leaving if we don't sit down."

"I think it's so odd that Stanford Cudlip hasn't called me, or hasn't had one of his secretaries call me," said Ormolu, beckoning her guests toward the dining room. "I have him seated to my right, forgodssake. Perhaps there's a crisis in the world we haven't heard about yet. You know how he's always going on about terrorist attacks. Do you think anything's happened?"

Just then Lord Cudlip rapidly walked in, assuming a supplicant's pose, full of apologies. "My dear Ormolu, do please forgive me. The phone was out on my plane, if you can imagine, or I would have called before I left Las Vegas."

"What in the world were you doing in Las Vegas, Stanford? You're seated over there next to me, and Mimi's on the other side. Lil, you're over there next to Addison. If you knew how much I miss my dining room, and I can't get that damn Ferdy Trocadero back to repaint. Don't tell me the next terrorist attack is going to be in Las Vegas?"

"No, no, my dear Ormolu. I was visiting Elias Renthal at the federal prison. He'll be getting out soon, a few months at most. And it's not true what you've heard at all the parties, that he has massages in prison. He doesn't. No special privileges at all, and he's just about done his seven years, and he hasn't complained. My hat's off to him."

"What a good deed, Stanford," said Ormolu. "You are a perplexing person. Now sit down, sit down. Percy said everyone was about to leave if we didn't sit down, and Lil Altemus has let me know that you never should wait for a late guest."

"Sounds like Lil," said Lord Cudlip.

Lord Cudlip didn't tell anyone that Simon Cabot in London had suggested the trip to Las Vegas in his private plane. It would make Lord Cudlip look like a loyal friend, visiting Elias Renthal in prison, and it would make Elias Renthal look like a man who was still important.

FROM A public relations point of view, it was Simon Cabot, "our man in England," as Ruby Renthal always referred to him when talking to Elias, who more or less orchestrated Elias Renthal's release from prison, or the facility, as Ruby insisted on calling it, sternly and quickly correcting anyone who used the word *prison,* a word she could not bear. Ruby's persistence, as well as a call from Baroness de Liagra in Paris on Ruby's behalf, as well as a call from Chiquita Chatfield, as in Duchess of, changed Simon Cabot's mind about representing someone in an American federal facility, an association he had feared that his other powerful clients in distressing situations might object to. Secrecy was part of the lucrative bargain they came to. Simon Cabot was a great one for e-mail and gave his ideas to Ruby without ever leaving England. The Renthals were most anxious that there be as little press as possible on Elias's departure from the prison in Las Vegas. "Oh, dear me, no," said Simon, advising Ruby not to wear the suit she described to him with the sable collar and cuffs that Baroness de Liagra had privately comissioned Karl Lagerfeld to design especially for her. "Play it down, like Perla Zacharias did at the trial of the male nurse in Biarritz after Konstantin's murder," said Simon. "Wear that black suit you were wearing when we met at Claridge's, and leave your ruby bracelet home," he said. "There's certain to be photographers there. Don't get out of the car to greet Elias. Don't have any sort of a public welcome-home situation. Pictures are less likely to be published if you're not in them. It's you they want to see. You make the picture more valuable to the tabloids. People are beginning to talk about Ruby Renthal again. Elias should be dressed in a business suit, with a white shirt and a striped tie, as if he were going to the office. Have him walk directly to the car. Tell him not to stop to pose when the photographers call out his name. Just keep walking to the car. If they yell, 'How was prison, Elias?,' which they probably will, or, 'Is it true you had to clean toilets, Elias?,' tell Elias to ignore them and, for god's sake, not to get angry in public. I have heard all about his temper. The driver should be holding the car door open for him, so that he can slip right into the car. It's all right for the chauffeur to tip his hat to Elias. Kiss him inside the car, after the door is closed. Put your arms around him, in case they shoot through the back window. It should be very discreet and proper. There may be more photographers and reporters at the airport after you leave the prison, so be forewarned. I know the *Financial Times* is sending someone. And, of course, the *New York Times* and the *Daily News,* Toby Tilden from the *New York Post,* and the *Wall Street Journal,* who have been very tough on Elias from the beginning. The driver will take the car out onto the tarmac, as close as possible to the stairs up to the plane. You get out first and walk up the steps, where you wait for Elias. Think of Jackie O and how she would have played the scene and do that."

"I TOLD you Simon was brilliant," said Ruby when Elias told her about Lord Cudlip's prison visit. "I told you. You didn't believe me. Was I right or was I right?"

"Lord Cudlip's the one who's brilliant," said Elias. "Or Stanford, as he told me to call him. I don't know why, but I got the feeling that he's going to ask me to go on his board of directors."

"Oh, my god, Elias. Wouldn't that be wonderful?" said Ruby. "That would show New York that you were back in the big time. His board of directors has some of the swankiest people in New York, London, and Paris on it. The Infanta of Spain. People like that. I'm sure that was Simon Cabot's idea too."

"Cudlip's like a real intellectual. He's writing a biography of Benedict Arnold, at the same time that he's running his empire. He's bought all the family papers from Benedict Arnold's descendants. Twelve million bucks he paid for the papers. It's going to be eight hundred sixty pages long. I don't know where he gets the time to write it, running that media empire of his."

"Just between us, Elias, you name me three people we know

who are going to read eight hundred sixty pages about Benedict Arnold," said Ruby. "Who gives a shit?"

They both roared with laughter.

GUS WAS at the office of Lance Wilson, his editor of many years at *Park Avenue,* handing in his prison interview with Erik Menendez, whose trial for the murder of his parents Gus had covered for the magazine years earlier. Erik and his brother were currently doing life without the possibility of parole in different California prisons, where Gus had visited him.

Stokes Bishop, hearing that Gus was in the building, popped into Lance Wilson's office. Lance stood up and welcomed Stokes back from his holiday in St. Bart's on Larry Yelster's three-masted schooner built for him in Germany. Stokes raved about the yacht.

"How's the case going, Gus?" asked Stokes. "Do you like your new lawyer?"

"I want to settle," said Gus. "I kid you not when I say I'm afraid of a heart attack."

"Don't settle, Gus. Take it all the way," said Stokes. "What a trial that will be. Christine Saunders, every big news person will cover it. Cramden doesn't have a chance in a New York courtroom. You saw his interview with Christine Saunders. He was a creepy little disaster."

Gus had stopped asking about Stokes's promise to cover his legal fees. He had long since realized that this matter was out of both of their hands.

CHAPTER 14

GUS BAILEY WAS SEATED AT HIS REGULAR CORNER table in the back room of Swifty's with Bobby Vermont, whom he always described as his oldest New York friend. Their wives had gone to the same school. Their offspring had known one another as children. They had worked together in the early days of television. Bobby was one of the few people Gus discussed his slander suit with.

"You must know that everyone's afraid to ask you about your lawsuit," said Bobby.

"Is everyone talking about it?" asked Gus.

"You know they are," replied Bobby. "With concern, I might add."

"I get pity letters from friends," said Gus. "Especially after that shit Toby Tilden wrote in the *Post* that I was hiding out in the country as much as I could, only attending the social events I have to, afraid to see anyone, and worried about money. I know they mean well, but I can't stand to read the letters, even though I do worry about money. 'Dickie and I are so sorry to hear of the terrible predicament that you find yourself in.' That sort of thing."

"The word is out that you don't want to see anybody. Who was it who gave you the false information about Diandra

Lomax's disappearance?" asked Bobby. "How did he get to you?"

For some reason, Gus found it difficult to talk about the man, whose real name was Cal Hornett. Their last conversation had taken place in England. By that time Gus had known he was a fraud who had told him a false story and cost him an enormous amount of trouble and money. Their phone call in England had been ugly. Gus had grown to feel fearful of him.

"Dear God," said Gus, momentarily diverted from the horse trainer with the powerful Middle East connections by someone he noticed across the room.

"What's the matter?" asked Bobby.

"Perla Zacharias just came in. She's not fond of me. I haven't seen her since the trial in Biarritz. I hope there's not a scene."

"Sable coat? Face-lift to the max? That one?" asked Bobby.

"That's Perla. God, look what she's done to her face. The left eyelid droops more than the right. She looks like she's in the witness protection program. I can't believe Robert's going to seat her right next to me on the banquette, but he is," said Gus. "I guess he doesn't read my diary in *Park Avenue* or the gossip columns."

"Just keep talking. Don't look," said Bobby.

"I CAN'T believe I'm sitting directly next to that odious Gus Bailey," said Perla after she had greeted Addison Kent, kissing him on both cheeks.

"He doesn't notice. He's deep in conversation," reassured Addison.

"He noticed," said Perla.

"Aren't you going to take off your sable coat, Perla?" asked Addison.

She slipped out of her coat and placed it on the banquette between herself and Gus, as if to build a sable wall between them. She never looked in his direction. They had not seen each other since the last day of the male nurse's trial in Biarritz, where they had also never looked at each other. Their last interaction had been when she called him at his house in Prud'homme. But Perla Zacharias was finished trying to appeal to that bastard. She had other avenues to pursue, and she would absolutely pursue them. Gus Bailey was but a minor speed bump on her rise to the top.

She raised her voice slightly as she said to Addison, "The Prince of Wales said to me the other night at Clarence House, when I told him I had bought so many things belonging to the Windsors at the auction, he said to me, 'My great-uncle was not a good man, a most peculiar individual.' Don't you think it's amazing that he made such a personal revelation to me?"

"How much did it cost to sit next to him?" asked Addison. Perla quietly gasped. She preferred to have people think she had been *invited* to Clarence House as the personal guest of the future king and his duchess, not that her exalted philanthropy to the prince's charity had earned her the best seat at the table. Addison Kent still had much to learn about being the walker of the third richest woman in the world.

CHAPTER 15

GUS STAYED HOME THAT WEDNESDAY NIGHT TO watch his television show, *Augustus Bailey Presents*. He usually watched rough cuts and final cuts of his shows before they went on the air, but this night the producer and editor had been working up to the last minute, making changes, and there hadn't been an advance screening. Gus's introduction and narration of the show had been shot only the day before at his home in Prud'homme, Connecticut. He felt a bit of anxiety, as he personally knew the imprisoned Elias Renthal, whose story of financial malfeasance was the subject of that evening's episode. It was Gus who had persuaded the president of the Butterfield Club to speak on camera about the reasons why Elias Renthal had been asked to resign from the prestigious men's club on Fifth Avenue before the trial that sent him to prison for seven years. It was Gus who had persuaded Lord Deeds, the delinquent, drugged, and disinherited son of the Duke and Duchess of Chatfield, Bunny and Chiquita, to say on camera that the fabulous social climb of the Renthals had had much to do with the new acre of roof for Deeds Castle, which Elias had paid for at a cost of over a million dollars, assuring him a permanent invitation to the famous shoots at Deeds Castle. It was Gus who had gotten Max Luby to speak on camera in defense of his imprisoned friend.

Gus, seated in front of a bookcase in the living room of his house in Prud'homme, addressed the television audience:

"Social climbers get a bad rap. I dabbled myself in the art of it, so I know. They are fascinating to watch. Many fall by the wayside, but others go the whole way and end up as old guard to everyone except the real old guard. Elias Renthal is a massively noticeable presence in whatever circumstance he finds himself, even prison. Stout, beautifully dressed in English bespoke suits and shirts and ties and shoes before his incarceration, he drew people in society to him with his welcoming smile and jolly manner, as if proximity to him would bring them the vast riches that he made for himself. By his side always was the beautiful red-haired Ruby Renthal, who divorced and remarried Elias when he was in prison. Elias took to the grand life as if he were born to it. He chartered large yachts for Mediterranean cruises with the swellest cast of characters you ever heard of. Elias became a part of that world. If you could have seen him in his shooting clothes from Huntsman in London at Bunny and Chiquita Chatfield's shooting party at Deeds Castle. He belonged. He was funny. He told wonderful stories. He was generous. He had given the new roof for the castle in a confidential agreement with the duke, which everyone eventually heard about. He created good times for the grandest people in the world."

OVER AT the Butterfield Club, Percy Webb turned to Herkie Saybrook, when they were playing backgammon, and said, "Elias is going to be pissed off at Gus Bailey about this show when he gets out of prison." And, the next day, during lunch at the Rhinelander Hotel, Lorcan Styne turned to Perla Zacharias and said, "Elias Renthal is not going to be happy about that show of Gus Bailey's last night."

And Lil Altemus, who was having her dreaded lunch with her stepmother, Dodo Van Degan, at the corner table in the back room of Swifty's, mentioned in passing that she'd heard someone had brought two TV sets into the dining room at a dinner party to watch the Elias Renthal story on Gus Bailey's show. But Dodo didn't seem very impressed, so Lil changed the subject, slightly.

Despite the considerable riches of her stepmother, of which she was envious, Lil was never able to think of her as anything but the poor relation she had once been.

"I do so hate the word *common*," said Lil. "It's so incredibly snobbish, and I'm not snobbish at all, as anyone who knows me can tell you, but sometimes, it's the only word that hits the situation, and Mrs. Renthal, The Convict's Wife Ruby Renthal, is common. That's all I have to say on the matter. Imagine, she literally *stole* my cook. Gert was with me for more than twenty-five years. She's going to let Gert use her husband's private plane to take her to Ireland for her family visits. Now that's common."

"I have another interpretation of that story," said Dodo, who was tired of hearing Lil repeat the story of Gert's betrayal.

"Which is what?" asked Lil, in a disinterested voice.

"I bet Maisie Verdurin told Ruby you blackballed her and Elias from getting into your old Fifth Avenue apartment building, and she's just getting even with you. Even a bitch like you, Lil, can't blame poor Gert for grabbing up the opportunity of a lifetime," said Dodo.

"I'll never speak to Gert again, ever, ever, ever," said Lil. "After all I've done for her."

"From what I hear from Brucie Random, the florist at the Rhinelander Hotel, who always knows all the latest news about everybody, Gert's also getting double what you paid her, and a sitting room all her own in the new Renthal mansion over on East Seventy-eighth Street. I don't blame Gert for not wanting to sleep in that little rat's hole of a maid's room behind the kitchen in your apartment. You canceled her annual trip to Ireland, for economic reasons, and you counted the change when she came back with the groceries from Grace's Marketplace. She'd have been a fool to turn down that job."

Lil always pretended not to hear Dodo's criticisms. "Such awful people, those Renthals. In my day, we didn't know people who went to prison," said Lil. "Now they're all around us, and they all seem to think they can just pick right up again where they left off before going to prison, as if nothing untoward had happened."

"Let's change the subject," said Dodo.

"How come I never see you around at any of the parties? Surely as the rich widow Mrs. Van Degan you must be invited, just for the name you now bear."

"Oh, I go to plenty of parties, Lil. We just travel in different circles. In fact, I've become a bit of a partygoer. I even have a walker."

"*You* have a walker?" asked Lil, hooting with laughter. "How hilarious! Do tell. Don't tell me it's Brucie Random, your friend the florist in the Rhinelander Hotel."

"No, it's not Brucie, but I met him through Brucie, at one of his parties where he sang show tunes, and his friend Jonsie from the wine shop on Madison played the piano. I had such a good time, and they all thought I was a riot. I was sort of the hit of the party." She left out that her impersonation of Lil counting the change after Gert brought back the groceries from Grace's Marketplace had had all the guys on the floor laughing. "Jonsie introduced me to Xavior."

"Xavior? That's your walker's name?" asked Lil.

"Francis Xavior Branigan, but he's called Xavior by his friends," said Dodo.

"And is Mr. Xavior Branigan a florist, too?" asked Lil.

"Mr. Branigan is the assistant funeral director at Grant P. Trumbull's on Madison Avenue," said Dodo.

"An undertaker? You're going around to parties with an undertaker?" Lil shrieked with laughter. "I haven't had such a good laugh in months. You know what they call women like you, don't you? Winkie Williams, I miss him so, told me this."

"What *do* they call women like me, Lil?" asked Dodo.

"Fag hags," said Lil, spitting it out.

"Well, as long as I'm happy in the role, and I am, that's all that matters," said Dodo, giving herself a moment to think of how to get even. She knew that bad language and dirty talk offended Lil.

"Your esteemed father popped my cherry when he was eighty-three and I was a thirty-eight-year-old maiden lady. Push and squirt. Over in an instant. I never enjoyed it much after that. Usually I just showed him a dirty movie and jerked him off."

Lil covered her ears with her hands and began humming. "I am *not* listening. I can't hear a word you are saying," she said.

"Xavior's so thoughtful. So kind. Xavior let me look at Winkie Williams in the casket the night before he was cremated. He was wearing the lavender tie from Turnbull & Asser you gave him for his birthday."

"I heard that from Addison Kent," said Lil, in a tone that indicated her source was of a higher social level than Dodo's source, even though Lil did not personally care for him.

"Jonsie told me Addison Kent and Xavior had sex in the men's toilet off the front hall of the Grant P. Trumbull Funeral

Home when Addison took over Winkie's clothes for the cremation," said Dodo.

"I hate you, Dodo," said Lil.

"Not as much as I hate you, Lil," said Dodo. "Why do we go
on with these ridiculous lunches that we both hate?"

"We have to keep up some semblance of a family," Lil
said, reminding herself as much as Dodo, as she did every time
their meals together became too much to bear. "The Van Degans. The Harcourts. The Grenvilles. The Rockefellers. We all
used to matter so much. Now only the Rockefellers do. When I
was growing up, people always used to say how rich the Van
Degans were, and we were. Back then if your family had forty
million dollars, like we had, it was like being in the financial
stratosphere. Now forty million dollars means absolutely nothing, even if we still had it, which we don't, thanks to my nephew,
young Laurance. Forty million dollars is what the Murdochs
paid for their new apartment on Fifth Avenue. And all those
ghastly new people you never heard of before have so much
more money than we ever had when we were at the top of the
peak. Gus Bailey told me that Perla Zacharias has more money
than you can imagine. Simon Cabot told Gus that Perla's money
was limitless." Lil sighed. "Is it my turn or yours to pay?"

"I gave Robert my American Express card when I came in,"
said Dodo. "The rich relative always takes the poor relative to
lunch."

"I am *not* poor," said Lil proudly.

"No, of course not," replied Dodo. "You're just living
in reduced circumstances. Maybe Adele Harcourt will leave
you a little something in her will, if she hasn't left everything to
the poor. By the way, how *is* Adele Harcourt? You never hear
much about her since she fell and broke her back in your
kitchen."

"It was her hip, not her back, as you know perfectly well,

and I've had the linoleum changed, no thanks to you," said Lil, gathering her things. "Poor Adele doesn't see anybody. Except me, on occasion. Her former butler, George, told Kay Kay Somerset, who lives on the floor below at Seven Seventy-eight Park, that she's very unwell."

CHAPTER 16

ADDISON KENT MADE A FATAL ERROR WHEN HE high-hatted Brucie Random in his very chic flower shop in the Rhinelander Hotel on upper Madison Avenue. Addison, dressed stylishly for a lunch party, with his top coat hanging on his shoulders, like a cape, had dropped in to send some jonquils—"masses and masses of them"—to Adele Harcourt, who was still laid up after tripping over some old linoleum in Lil Altemus's ghastly new apartment and breaking her hip. "The card shouldn't be addressed to Mrs. Adele Harcourt, which people always call her," Addison said to Brucie, in what Brucie Random told his friend Jonsie over at Thierry's Wine and Liquors had been a condescending voice, explaining the proper ways of society to a florist whose shop catered to people in society. Brucie kept a copy of the Social Register right next to the cash register and didn't have to be told how to properly address Adele Harcourt, who had been a customer of his flower shop ever since Brucie had started there when he couldn't get any more work on Broadway after *Company* closed in 1972. One of the great excitements of his life was that he was in the chorus on the album of *Company,* which happened to be playing at that very moment in the shop.

"Yes, yes, I know," said Brucie. "It's Mrs. Vincent Belmont Harcourt, not Mrs. Adele Harcourt. Mrs. Harcourt is one of my best customers. I don't know if it matters, but Mrs. Percy Webb, the divine Ormolu, for whom I'm going to name a scented candle, has just ordered three dozen jonquils for Mrs. Vincent Belmont Harcourt, which are being delivered to her Park Avenue apartment at this very moment. Mrs. Harcourt is very unwell, I hear."

"Change my order to the tangerine-colored roses, then," said Addison, who picked up a scented candle and breathed in its aroma. "Lovely, lovely."

"That's what Winkie bought before he died," said Brucie.

"Yes, I know. I saw it next to his bed when I discovered his body that morning," said Addison.

"I heard you discovered the body," said Brucie.

"Such a shock, when I arrived there and found him dead," said Addison, leaning over to inhale the scent of the candle again.

"Yeah, I bet it was a real surprise for you."

Immaculata, Winkie's cleaning lady, who was also Brucie's cleaning lady, had heard the next morning from Albie, the superintendent of Winkie's building, that Mr. Addison Kent had been in the apartment. Immaculata had found the empty bottle of Seconal in the wastebasket in Winkie's bathroom, where Addison probably had dropped it before leaving, because Winkie certainly couldn't have navigated his way into the bathroom, or so Brucie and Jonsie figured, after having swallowed a whole bottle.

"Actually, he wore one of the tangerine roses in the buttonhole of his gray suit in the casket when he was cremated. He looked very smart," said Addison, who realized he had offended Brucie and thought a flower compliment would make things right.

"So I heard. Xavior, from the funeral home, is a friend of mine," Brucie said pointedly.

"Oh, Xavior," said Addison vaguely. "Yes, I met Xavior at the cremation."

"You did more than meet him is what I heard," Brucie said. Addison blushed.

Thereafter, Brucie Random, Jonsie, and Xavior always referred to Addison Kent as Miss Kent behind his back. "Miss Kent was in. She ordered tangerine-colored roses for Adele Harcourt," said Brucie over the phone. "She had dick on her breath. I almost told her to gargle with Listerine before kissing all those society ladies at lunch, but I refrained. Hey, that fifty-five-dollar scented candle she was sniffing all of a sudden isn't here anymore. Better watch out for Miss Kent. She's a klepto."

"THAT GOLD cigarette case that Cole Porter left Winkie in his will, I can't find it anywhere," said Lil Altemus. "Cole Porter had it engraved in his own handwriting, 'To Winkie Williams, the Extra Man himself, Love, Cole.' You can imagine Winkie's excitement when he got it. I know for a fact that Winkie wanted to leave it to the Costume Institute at the Metropolitan Museum. I heard him tell that to Diana Vreeland years and years ago when she was still in charge of the whole thing. It would be so divine in a vitrine. You didn't see it, did you, Addison?"

"No, I don't know where he put it," replied Addison.

"I bet that maid took it," said Lil. "Immaculata. I never trusted Immaculata. She once tried to sue me."

"ELIAS, I think you're going to have to start going to temple on a regular basis when you get out of this facility."

"Since when do you have such a big interest in me going to

temple? It used to drive you crazy every time you saw me with a yarmulke on at some funeral or other."

"Well, church and temple were Simon Cabot's idea. The Zendas are regulars, and Perla Zacharias, when she's in town, and Nazim Zacharias, Konstantin's brother, when Perla's not in town, and all the important people. It's good for you to be seen there. Sometime, at some party, your name will come up, and someone will say, 'Oh, I saw Elias at temple this morning.' It's a good kind of thing to have said about you."

"Are you planning on accompanying me?"

"No, I'm going to start going to Mass every Sunday at St. Ignatius Loyola on Park Avenue and Eighty-fourth Street. That's where Jacqueline Kennedy Onassis's funeral was, and Mark Hampton's. That's where the big-time Catholics go," said Ruby.

"Oh, and I'm going where the big-time Jews go, is that it?" asked Elias.

"It sounds awful when you say it that way, Elias. Actually, it's a very nice thing for us both."

"Do the fashion photographers from the *Times* and *W* stand outside St. Ignatius Loyola and report on your latest eight-thousand-dollar suit from Galliano's spring collection?"

"It's not that at all, Elias. There's no publicity involved."

"Then what's the point?"

"I wouldn't mind one of those very rich Cord sisters saying about me at Swifty's or someplace, 'Oh, I saw Ruby Renthal receiving communion this morning at St. Ignatius Loyola.'"

"It's the very meaning of religion," said Elias, and they both laughed.

"It will be good for us," said Ruby. "I used to be the smartest girl in Sunday school when I was a kid."

"Do you even know the Cord sisters?"

"Not yet."

GUS WAS having dinner with his editor, Lance Wilson, at Donohue's, an Irish steak house and bar on Lexington Avenue that was a popular hangout for people in the media. They often had dinner together on the day that Gus turned in his monthly diary; they read it over together, and Lance made suggestions for rearrangements of the various topics.

"Gus, I think you've said enough for the time being about Gerald Bradley Junior," said Lance. "He's been in your last two diaries. I like the story you told me about the young antiques dealer on the Upper East Side, who's been indicted for theft that you don't believe he committed. I think you should lead with that and end with Gerald Bradley Junior, but cut it down."

"Okay," said Gus. "Lance, strictly off the record, I want to ask you something."

"Go."

"Do you think Stokes Bishop wants to get rid of me? Do you think I should resign before he lets me go?" asked Gus.

"Don't be silly, Gus," said Lance.

"I just worry that this slander suit has come between us."

"MR. BAILEY, would you mind terribly if I asked you a few questions about the Zacharias murder in Biarritz?" asked Baroness de Liagra. "My husband often did business with Konstantin Zacharias, and my friend Ruby Renthal speaks highly of you, and of course I read you in *Park Avenue*."

They were at a small dinner in the back room of Swifty's that the much-married Yehudit Tavicoli was giving for the baroness, whom she had known during her years in Paris.

"I'm sure you know as much as I do, Baroness," replied Gus.

"I've gone to Biarritz every summer for my whole life. When

I was a child, my father used to rent the same villa year after year. It was so divine in those days. I used to play with Lola de la Grange at that beautiful villa the Zachariases bought. It was built for Empress Eugénie, did you know that? My father rarely went back to the villa after the Zachariases bought it. We didn't even go to their famous ball, and we were in Biarritz at the time. My father, who was a dashing sportsman who enjoyed social life, used to say the Zachariases had too much money and that it's not good to be that rich. That something bad would happen in that household."

"Your father was right," said Gus.

CHAPTER 17

"I HEAR PERCY WEBB LOST A BUNDLE WHEN LORCAN Styne's company went belly-up," said Lil Altemus at Polly Winter's lunch party at the Colony Club.

"Oh, I wouldn't worry about him. There's plenty more where that came from," replied Gus. "There's broke and there's rich broke."

"They say he just sits in front of the money channel on TV for hours. He never talks to anyone except his broker. It's driving Ormolu crazy. He wouldn't go to Bratsie Bleeker's lunch at the Butterfield yesterday. Backed out at the last minute."

GUS WAS having dinner at Le Cirque with his son Grafton and his granddaughter, Sarah. It was Sarah's birthday the next day, her fourteenth, and parents and grandparents were most definitely not invited to her party the next evening, so Gus was having a little private birthday dinner for Sarah, with presents. The main course over, together they enjoyed slices of a divine chocolate mousse cake with hazelnuts.

When Sarah excused herself to go to the ladies' room, Grafton took the opportunity to ask Gus about the lawsuit. "How's things on the case, Dad?"

"Depositions coming up," replied Gus quickly, signaling that he didn't want to talk about it.

"How's the stress?" Grafton eyed his father carefully, noting the weariness in his face. He was concerned.

"A constant in my life. The novel is the only thing keeping me sane right now. I can forget about all the other unpleasantness when I'm working on it. I think it's going to be my best yet."

"Has the magazine come up with any money to help you out with the lawyers' bills?"

"No."

"Want me to call Stokes Bishop? I saw him the other night at Il Cantinori."

"No; I'm sure this is bigger than him. This is what happens when you make powerful enemies."

Gus was saved when Sarah rejoined them at the table and ate up the last crumbs of the delicious cake from her plate.

"Well, we'd better be off," said Grafton. "School night. Get your stuff together, Sarah, and put the presents in this shopping bag with the cards."

As they rose to leave, a man from another table called out, "Hey, Mr. Bailey. Hold on a minute."

Gus turned to see a man getting up and approaching him from his table. Although he was seated at a table in the section of the room where prominent people were seated, he was not dressed properly for that location, especially in a restaurant with a strict dress code. Later Gus modeled a character in his novel after this man, and he described him as follows: "He was dressed like one of those hoods in Tony Soprano's gang on television. He looked out of place, but he was very sure of himself."

The stranger went on talking. "We were just speaking about you at our table over there. One of the guys recognized you. We were wondering why you don't write about the Zacharias case in *Park Avenue* anymore. You were the only one writing about it, and then you stopped."

"Yes, I did," said Gus. "The trial was over."

"But the story wasn't."

"That's right."

"Then why did you stop writing?"

Gus looked at the man before he answered.

"I got a warning."

The man turned back to his table and called out to one of the men sitting there watching them. "Joe—Joe, come over here," he said, waving to another gentleman. "Joe's the one who recognized you. He was telling us things about the case. He wants to speak to you. Joe, this is Gus Bailey. Joe Carey. I asked Mr. Bailey why he stopped writing about the case, and he said that he got a warning."

Gus told Grafton and Sarah to go on after saying his good-byes. He had a feeling this was going to take some time.

Gus and Joe Carey shook hands as Joe nodded his head in understanding. Gus saw instantly that Joe Carey was someone to be reckoned with. Later, in his novel, Gus would describe the character based on Joe Carey as "a handsome, mid-forties, twice-divorced, slightly mysterious man." Unlike his badly dressed tablemates, Joe Carey was wearing a dark blue suit and a Turnbull & Asser striped tie that fit in perfectly with the dress code of the exclusive restaurant.

After his thuggish friend left, Joe and Gus sat back down at the table Gus had just shared with his son and granddaughter, and Joe began talking.

"Konstantin was my friend," he said. "I knew him before he married Perla. She never liked me. She never liked anyone who got too close to Konstantin. I never got invited to any of the parties, but I'm one of the few people he ever confided in. Konstantin didn't trust many people. I was there in Biarritz the night of the fire. For two days he had wanted to talk to me alone. He was very medicated for his ALS and his anxiety. I could see in his eyes he had something he wanted to tell me, but Perla would never let me be alone with him. She knew that anything negative that was said about their household could tarnish their social standing, and she was careful to control all information. I no sooner got into Konstantin's room than she walked in and stayed until I left. He didn't want to sell the bank. He wanted that bank to stay in the family and go to his brother. Perla's the one who pushed for the sale. Believe me, she doesn't want to have to have any dealings with Konstantin's brother, who never liked her and had discouraged Konstantin from marrying her."

Joe paused for a moment to catch his breath and then added, hesitantly, "There's something wrong, you know. Konstantin was a dear friend, and it kills me that Perla's obsession with making this story die down so she can be Adele fucking Harcourt is standing in the way of giving all of us who cared about Konstantin some peace and letting us understand what really happened. Has she tried to stop the publication of your book that I saw announced in Kit Jones's column?"

"No, I don't think so."

"She will. Who's the billionaire who owns your publisher?"

"I'm not sure."

"Well, whoever he is, she'll get to him. Those billionaires all know each other. They stick together."

Gus's stomach churned at the thought. He had already been forced to stop writing about the Zacharias case in the magazine, he had this terrifying lawsuit pending, and he just generally wasn't feeling like himself lately. He did not have a personal life. He had two sons and a granddaughter he loved dearly but didn't see enough. There was no companion to keep him company. The book was the only positive thing in his life right now that was all his own. He couldn't stand to lose it.

"Has she offered you any money?" Joe Carey pressed.

"No."

"I wouldn't be surprised if she offered you as much as two million not to write," said Joe.

"I might be tempted," said Gus, joking. "These legal bills are looming in my slander suit."

"She's afraid of you, Gus. The word's out that people from Johannesburg and Paris are phoning you. Your core audience is the kind of people she wants to be in with. If you need any help with that lawsuit when the time comes, let me know," said Joe. "I read about it in Toby Tilden's column. You could have been set up on that, you know."

"Come to think of it, she has been suspiciously quiet recently. When she first heard about the deal she tried to arrange an interview with me before it was killed by her lawyer, Pierre La Rouche. Then Perla had one of her lesser legal minions invite me to his office in Gramercy Park to meet and discuss the book I intended to write about the case."

"Did he hint at an offer?"

"Not exactly, but he did give me some first editions of very rare books, which I happen to collect. I guess they wanted to try honey before vinegar. Two of my favorite English novels were among them: Anthony Trollope's *The Way We Live Now* and Evelyn Waugh's *Brideshead Revisited*. She'd done her research on me. I opened the wrapping paper. I held the books in my hand, yearned for them briefly, and then didn't want them anymore. I haven't heard anything since then, but I can't imagine she would have given up. That's just not the kind of woman she is."

"Gus," Joe said quietly, "there's a very hush-hush rumor that Perla is going to make a very substantial contribution to the Manhattan Public Library, but there are strings attached."

"What sort of strings?"

"She wants the library to be renamed the Perla and Konstantin Zacharias Library. She wants their names carved into the stone on the Fifth Avenue side."

"That will never happen," said Gus.

"It might if she pays the hundred million in one lump sum, not in increments of ten million a year for ten years, or something like that."

"That'll be enough to send Adele Harcourt to her grave. Listen, Joe," Gus continued. "Here's my card. It has all my phone numbers and fax numbers and my e-mail address. I'd love to meet you for lunch or dinner. We have a lot to talk about."

Joe motioned with his hand that he had one more thing to say. He leaned in.

"I made a condolence call the day after the fire. There was no sense of mourning whatsoever in that household. She has this fancy Johannesburg butler in livery who showed me to the library. I thought she'd be dressed in widow's weeds, fighting back tears, receiving her friends. Instead, she was sitting at a desk and making out a list of people to be invited to the funeral, as if she were making out a guest list for a party. I told her how sorry I was about Konstantin. She simply said, 'So sweet of you,' clearly wanting to get back to her invitation chores. Maybe it doesn't mean anything, maybe she's just ice-cold, but she avoided answering my questions about the fire. In a very matter-of-fact voice, she revealed the astonishing news that the male nurse, whose name she couldn't remember, had confessed to setting the fire and had already been arrested and put into the Biarritz jail. Then she more or less dismissed me from her presence. On my way out, she asked me to tell her secretary that she needed the address for the Infanta of Spain, whom she wanted to invite to the funeral."

Joe leaned back in his chair.

"By the way, I didn't get invited to the funeral."

"But the Infanta of Spain did, I bet," said Gus.

"Yeah, and her picture was in *Hello!*" They both laughed.

Joe Carey telephoned Gus the next morning to set up a date

for lunch, and Gus found it amusing how specific he was as to where he did *not* want to meet.

"I don't want to go to Swifty's, or Michael's, or '21,' or the Four Seasons, or Le Cirque, where you seem to know all the people. I was watching you last night at Le Cirque. People kept stopping at your table," said Joe. "I'm a background player. It's not a good thing for you and me to be seen together."

"I understand that," said Gus. "Tell me where you want to go, and I'll meet you there."

"I'll have my driver pick you up at your building at twelve thirty, and I'll take you to lunch where you won't see a soul you know, and no one will know you either."

"I KNOW it doesn't look like much, but the food's good," said Joe, after Gus joined him in the back of the somewhat dingy steak house. It was slightly dark and depressing, without any sort of atmosphere at all. They could talk freely there.

"Everything's fine," replied Gus. "I like it here. This lunch isn't about food or being recognized. Tell me about Konstantin."

Joe let out a heavy sigh and began talking.

"Konstantin was like a father to me. Ever since he ratted out the Russian mafia to the FBI for money laundering, he knew that what happened to him was going to happen at some time. He was frightened. He became paranoid. He thought assassins were hiding behind the curtains in the villa in Biarritz. All the doctors he felt safe with were fired, and the new doctors kept him overmedicated. And, as I mentioned yesterday, Perla was always in the room with him whenever anyone came to visit. If he ever got to talk on the telephone, she was listening on another extension."

"Why did he rat out the Russian mafia to the FBI?" asked Gus.

"It was like a trade-off. The FBI stayed away from him and his assets. Are you aware that a billion dollars is missing somewhere between Konstantin's bank in Biarritz and Moscow? I didn't think you knew that. Let me tell you something, Gus. You don't fuck with the Russian mafia, if you know what's good for you."

"How about the nurse who confessed, and the fire in the penthouse?" asked Gus.

"I'm confused about him. Could be part of the Mafia's plot, but I don't think so. Listen, Gus, you have to be careful yourself. You've pissed off some very important people with the way you've covered this case. I happen to know from my spy in that household that the lady doesn't like you at all, and she has a reputation for getting even. "

Gus nodded, taking a bite of his slightly tough steak.

"Are you aware she has a brother?" Joe added.

"No," said Gus, surprised.

Joe replied evenly, "Perla has a much younger half brother from her father's fifth marriage who was briefly her ward when their father died. He is never spoken of. His name is Rocco."

Gus chewed his food quickly and swallowed.

"You're kidding, right?"

"She doesn't show him off. She makes sure he stays in Johannesburg. And listen, Gus—for what it's worth, brother and sister are not fond of each other. It seems to me if she's looking to be the next Adele Harcourt, it would not be to her advantage if this kind of information were to leak out in the wrong circles."

Joe Carey gave Gus a knowing look and nodded his head. Gus felt fortunate to have met him. The information that Joe Carey knew about Perla could not only help Gus to write his book, but it might also help him keep Perla, that infamous lady, from getting the plug pulled as she had at *Park Avenue.*

"Gus, I want your book to be published. I want people to ask more questions. I lost a very dear friend, and that bitch, in her quest to become the toast of Manhattan society, is keeping me from finding out the truth. I am going to help you pursue that truth, and I am prepared to do whatever you need me to, to make that happen."

CHAPTER 18

ELIAS RENTHAL'S RELEASE FROM THE FEDERAL prison in Las Vegas, Nevada, did not make the front pages of any of the New York papers. While Elias was living his final moments as a convict, Adele Harcourt died at her apartment on Park Avenue, all alone except for Lil Altemus, who had just told Adele of the name change of the Manhattan Public Library, which was to be called the Konstantin and Perla Zacharias Library in return for a one-hundred-million-dollar gift, to be paid in the full amount, not in increments, from the Konstantin Zacharias Foundation. "She just closed her eyes and died, poor darling," said Lil.

The next day Adele was on the front page of every New York paper, as well as being the lead story on all the local news channels on television. To the relief of Ruby Renthal, who had social aspirations, Elias's release-from-prison pictures were on the financial pages only and took second place in that section to the story of Leonard Watson's prison sentence of twenty-four years for robbing his stockholders of one hundred million dollars.

Simon Cabot, in London, heard the news of Adele Harcourt's death from Perla Zacharias, whose cook was a friend of

Adele's former butler, George, who had been relieved of his job by Mrs. Harcourt's nephew from Wyoming, who felt that since Adele no longer went about in society, she didn't need a butler. George, who Ruby recently hired to be her butler at the house on Seventy-eighth Street, kept up with hourly telephone calls with the maids still in Mrs. Harcourt's employ, so concerned was he about the great lady whom he had served for so many years. George called Perla's cook one minute after Adele drew her last breath, and one and a half minutes later, Perla Zacharias, who admired Adele Harcourt over any person and wanted to assume her mantle in New York society, loved having the news of such a piece of social history to pass on to Simon Cabot.

Lil Altemus, who had arrived at the last minute, pushing her way in, was the only one in the room. She had heard from George that it was about to happen. "She was like a second mother to me," Lil said to the nephew and his wife, who lived on an avocado ranch in Wyoming, and were said to have planned to take over the apartment and the country houses and to fire the help and remove the Vigée Le Brun portrait of Marie Antoinette that was Adele's favorite picture in her collection although it had mysteriously gone missing recently. "All that going on just as Mrs. Harcourt 'passed over,' " said George as he described the moment to Perla's cook. As soon as Simon hung up from talking with Perla, he telephoned Elias Renthal's plane.

Inside the plane, Elias was beaming from ear to ear. He couldn't believe his good fortune that he was out of prison after seven years and·was lying back relaxing in the luxury of his private jet.

"The plane looks beautiful, Ruby," said Elias.

"It had better look beautiful, after what you paid to have it done over," said Ruby. "I used Nicky Haslam. He does the London houses for all those rich Russian oligarths, or whatever they're called. I hear Yehudit Tavicoli's after one of those oli-garths."

"I heard from Max Luby that this renovation of yours cost something like three million," said Elias.

"Max Luby read that in Gus Bailey's diary in *Park Avenue*," said Ruby. "Besides, you can afford it."

"Gus Bailey had better watch his back. He is on my shitlist for running that television show about my case just when I was getting out," said Elias. "Speaking of Max Luby, save the date of March twelfth in your book for him."

"Why in the world would I save a date for Max Luby?" asked Ruby. "He doesn't like me. I don't like him."

"Max Luby's the best friend I ever had. He looked after my money the whole time I was away. If it weren't for Max, you wouldn't have had the three million to do over the house," said Elias. "He flew out to see me every week that I was in prison. I'll never forget that."

"I don't need his oral history, Elias. What's the big date you made for March twelfth?" asked Ruby.

"He's being honored by the Chamber of Commerce in Brooklyn as Man of the Year, for all he's done for the poor kids over there. It's a big deal for him. I've known Max for forty years, and I've never seen him so excited about anything. He's got all the Cleveland relatives coming in. He's losing weight working out in the gym, and he's having a new toupee made for the occasion that's costing him a thousand dollars."

"Does Max think that people will think that rug pasted to his head is real?" asked Ruby.

"He wants you and me to be there and sit on the dais," said Elias, ignoring Ruby's comment. "He said you'd add class to the evening."

"It won't be in the papers, will it?" asked Ruby.

The telephone rang. Selena, the flight attendant, asked, "Would you like me to answer that?"

Elias said, "No. Let the voice mail pick up. It might be a reporter." He felt good giving orders again.

The telephone rang three rings before Selena checked the caller ID, just in case. "Ma'am, it's Simon Cabot calling from London."

"I'll take it. I'll take it," called out Ruby, racing for the phone. "Simon, I'm here. We're not picking up the phone in case it's a reporter who somehow got the number. Everything's gone extremely well so far. Elias was simply a star the way he walked over to the plane after we left the facility. He waved to the photographers, but he never stopped. And I wore the old Adolfo black suit, just like you suggested, not that anyone noticed, I was so hidden in the backseat of the limousine, and the windows were black."

"I wanted to tell you that Adele Harcourt died," said Simon. "Perla Zacharias called me from New York. There will probably be a huge amount of coverage of that."

"Oh, Adele died, huh? End of an era, right? You know, she took that fall that eventually killed her in Lil Altemus's kitchen when she tripped over the old linoleum that Lil didn't have enough money to change when she moved into the apartment," said Ruby. "Let me just tell Elias, Simon." Her voice took on the solemn tone of announcing a death. "Elias, Adele Harcourt died."

"She was a hundred and five, for Christ's sake," said Elias. "Max Luby said she was gaga."

"You're missing the big picture, Elias," said Ruby. "The point is Adele Harcourt will get all the press in tomorrow's papers, which is great for us."

"Yeah, you're right," said Elias. "Didn't I give her a couple million dollars for the Manhattan Public Library and some more for the Adele Harcourt Pavilion at New York–Presbyterian Hospital?"

"Yes. The library was when she had us to dinner," said

Ruby. "Simon, thank you for calling. Elias just reminded me that he once gave Adele a very generous gift for the Manhattan Public Library and for the Adele Harcourt Pavilion at New York–Presbyterian Hospital."

"I think it would be a good thing if you attended the funeral," said Simon. "It would be a good place for Elias to be seen in public in New York after just getting out of prison. And you can wear the suit with the sable collar and cuffs that would have looked wrong outside the prison."

"A funeral like that will probably be by invitation only," said Ruby.

"That can be arranged," said Simon. "One of the ushers is a friend of mine. He was the walker for Adele Harcourt in the last year of her life." Former quickie trick would have been a more apt description of the friend, Addison Kent, but Simon Cabot was always a gentleman and kept that part of his life under lock and key.

THERE WAS sadness but not shock when the announcement of Adele Harcourt's death was made. Her passing was not unexpected. She was, after all, as Elias Renthal had pointed out, a hundred and five years old, and she had not been seen in public since she had tripped on the linoleum in Lil Altemus's kitchen and broken her hip. Her broken hip had led to pneumonia. She had refused to go to the hospital. She knew she was at the end of the line, and she wanted to die in the Park Avenue apartment where she had lived for so many years.

Things had begun to change in the apartment, but, alas, she did not notice. George, her trusted butler of so many years, had been let go. The weekly delivery of flowers for the whole apartment from Brucie's shop in the Rhinelander Hotel was canceled. When she was unconscious, her nightgowns and bed jackets were not changed, nor were her Porthault sheets changed daily, as they once had been. Her closest friends knew the end was near, but they kept discreetly silent on the subject out of loyalty. The ever-faithful George, who had always organized the seating and written out the place cards and menu cards for Adele's dinner parties, called every day to check with the maids on Madame's condition. When he had moved out of the servants' quarters where he had lived in contentment for so many years, he had said to the two weeping maids, Floriana and Ascensión, who hated to see him leave, that he suspected the fagola from Boothby's auction house, who often took Madame to the movies, had carried off the tiny portrait of Marie Antoinette by Vigée Le Brun that had been Madame's favorite of all her pictures.

IN THE backseat of Ruby Renthal's dark green Mercedes limousine, with the glass window raised between the chauffeur and the occupants, Ruby said to Elias, "Well, that wasn't too bad. There weren't that many photographers, and wasn't Jacques marvelous, rushing us right by them and into the backseat?" She picked up the telephone and buzzed. "Jacques, I was just saying to Mr. Renthal what a wonderful job you did there in the airport whisking us past the photographers. We're so appreciative. Now, will you phone ahead to the house and tell George, the new butler, to have all the lights on and the fireplaces lit? Tell him that as soon as the car pulls up in front of the house, he is to open the door so that we can run inside in case there are photographers waiting outside. Oh, and another thing, ask George to tell Gert that it will take me about forty-five minutes to show Mr. Renthal around the new house, and then we'll have dinner. In the small dining room, but Gert knows all that. Make sure there's ice in the silver bucket on the bar, and Mr. Renthal likes his lemon twist cut very thin for his martini." She hung up the phone and leaned back on the seat next to her husband. "I love giving orders to the help. Are you excited, Elias?"

"I can't believe it. I'm back in New York City," said Elias.

"You're free. That's all that matters," said Ruby.

"I'm out of prison, but you know I'm not necessarily free, I mean *really* free. I'm on what they call supervised release. It's a fancy way of saying probation."

"What does it mean? You have to report to a parole officer?" asked Ruby.

"That's right. If we travel anywhere, I have to get written permission."

"Written permission to fly on our very own plane?" asked Ruby in a shocked voice.

"You got it," said Elias. "The parole officer can drop in on me at any time, which could be embarrassing if we should be having dinner at Swifty's, or entertaining at home. They hate rich people. They like to embarrass people like us. Max tells me it's even worse since all the bailouts. People seem to be taking their frustrations out on us as a group."

"Wait until the parole officer sees the house you're about to move into," said Ruby.

"Or they can call you on the phone at two o'clock in the morning, just to make sure you're there."

"But you served your time. You took your medicine. It's not fair. Does that mean we have to act humble? Dear God, wait until you hear about the party I'm planning to give."

"Tell me," said Elias.

"Later. I have a present for you," she said. She took a small black velvet box out of her bag.

"Oh, my," said Elias. "Jewels for the ex-convict."

"Don't jump to conclusions about jewels, and don't call yourself an ex-convict, even as a joke. Open it."

"A key," said Elias.

"A solid gold key with a ruby, my stone, set in it," said Ruby.

"What's it for?" asked Elias.

"It's for the front door of the most beautiful house on the Upper East Side of New York City, which happens to be the new home of Mr. and Mrs. Elias Renthal," said Ruby.

As the dark green Mercedes limousine pulled up in front of the house that was still known as the Tavistock mansion, the bronze front door opened. There stood the new butler, George—who had been Adele Harcourt's ever-faithful butler for so many years until he had been fired by Adele's nephew and his wife—waiting to welcome his new employers. Jacques, the new chauffeur, hopped out and ran around to open the rear door. Ruby got out of the car first and then she turned back and directed Jacques in helping Elias get out of the car. Just as he stood on the sidewalk and looked up at his new house, a couple walked past them. It was Ormolu and Percy Webb walking to their apartment on the corner of Fifth Avenue and Seventy-eighth Street after leaving an impromptu buffet evening at Christine Saunders's, where they all had found themselves since they were free after the cancelation of the American Ballet Theater's performance and gala because of Adele Harcourt's death. Just before the moment when the two couples came face-to-face, Ormolu, who hadn't wanted to walk home in the first place, whispered to Percy, "Oh, my god, it's the Renthals, home from prison." As the two couples's paths crossed, neither knew what to say.

"Hellohowareyou?" said Ormolu, giving the smile she saved for people who were lesser than she. She and Percy kept on walking without stopping.

"That's what I call being snubbed," said Ruby. "I hate that bitch."

"Is that the way it's going to be?" asked Elias.

"We can handle it, Elias." She took his arm. "Ormolu is pissed at me because I've tied up Ferdy Trocadero for the last four months doing his special brand of seventeen coats of paint in all the public rooms, and Ormolu wants Ferdy Trocadero to repaint her dining room."

"Who the fuck is Ferdy Trocadero?" asked Elias.

"And this is George, our new butler. He used to be with Adele Harcourt. He's in mourning, so be nice."

"Sorry for your loss," said Elias, passing George to enter his new home.

Ruby took Elias by the hand and led him from room to room in the magnificent house on East Seventy-eighth Street that was to be their home. "My God, Ruby," Elias kept saying. "This is beautiful. I had no idea I was coming back to live in a palace like the Vanderbilts used to have, and the Rockefellers, and those kind of people. Where did you buy all this fancy French furniture?"

"All the eighteenth-century French pieces I got at Perla Zacharias's auction at Boothby's," said Ruby. "She got rid of all the furniture that didn't get burned in the fire at the villa in Biarritz."

"I recognize some of the pieces that we used to have," said Elias.

"They didn't sell everything in the auction of all our stuff when you went to the facility, so I put everything that didn't sell in storage, waiting for the day you'd be out," said Ruby.

"These curtains, these rugs, these pictures. How did you put it all together with no publicity?" He looked in all directions in wonder. Every room looked rich, rich, rich, a look they loved.

"That was the whole point. No one knew what was going on in this house for the past ten months except Maisie Verdurin and my friend Charlotte de Liagra, who lives in Paris and knows more about decorating than anyone."

"So the muff diver's still in the picture, huh?"

"Don't screw up our first night in our new house, Elias," Ruby said with an edge in her voice.

"Oh, sorry."

"Now comes the real surprise," said Ruby as she led him into the elevator and pushed the down button.

"How come I smell chlorine?" asked Elias.

"Because you are about to see the largest indoor swimming pool of any private house in the city of New York," said Ruby.

"Holy shit," said Elias in delight. "This is not like any ordinary swimming pool."

"The columns and everything were copied after the pool at the Hearst Castle in California," said Ruby. "It was Baroness de Liagra's idea. Like I said, the baroness practically decorated the whole house. That woman has taste."

"You're not still sniffing her pussy, are you?" asked Elias.

"Oh, for god's sake, Elias. I told you that was a onetime thing for the experience. Now we're just best friends."

"But you liked it that one time, you said," said Elias.

"What I said was, it was not unpleasant. You know what my preference is. I can still take both your nuts in my mouth at the same time, if that will get you out of your suspicious mood and make you enjoy this palace that is our home."

"I like you when you're cheap," said Elias.

"So you've told me in the past," replied Ruby. "It's not my favorite compliment."

"Where is the baroness? She's not tucked away in one of the fourteen bedrooms, is she?"

"No, she has a horse running in Chantilly this Saturday," said Ruby.

"Oh, excuse me," replied Elias.

"Charlotte thinks we should hire the Aquacade show at the Seraglio Hotel to perform in the pool when we give the party of parties to open this house to New York. The pool filled with gardenias. High dives by great-looking guys. Water ballet out of the Esther Williams movies with beautiful young women, and the guests can stand on that balcony up there. We'll be the talk of New York again. We'll be where we were."

She kissed Elias and began rubbing her hand over his trousers. "You just lean up against that eighteenth-century ormolu cabinet I bought from Winkie Williams's sale at Boothby's and unbutton those fly buttons on your Savile Row suit and let me attend to my carnal tasks," said Ruby.

Elias laughed in delight. "That's the Ruby I missed, the raunchy Ruby I first fell in love with." He reached into his open fly and took out his penis. "Here, take it, baby. It's been a long, long time."

"Dear God," she said, looking at the task ahead of her. "How many Viagras did it take to get this?"

Unable to wait one second more, Elias put his hand over her beautiful red hair and pushed her down to her knees.

"Don't forget. We have to go to Adele Harcourt's funeral in the morning," said Ruby.

"Her dying now, just as I get out of prison, was probably her way of thanking me for the couple of million dollars I gave her for the Manhattan Public Library and the Adele Harcourt Pavilion," said Elias.

"Let's not go that far," said Ruby. "I think her age and her broken hip in Lil Altemus's kitchen had a little more to do with it."

"That's going to be some funeral, from what I read in the papers. You're sure we're definitely invited?"

"Simon Cabot arranged the whole thing."

"I can't wait to take a swim in the morning in my new indoor swimming pool."

CHAPTER 19

NEW YORK SOCIETY HAD GONE INTO MOURNING.
Dinners were canceled. The American Ballet Theater's opening-night benefit at Lincoln Center was
canceled out of respect to Adele Harcourt. Mrs. Zenda, the
chairperson, was distressed after seating all those tables, but she
understood. Mrs. Zacharias called Simon Cabot in London to
arrange for her to be invited to the reception at the Butterfield
Club after the funeral. A great deal of the population of New
York went into their own sort of mourning, as Adele Harcourt
had done more for the city in a philanthropic way than any other
person. She had given her entire fortune, which was considerable, to the city of New York over the years. She was possibly
New York's most beloved public figure, a role she cherished,
and the *New York Times* carried the story of her death on the
front page above the fold, with a long continuation of her good
deeds and strenuous social life on the page before the editorials.
Her generosity had made her famous, and her name was as well
known in certain barrios and slums as it was on Park Avenue,
where she lived and went forth each evening in beautiful gowns
and jewels to enjoy her role as queen of society.

"I was in the room with Adele when she died," said Lil Altemus, whenever the subject came up between Adele's death and her funeral at St. James' Church on Madison Avenue and Seventy-first Street. When she recounted the moment of death, she did not repeat that she had just told Adele that the Manhattan Public Library was to be named after Konstantin and Perla Zacharias because Perla had given a lump sum of a hundred million dollars to the library, which had been Adele Harcourt's favorite charity. "It was so peaceful," said Lil. "She had such a lovely smile on her face. Beatific, really, and then she simply stopped breathing." Addison Kent told Ethan Trescher, who had quietly handled Adele Harcourt's public relations for so many years, and Ethan passed on Lil's quote to Kit Jones, the gossip columnist, who led off her column with Lil's touching words.

"How in the world do you suppose that got into Kit Jones's column," said Lil, who was secretly thrilled, although she always criticized people she knew whose names were in the paper too much. "At least Kit Jones always handles it so well for people like us now that Dolores De Longpre has retired."

IT WAS Ethan Trescher who ran Adele Harcourt's funeral at St. James' Church. St. James' was the church of choice for the old Protestant families of New York. Van Rensselaers, Vanderbilts, Van Degans all worshiped at St. James'. It was the church where Billy Grenville's funeral had taken place after his beautiful wife from the wrong side of the tracks shot him to death as he emerged nude from his shower. It was where the funeral of Hubert Altemus, the son of Lil Altemus, had taken place after his death from AIDS, which his mother had never acknowledged as the cause, even when his Puerto Rican lover had shown up uninvited and had been offered a seat in the family pews by Dodo Van Degan. It was the church where the heiress Justine Altemus, the daughter of Lil Altemus, had been married in a disastrous and very brief union to Bernard Slatkin, the television reporter who was now enjoying great success covering the Middle East for NBC. Justine had moved to Paris to live with a new husband and taken her daughter, Cordelia, by Bernard Slatkin, with her.

Outside, Madison Avenue in the Seventies had to be closed off with barriers to deal with the throngs of people who simply wanted to watch Adele Harcourt's casket—covered with thousands of lilies of the valley, arranged beautifully by Brucie, the florist in the Rhinelander Hotel—pass by in the newest of hearses, provided by Grant P. Trumbull's, the most prestigious mortuary in the city. In the driver's seat of the hearse sat Francis Xavior Branigan, the assistant funeral director and secret lover of Dodo Van Degan, whose heart beat with excitement at the importance of his position in what he would later tell his friends Brucie and Jonsie had been the funeral of the year. "The spray of lilies of the valley on the casket was bliss, Brucie," he would say.

Ethan Trescher stood in the back of the church watching every entrance, waiting to spot the people who were to be given special treatment, making eye contact with the sixteen ushers who were seating people. Ethan Trescher was the master of seating. He was a gentleman of the old school. Adele Harcourt had counted on him for years to arrange her great charity events and to call Dolores De Longpre when it became absolutely necessary to deal with an issue.

He had instructed the ushers, of whom Addison Kent was one, that dignitaries such as former first lady Laura Bush, as well as the Duke of Chatfield, who was representing Prince Charles, a very special friend of Adele's, were to be seated in the first row on the left side of the aisle. The mayor, the governor, the two senators, the president of the Metropolitan Museum of

Art, the president of the Manhattan Public Library—whose
board, as Toby Tilden had announced in that morning's *Post,*
had approved its change of name to the Konstantin and Perla
Zacharias Public Library since Perla Zacharias had donated one
hundred million dollars in one lump sum. It was a matter causing great dismay in upper-class circles, many members of which
whispered thanks that Adele Harcourt had not lived to hear the
news. There were also various dignitaries of the city, whom
Ethan would recognize, who were to be in the twelve rows behind Laura Bush and Bunny Chatfield, who was accompanied
by his duchess, Chiquita. Everyone loved Chiquita.

"The prince was so sorry not to be able to come and sends
you his warmest regards," said Chiquita to Ethan when he was
personally showing the duchess to her seat. Chiquita chatted all
the way up the aisle. "Camilla sends her love. She's been staying
with us at Deeds Castle. Diana's butler, that awful Paul Burrell,
shudder, shudder, shudder, is taking the stand tomorrow at that
awful trial at the Old Bailey—they say he stole all those things
from darling Diana—and the prince simply can't be out of England, even though he adored Adele." Ethan, who was used to
that kind of conversation, later passed it on to Kit Jones for her
column.

The right side of the aisle was reserved for family and close
friends. Under normal circumstances, Adele Harcourt would
have lain in state at the Armory on Park Avenue and Sixty-sixth
Street, where she had celebrated her ninetieth birthday, but the
Winter Antiques Show had booked the space and couldn't be
moved on such short notice. However, out of respect for Adele,
who always attended the opening night, the Antiques Show
closed its doors for the hour and a half of Adele Harcourt's
funeral.

"She was like our own Queen Mum," said Gert Hoolihan,
standing in the crowd as the hearse went by, to a young lady by

her side. She took a Kleenex from her bag and wiped the tears in her eyes. Gert had cooked many a meal for Adele Harcourt over the years, when she had been Lil Altemus's cook. "Mrs. Harcourt always loved my fig mousse. She'd come back to the kitchen after dinner to tell me. 'Gert, you outdid yourself,' she'd say. No airs from her, like some of these people have, no names mentioned here. Let's move up closer to the entrance so we can watch the important people go in."

Lil Altemus, even when she was still rich, never used limousines, which she thought were vulgar. "They're all right for movie stars and rock stars and all those new people nobody ever heard of before who have so much money these days and are ruining Southampton," she often said. Instead, she used her Buick station wagon, which was driven for years by her chauffeur, Jimmy. After leaving her Fifth Avenue apartment, she had to sell the Buick station wagon and let Jimmy go. She had become dependent on old friends for rides to the theater, to the opera, and to weddings and funerals. On the day of Adele Harcourt's funeral, she arrived at the church with her friend Kay Kay Somerset in a Lincoln Town Car from a car service, which Kay Kay was paying for.

"My word, look at all these people," said Lil as she stepped out of the car. "Did you tell the driver to wait for us and take us to the reception at the Butterfield Club?"

"Yes, Lil," said Kay Kay. "It's the fourth time you've asked me that."

"This is the biggest funeral they've had here at St. James' since Ann Grenville killed Billy," said Lil. "Ann was so trashy she wanted to come to the funeral after she shot him with a twelve-gauge shotgun, but Alice simply wouldn't allow it. Just look at these people behind the barriers. Everyone's behaving so well. The people loved Adele. It's really so touching, isn't it?"

"End of an era," said Kay Kay. "I'm going to run over and say hello to Petal Wilson and tell her I can't go to the matinee tomorrow because my daughter's coming to town unexpectedly from St. Louis. Something must be wrong with the marriage, I suppose. This is her third marriage, for god's sake, and she's only thirty. You'd think she'd learn to get it right eventually. I'll look for you in the vestibule, Lil. Don't go up to the seats without me."

"Oh, no, I won't. Addison Kent is saving us places. I'll look for him," said Lil.

"Mrs. Altemus?"

Lil recognized the voice and turned around to see Gert standing in the crowd. She had not seen or heard from her since Gert's unpleasant leave-taking to go into the employ of Ruby Renthal, who had offered her more money and a room with a sitting room and free trips to Ireland on Elias Renthal's G550, which Lil had considered a betrayal. Several times she had felt guilty that she had screamed at Gert, and fired her, and told her to get out of her apartment right then and there after Gert had been with her for so many years, but always the outrage of Gert's perfidy squashed the competing thought. She firmly believed that Gert had betrayed her by going to work for the Elias Renthals. She had often wondered what she would do if she ran into Gert at Grace's Marketplace, where Lil now did her own marketing. In her thoughts of the imagined meeting, she snubbed her, walked right by pretending she didn't see her.

"Oh my goodness, hellohowareyou?" said Lil, in a distant tone of voice she sometimes used with servants.

"I had to come, Missus," said Gert nervously, who understood Lil's tone of voice from the many years she had worked for her but was determined to go on with what she had to say. "I had to pay my respects to Mrs. Harcourt. She was always so good to me, and she fell and broke her hip in my kitchen. I mean *your* kitchen, excuse me. I feel that somehow I played a little part in her story."

"Yes, I suppose you did," said Lil. "Knowing Mrs. Harcourt as I did, I'm sure that she would have been very touched that you came. Actually, I was with her when she died."

"I read that in Kit Jones's column," said Gert.

As Lil started to move off to the steps of the church, Gert said quickly, "Mrs. Altemus, before you go into the church, I'd like you to meet my niece, and your namesake, Lillian Hoolihan, who has just moved here to New York from Roscommon in Ireland, where the whole family is from."

Lil turned toward the young woman, whom she had not looked at before.

"Hello, Mrs. Altemus," said Lillian Hoolihan. "My late mother, bless her soul, always said it was Gert who wanted me to be named after you. At home in school, at Our Lady of Sorrows, they called me Lil, just like you. It's an honor to meet you, ma'am."

Later, Gert said to her niece that she thought she had seen the beginning of a tear in Mrs. Altemus's eyes. "Thank you, Lillian. Thank you. That's very nice," said Lil, looking ahead. "Oh, Kay Kay, wait up a second, and we'll go in together. Addison Kent is an usher, and he knows exactly where I'm supposed to be seated. Third row, right-hand side, directly behind Adele's nephew and his wife from Wyoming or someplace. Good-bye, Gert."

"Bye, Missus."

"Wasn't that Gert you were talking to?" asked Kay Kay Somerset. "I thought you were never going to speak to her again, ever, ever, ever, after she walked out on you to work for Mrs. Renthal, leaving you high and dry."

"You can't imagine what happened. That girl with her is her niece, the one she was always going to Ireland to visit every year, and she's named Lillian after me, but the girls in her school called her Lil. Don't you love it? I didn't know which way to look. I will say that Adele always loved Gert's fig mousse."

"Adele's butler, George, told my maid that Adele thought Gert's fig mousse was good for her bowels," said Kay Kay.

"Make sure you tell that to Gert on the way out after the service," said Lil.

"Oh, hello, Addison. I hope you've saved us our seats. Third row, right-hand side, right behind the Wyoming nephew and his wife. I knew you would. You know Kay Kay Somerset, of course. It's just too sad. It's too sad for words. I can't imagine New York without Adele. You were so sweet to her, Addison. Taking her to the movies in the afternoon, all those nice things you did. Do I take your arm to go up to my seat or just follow you?"

Still rattled by her encounter with Gert and caught up in mourning for darling Adele, as well as excitement over her plum seating assignment, Lil chose to be warm to Addison Kent, whom she normally found contemptible.

"I have something for you, Lil," said Addison as he took her arm and walked up the aisle. "Adele asked me to give it to you, and there's one for Loelia. Here. Just slip it in your purse." He handed Lil a small leather box.

"What is it?" asked Lil.

"An emerald and diamond ring that Adele wanted you to have," said Addison, happy to be in such an enviable position. "Loelia got the ruby and diamond one. This way there's no tax and no wait and no family and no lawyers involved."

"Well, I certainly hope the police won't be tracking me down looking for stolen goods," said Lil, who would have preferred to have received the emerald and diamond ring from a lawyer, saying it had been bequeathed to her by Adele Harcourt, accompanied by a lovely note from Adele on her blue Smythson stationery, telling her the history of the beautiful jewel. Receiving it from Addison Kent in such a manner was furtive, she felt, especially while walking up the aisle to her seat at Adele's funeral.

Once seated in the third row, she nodded to the young couple from Wyoming, who returned her greeting. "Topher and Diane Abernathy, this is my great friend Kay Kay Somerset. Topher is Adele's nephew. Your aunt Adele is watching over us today. You can be sure of that. She told me all about your avocado ranch. Tell me about your mother. She and I were in the same class at Farmington. We called her Ticky in those days. I didn't make the fiftieth reunion, I'm afraid, or I would have seen her. I read all about it, though, in the alumnae bulletin, and I saw that Ticky was there. Do please give her my love."

She settled back into her seat next to Kay Kay and showed her the leather box.

"What is it?" asked Kay Kay.

"Oh, look. There's Laura Bush. She looks good in purple, don't you think? She's so much better dressed than when she first came east from Crawford. A little Crawford goes a long way for me. Once Oscar started dressing her, he gave her a whole new look."

"What's in the leather box?" asked Kay Kay.

Lil opened the box and was overcome by the beauty of the ring. She remembered having admired it many times when Adele had worn her emeralds.

"Put it on," whispered Kay Kay.

"Don't you think it would be a little much to wear it at her funeral?" asked Lil. She indicated with her head the young relatives from Wyoming and mouthed the name Topher.

"Just to see how it looks, and then take it off again and put it in your bag," said Kay Kay.

Lil put it on. "Look," she said, holding her hand low behind the pew lest anyone see what she was doing and find it distasteful.

"It's beautiful," said Kay Kay. "Why aren't you more excited?"

"Do you know what I don't like about Addison Kent? He's far too inside for such an outsider, if you know what I mean. Imagine him handing me this ring from Adele when he's walking me up the aisle at her funeral," said Lil, abandoning the feeling of kinship she'd had with Addison just moments earlier. "Of course I'm going to keep it, but I wonder how much I could get for it."

"Shhh," whispered Kay Kay, pointing with her finger at the pew in front of them.

"Oh, listen to that music," said Lil, shifting the conversation. "Isn't it heavenly? I hear Renée Fleming's going to sing the Ave Maria. Adele adored Renee Fleming. She went to every Renée Fleming concert, and she went to every opera she sang at the Met. She used to have her to tea, even. Oh, look at those choirboys in their red cassocks and their white surplices. Aren't they adorable? Adele planned the whole thing, you know, with a little help from Ethan Trescher, of course, who knows how to run big events like nobody else. Look how beautiful the altar looks. The flowers are to die for. I see the fine hand of Brucie arranging all the flowers. There's Lita and Otto Aksam. There's Bunny and Chiquita Chatfield in the same pew with Mrs. Bush. Have you met Chiquita? She's a riot. She's his fourth, I think. They must have come all the way from London for the funeral. There are the Sandovals, back together again, thank God. Ormolu and Percy Webb."

"Wonderful suit on Ormolu, don't you think?" asked Kay Kay.

"It's Oscar's. There's Perla Zacharias with the face-lift of the decade," said Lil, assuming a look of disapproval. "She has no shame, that woman. She thinks her money can buy her way in anywhere. There's such a thing as too much money, you know. This business at the library is really too much. I told you Adele's reaction when I told her. She just died, there and then. Ethan had to invite Perla. Oh, listen. The music's changing. They're bringing in the casket soon. I don't know if I can look at the casket. Poor Adele. I'll miss her so. I think I'll just look at the lilies of the valley. Oh, my god, there's Xavior Branigan, the one walking in front of the casket. He's the assistant funeral director at Grant P. Trumbull's."

"How in the world do you know the name of the assistant funeral director at Grant P. Trumbull's?" asked Kay Kay.

"Well, I'll tell you how I know his name," said Lil, leaning over to whisper in Kay Kay Somerset's ear. "He's having an affair with my stepmother. Can you imagine?"

"With Dodo? I can't believe it. It's too hilarious," said Kay Kay.

"Isn't it killing? And she's mad about him." They shook with silent laughter at the absurdity of poor Dodo, the widow of Ormond Van Degan, one of the great men of New York, being besotted with Francis Xavior Branigan, the assistant funeral director of the Grant P. Trumbull Funeral Home. "He looks a little light on his feet if you ask me," said Lil. "Oh, my god, I can't believe my eyes, what I'm seeing. I just might faint."

"What do you see?" asked Kay Kay.

"Elias Renthal, fresh from prison, looking for a seat far too near the front so everyone can see him," replied Lil. "Look at the look on Ethan Trescher's face. He's furious, simply furious. Renthal just pushed by him as if he didn't exist. Prison manners, that's what I call it."

"Look, he's trying to say hello to you, Lil," said Kay Kay. "He's even waving, with a big smile on his face."

"I looked right through him, as if I didn't know who he

was," said Lil. "Who do these people think they are? They're nobody anymore, but they don't seem to know it yet. Elias Renthal didn't even know Adele. Isn't it typical he'd come here on his first day out of prison?"

"You're wrong, Lil. He did know Adele," said Kay Kay. "He gave a large donation to the library, several million I think it was, and Adele had him and Ruby to dinner. You were there. I remember seeing you."

"He was there exactly one time, as a payback," replied Lil. "At least he won't have the nerve to go to the Butterfield Club for the reception afterward. They only invited three hundred, and the Renthals were definitely *not* on the list. They kicked Renthal out of the Butterfield, don't you remember? It was my dear brother, Laurance, who wrote the letter."

"Ruby's still quite pretty," said Kay Kay. "I haven't seen her for years. I wonder who did her face. Whoever it was did a fabulous job. That's a marvelous suit she's wearing, with the sable on the collar and cuffs."

"Karl Lagerfeld for Chanel Couture, eleven thousand dollars. Addison Kent told me. That Baroness de Liagra orders Ruby's clothes for her in Paris. You've heard the *on-dit* on the baroness, haven't you?" Looking directly at her old friend, she mouthed but did not say the word *lesbian,* about the baroness. Again they shook with silent laughter.

"Lil, how do you know all these things?" asked Kay Kay.

"Winkie Williams would have loved this funeral," said Lil, ignoring her friend.

RUBY, MARCHING up toward the front on the arm of Addison Kent, looked straight ahead. "Just don't seat us in the same row with Perla Zacharias," said Ruby to Addison. "We can't give people that kind of ammunition on our first day back. Elias, be more careful and dignified. It looks like you're climbing over people just to get to our seat."

"Lil Altemus didn't acknowledge me," said Elias to Ruby, when they were settled in a third-row seat over on the far right under the rose window. Simon Cabot had made the seating arrangement for the Renthals from London over the telephone with Addison Kent, who had become the full-time walker of Perla Zacharias since Adele Harcourt had taken ill and stopped going out socially. "I leaned over and waved to Lil and she saw me and then looked straight ahead. Is that's the way it's going to be for us?"

"How did you like your first dinner in the new house last night? All your favorite things: crown roast, asparagus," said Ruby.

"Great, great. I told you last night it was great. What the fuck does that have to do with what I'm talking about, that Lil Altemus just snubbed me?"

"Shhh. Forgodssake, don't say 'fuck' in St. James' Church. That's the rose window that Alice Grenville gave after Ann Grenville shot Billy Grenville," said Ruby, pointing upward.

"That doesn't answer my question," said Elias, impatiently.

"Well, the delicious meal last night, where you had three helpings of the crown roast, three helpings of asparagus hollandaise, and two pieces of apple pie, was cooked by the famous Gert Hoolihan, who was Lil Altemus's cook for twenty-five years, or something like that, when Lil lived in the big apartment on Fifth Avenue," said Ruby.

"That was Gert who cooked? Gert who used to make the fig mousse at Lil's, and all the guests clapped for her after dinner?" asked Elias.

"Yes, that was Gert," said Ruby.

"And how did Gert end up in our kitchen, please?" asked Elias.

"I saw her walking wearily down Third Avenue one day burdened with groceries from Grace's Marketplace, and I gave her a ride in the Mercedes because she had to go back to Clyde's pharmacy because she'd forgotten to pick up Lil Altemus's special order. I doubled her salary, gave her a little sitting room, and promised that you'd drop her off in Dublin when you fly on the G Five Fifty to London."

"No wonder Lil didn't speak to me," said Elias.

"I suppose it's a combination of me stealing her cook and you being an ex-convict, which is what I hear she calls you," said Ruby.

Elias blushed. He knew that whatever he did in his new life the word *ex-convict* would always be used to describe him. Gus Bailey, whom Elias so disliked, had written in his diary in *Park Avenue* that the word would be in the first line of Elias's obituary when he died.

"Gert is much better off with me," said Ruby. "She was wasting her talents in that dinky little kitchen of Lil Altemus's where Adele Harcourt tripped on the linoleum. With us she has an enormous kitchen and exactly the same stove they have at Le Cirque. A big stove is what she missed most after Lil had to give up the Fifth Avenue apartment and moved to the place on East Sixty-sixth Street. And the maids do the washing and cleaning up. She doesn't have to do any of that."

"Why didn't you buy Lil's old apartment when she moved out? That would have been a good place for us," asked Elias, still smarting from the snub.

"Because Lil blackballed us when she was still on the board," said Ruby. "Maisie Verdurin told me so."

Lil looked over and waved to Gus, a gesture not lost on Elias Renthal. He loathed Gus. He was still livid that Gus had put on a television show about Elias's case just at the time Elias was getting ready to leave prison, bringing the whole thing up again, after most people had forgotten about it after Elias's seven years of incarceration, or so Elias liked to believe. He flashed Gus a withering look, as if he were expecting Gus to shrink in fear of him. Gus looked at him as if he'd never seen him before. He was also aware that Perla Zacharias was seated directly behind him, but he did not turn in her direction.

"THE LAWSUIT'S changed Gus, don't you think?" said Lil.

"Tremendously," replied Kay Kay. "He used to be so funny and full of stories. Now he hardly opens his mouth at dinner; I have to pry information from him. The spark's gone out. I sat next to him the other night at Maisie's. Then he pretended he was going to the men's room and he never came back. He just left."

"He's devastated by this horrendous situation. He switched to another lawyer here in New York, after *Park Avenue* hired that woman from Washington."

"Look, there's Lord and Lady Cudlip, or Stanford and Mimi, as Christine Saunders called them on her television program," said Kay Kay.

"I heard he's going to go belly-up," replied Lil.

"Oh, no, it couldn't be. They're much, much too rich."

"And overextended. You wait. It's all going to come out. On one of the rare occasions recently that he did open his mouth, Gus Bailey told me about it the other night. It's just a matter of time. I heard Lord Cudlip flew out to Las Vegas to visit Elias Renthal in jail again just last week, just as Elias was about to be released, that's how desperate he was, and asked if he could borrow thirty million dollars, and Elias Renthal turned him down."

"Oh, look, the bishop, Bishop Kinsolving. Look at those gold vestments," said Kay Kay.

"The bishop was such a good friend of Adele's. She always

had him to her big dinners, seated right next to her on her left. He was in my brother Laurance's class at both St. Paul's and Harvard. We used to call him Teddy in those days."

"Look. Lord Cudlip just cut Elias Renthal dead," said Kay Kay. "No money, no talkee."

"Oh, listen, Renée Fleming is singing the Ave Maria. Isn't it heaven? Isn't it thrilling? Do you think it's all right to turn around and look up at the choir loft? Adele adored Renée."

"You already told me that, and I already knew it before you told me," said Kay Kay.

"NOBODY CAN leave the church before Laura Bush," said Ethan Trescher, speaking to the ushers, who were gathered in the vestibule during Bishop Kinsolving's eulogy. "Immediately at the end of the service, even before we escort the casket out to the hearse, the Secret Service will take Mrs. Bush out the side door on East Seventy-first Street. I understand she is returning directly to Texas. She will not be coming to the Butterfield for the reception."

"Ethan?" said Addison Kent. "Is it all right if I go back in? I want to listen to Renée Fleming sing the Ave Maria."

"Oh, there are the Kissingers," said Ethan. "They've finally arrived. Their plane was late from London. I'll take them to their seats."

"Better late then never, I suppose," said Addison, snidely, who had never met the Kissingers, as he opened the door to listen to Renée Fleming sing.

"YOU GOTTA hand it to the Protestants, when it comes to this kind of service," said Elias. "I feel like I'm in Westminster

Abbey. Who's that singing? Good voice on that lady. May I make an observation?"

"If you keep your voice down," said Ruby through clenched teeth.

"There's not one man wearing a rug in this entire church. I gotta tell Max Luby to stop wearing his brand-new thousand-dollar rug before his testimonial dinner on the twelfth. Don't forget to mark that down. Oh, my god, there are the Cudlips," said Elias.

"They always look so rich," said Ruby.

"You look pretty rich yourself, with those sable cuffs."

It was a compliment Ruby loved. It gave her confidence.

"Sometimes you can be very sweet, Elias."

"Did I tell you he flew out to see me again at the facility in Las Vegas last week?"

"Again? No, you didn't tell me that."

"In all the excitement of leaving the facility, I must have forgot."

"I didn't know you and he were that close. Did he put you on his board?"

"It wasn't that kind of visit. He wanted to borrow thirty million dollars."

"Thirty million dollars?" asked Ruby.

"Don't worry. I turned him down. Lending him money is like flushing it down the toilet bowl. He's in big trouble. I wouldn't be a bit surprised if he's not going to the same place I just got out of."

"I'm shocked," said Ruby. "They've been taking New York by storm. Ormolu Webb just gave a big party for them. What did he do?"

"Turns out he's just another corporate tycoon charged with criminal fraud, racketeering, obstruction of justice, money laundering. Stuff like that," said Elias.

The exit of the former first lady was handled with dispatch immediately after the service. People sitting several rows back were not even aware that she was being whisked out a side door onto East Seventy-first Street. The music in the church was triumphant as the ushers, led by Francis Xavior Branigan, escorted Adele Harcourt's casket down the aisle while the congregation stood. Outside, the crowds clapped courteously for the great lady of New York as her casket was placed into the Grant P. Trumbull hearse. Most people did not notice that the lady sitting in the front seat of the hearse was Dodo Van Degan. Francis Xavior Branigan said, "I hope this won't make 'Page Six.' " Within minutes the funeralgoers inside the church began to pour out of the three main doors of St. James'. Some stood on the steps and the sidewalk to greet friends. Others stopped to sign the books inside each entrance.

Although there were eleven hundred people attending the service, only three hundred had been invited to the reception at the Butterfield Club on Fifth Avenue. Photographers, angry that they had missed the former first lady, pushed forward to take pictures of the other celebrities. "Mayor Bloomberg, turn this way." " Mr. Kissinger, look over here." "Miss Fleming, look this way, please." "There's Elias Renthal. He just got out of prison yesterday." "Hey, Ruby, look over here." "What's it like being out of prison, Mr. Renthal?" "Did you have to wear a striped suit, Elias?" "Did you see Gus Bailey's television show about you?" "Did you really pay a million dollars to put a new roof on some English castle?" "Is it true you had to clean toilets?"

LIL ALTEMUS and Kay Kay Somerset made their way to their car, straight-faced as they passed the Renthals being screamed at by the media. "At least they weren't invited to the reception at the Butterfield," said Lil in passing, even though she'd already said it to Kay Kay in the church. "Hello, Gus. Wasn't it lovely? It was like Adele was there. She planned the whole thing, you know. Would you like a ride to the Butterfield with Kay Kay and me?"

"Thanks, Lil, I think I'll walk," said Gus. "I see on my cell phone that my lawyer has called, and I want to return that. I'll see you there."

As he walked down Madison Avenue, Gus dialed his lawyer Peter Lombardo's private number.

"I've been to a funeral," said Gus when Peter answered.

"Adele Harcourt's. I imagined you were there," said Peter.

"I'm on my way to the reception at the Butterfield. What bad news on my slander case has happened?"

"I heard from Win Burch."

"His name sends chills through me."

"They've set the date for the deposition."

Gus had been a nervous wreck for the last several months, while waiting for the deposition. Strangers who had been cross-examined by Burch in other slander cases wrote or e-mailed Gus letters about the terrifying experience it had been. They said he was called the Pit Bull. This could ruin Gus if it didn't go his way, not just financially, but it could mean his career was over— and he didn't have it in him to start again. The whole mess made him feel tired and ill. He just didn't know if he had the strength for this.

JACQUES OPENED the back door of Ruby's dark green Mercedes-Benz and Ruby and Elias got in as quickly as possible. Elias was breathing heavily. He leaned his head back on the upholstered seat. He closed his eyes. His mouth hung open.

Ruby looked at him, aghast. "Elias, are you all right?" she asked. "Open your eyes."

"Yeah, I'm all right," he said.

"Your heart's beating a mile a minute," said Ruby, putting her hand inside his suit jacket.

When Elias spoke, he spoke slowly. "That was a terrible experience, having those reporters screaming at me, asking me questions about the facility. Only they called it prison. Did you see the look on Lil Altemus's face?"

"Stop worrying about her. Lil Altemus doesn't even have any money anymore—she takes the Madison Avenue bus—but she still has the hoity-toity attitude," said Ruby.

"When they write up Adele Harcourt's funeral in the paper tomorrow, that's what they'll write about," said Elias.

"Yes, it was terrible, Elias," said Ruby, in a consoling voice. "But at least you didn't lose your cool; like Simon Cabot said on the telephone yesterday, no matter what they say, don't get angry. That's the picture they want to get of you."

"What about this reception at the Butterfield Club?" asked Elias.

"Simon Cabot couldn't work that one out. He got us into the funeral at St. James' through Addison Kent, whom he knows through Perla Zacharias, but he couldn't get us on the list for the reception at the Butterfield. That's Ethan Trescher's list, and I heard he drew a line through our names with a black marker."

Elias was quiet for a moment, then he leaned toward the front seat and barked, "Jacques, take us to the Butterfield on Fifth Avenue and Sixty-fifth Street, to the entrance on Sixty-fifth."

Turning back to Ruby, he glared. "I used to be a member of that club. I used to play backgammon there in the afternoon. I used to have lunch there with very important people, like Laurance Van Degan, who was the one who put me up for membership, after a little arm-twisting on my part. He was also the one who wrote me the letter saying in print that I was no longer a member of the club. I remember going there after the scandal came out in the papers, before I was indicted even; the day that poor young man Byron Macumber jumped out of the window, I went to the club that day for lunch. Not one person spoke to me. Not one. Every one of those snobs turned away from me. They had this old guy there, Doddsie his name was; he's probably dead now. He'd worked at the club for forty years, and everyone in the club loved the guy. He knew what everyone wanted to drink. Even Doddsie snubbed me, the fucking hired help looked the other way. I'll always remember that. When I walked out of there for the last time, in that marble front hallway, I let out a fart that they could have heard in New Jersey."

"Mightn't it be a little embarrassing for you to walk into the Butterfield to a reception we haven't been invited to?" said Ruby, checking her makeup for the reception they were about to crash.

"Attitude is everything, as Loelia Minardos used to say to you," said Elias.

"Yes, Loelia did say that, didn't she? Well, I'm ready."

For a man who had been released from prison two days earlier, who had just been taunted by the media as he left Adele Harcourt's funeral at St. James' Church, and who was about to enter a club from which he had been asked to resign in order to attend a reception he had not been invited to, Elias Renthal emerged quite smilingly from his dark green Mercedes limousine, as if he hadn't a care in the world. He gallantly held out his hand to help his beautiful wife out of the car. He beamed at her in approval, glad she was wearing an eleven-thousand-dollar suit designed by Karl Lagerfeld with sable cuffs. "You look rich," he whispered in her ear.

People entered the club around them, giving them looks as they passed. "I didn't know he was out of prison," said Herkie Saybrook to Petal Wilson as they entered the club, speaking about Elias Renthal as if he weren't standing there waiting to enter. Elias took Ruby's arm as the door was opened for them by the very much alive Doddsie, the beloved club steward in his blue uniform with the gold piping who had been a fixture at the Butterfield for almost fifty years.

"Well, Doddsie, how nice to see you again," said Elias in a hearty voice. "Surely you remember Mrs. Renthal. This is the famous Doddsie, who's been at the Butterfield for, how many years is it, Doddsie?"

But Doddsie had let go of the door and turned away without acknowledging either one. Doddsie was of the old school. For him, the Butterfield was a bastion for gentlemen of old New York, where Adele Harcourt had been the only honorary female member. Doddsie, who put propriety above everything else, had never forgotten nor forgiven Elias Renthal's reverberating fart on his exit from the Butterfield nearly eight years earlier, after he had been kicked out of the hallowed establishment by Laurance Van Degan, Lil Altemus's brother, whose reputation in the financial world Elias had sullied.

Elias and Ruby stood in the line leading to the stairway that many people thought was the most beautiful stairway in New York. Adele Harcourt's social secretary, Emma Peasley, a maiden lady who knew her New York genealogy, sat at a small table at the foot of the stairs and checked off the mourners, most of whom seemed to know each other, on an alphabetized guest list before they ascended to the second floor, where the reception was being held. Emma's voice could be heard saying, "Yes, yes, Mrs. St. Vincent, go right up. Hello, yes, Mr. and Mrs. Percy Webb. Go right up. Oh, the Aksams, yes. Oh, Mrs. Altemus, how lovely. She was so fond of you."

"I was in the room when she died," said Lil.

"Yes, I read that in Kit Jones's column. Go right up," said Emma.

"Mr. and Mrs. Elias Renthal," said Elias, walking past Emma's table and list and ascending the stairs. "Remember these stairs, honey?" he said to Ruby. "The most beautiful staircase in New York, they used to call it, probably still do. Remember when we had it copied at Merry Hill?"

"This stairway never looked quite right in our house," said Ruby. "It looked nouveau riche in our house."

"Better nouveau than never, I always say," replied Elias. He stopped on the stairs and grasped the railing.

"Are you all right, Elias?" asked Ruby.

"Yeah, fine. Maybe we should have taken the elevator."

By that time, they were at the top of the stairs and had entered the crowd, moving through to the far side of the room. Waiters came forward with trays of champagne glasses and cucumber tea sandwiches. At the bottom of the stairs Emma was aghast. She beckoned to Doddsie. "Mr. and Mrs. Renthal crashed the reception. They walked right past the table."

"I WAS hoping to see Prince Charles," said Perla Zacharias in her charming Johannesburg accent to Ethan Trescher at the reception. "I know how close the prince and Adele Harcourt were. I was told he was coming for the funeral." Perla Zacharias paid a fortune each year to sit next to Prince Charles at Buckingham Palace or Clarence House, whichever royal residence was available on the night of the Prince of Wales Trust benefit. She had been known to call the prince and his wife Charles and Camilla. "Oh, Camilla's divine," she would say. "Charles is simply mad about her. Camilla will be a marvelous queen one day."

"No," replied Ethan. "The prince couldn't come. He sent the Duke and Duchess of Chatfield to represent him."

"Oh," said Perla. "Bunny and Chiquita are here? I long to see them. Oh, there you are, Addison. You were a splendid usher. What was in that velvet box that you handed Lil Altemus as you were taking her up to her seat?"

"WHO IS that woman simply beaming at me?" asked Bunny Chatfield. "She seems to be heading in our direction."

"Mrs. Zacharias," replied Chiquita.

"Oh, dear. Biarritz? Fire? Death? That one? With all the money? I would never have recognized her," said Bunny Chatfield.

"It's the face-lift. Too extreme by far. She's making a bee-line for us. Quick. Let's go say hello to the Renthals. No one is talking to them," said Chiquita, steering her husband away. "I wonder who did Ruby's face. It's fantastic. Whoever it is, is who I'm going to."

The Renthals were thrilled that the Chatfields came to speak to them. They felt safe in the company of the grand English stand-ins for the Prince of Wales and his duchess. The duchess kissed Ruby on both cheeks and then did the same to Elias. "You look divine, Ruby," said Chiquita. It was the first time they had seen each other since Ruby had been turned down for membership at the Corviglia Club in St. Moritz, where she had been proposed by the Chatfields, denied a place in the exclusive club because her husband was in prison.

"Welcome back to civilization, Elias," said the duke, who often said the wrong things but was never corrected because of the magnificence of his title. "What was it like in prison all that time? I talked to Cudlip, who flew out on his private plane to visit you. He complimented you for not complaining and making the best of it."

"It's not a topic I like to discuss," said Elias, hoping the conversation was not being overheard in the crowded room. "I'm more interested in hearing about your shoots at Deeds Castle. Are you still having them?"

"Indeed we are. As a matter of fact, now that you're out and free to travel again, why don't you plan on coming over on your plane to stay with us on the weekend of March twelfth? Don't you think so, Chiquita? I have an awfully good group coming, who would be happy to see you again."

Elias looked at Ruby. They both knew that Elias had promised Max Luby, his oldest friend, who had visited him every weekend for seven years at the facility in Las Vegas, Nevada, that he and Ruby would be present at his testimonial dinner in Brooklyn on that date. As he looked Ruby in the eye, he remembered saying to her on the plane after his release, "I've known Max for forty years, and I've never seen him so excited about anything."

"Yes, yes, I'm sure we'd love to come, Bunny," said Elias. "Wouldn't we, Ruby?"

"Oh, yes, yes. It sounds divine," replied Ruby.

Just at that moment Ethan Trescher and Doddsie walked up to the group. "Excuse me, Your Grace," said Ethan. "I would like to speak to Mr. Renthal for a moment."

"Can you hold it up just a bit, Trescher," said Elias. He saw in Doddsie's face that he and Ruby were about to be asked to leave the reception they hadn't been invited to. "I'm going to pop in that elevator and go down to the men's room. Excuse me, Bunny and Chiquita. I look forward to seeing you at Deeds Castle on March twelfth.

"I'll meet you downstairs, Ruby. It's time we were off." Breathing heavily, he moved swiftly toward the self-service elevator, ignoring Ethan Trescher and Doddsie.

Elias took up half the space in the tiny elevator. He was devastated by the snubs at the funeral, and by the fact that Ethan Trescher and Doddsie had been about to evict him from the Butterfield Club in front of the Chatfields, the only people who had spoken to him and Ruby at the reception. His heart was beating very fast again. He was planning how he would explain to Max Luby that he and Ruby would not be able to attend the Man of the Year dinner in Brooklyn on March 12. He held his hand over his heart until the elevator stopped on the ground floor. He pulled back the elevator gate and walked directly to the men's room, still breathing heavily.

CHAPTER 20

STANDING AT ONE OF THE FIVE URINALS IN THE
men's room was Gus Bailey, who had arrived late at the
reception after his cell phone call with Peter Lombardo
about the dates of the depositions in his upcoming slander suit,
as agreed to by Kyle Cramden's lawyer, Win Burch. The deposition occupied his mind as he was urinating. He knew that Win
Burch might reveal secrets of his life, which had nothing whatsoever to do with what he had said on Patience Longstreet's
radio show about former congressman Kyle Cramden and his
relationship with the famous missing intern, Diandra Lomax.

He had not as yet gone upstairs at the Butterfield, although
Emma, Adele Harcourt's social secretary, who did not know him
personally but recognized him from his television appearances,
had checked off his name on the list. "I never miss reading you
in *Park Avenue,*" she said when he first walked in. "I loved your
articles about the Zachariases in Biarritz."

"Thank you," Gus had replied.

She lowered her voice, looked in both directions to be sure
no one could hear her, and whispered to Gus, "Do you think
Mrs. Zacharias had anything to do with the whole thing? I do."

"There is nothing to bear out that theory," replied Gus.

"She's here," said Emma in a quiet voice that only Gus

could hear. "Perla is upstairs." Her eyes indicated the top of the beautiful staircase where the reception was going on. People always told Gus things, in whatever circumstance he was in, and Emma whispered to Gus that the Elias Renthals had crashed the reception and that Ethan Trescher and Doddsie were upstairs at that very moment to ask them to leave, as they were not friends of Adele Harcourt's and had not been invited to this private reception.

As Gus was zipping up his fly, he turned and found himself face-to-face with Elias Renthal, who, in his haste to get to the urinal, was unbuttoning the fly buttons of his Savile Row suit from Huntsman in London as he pushed open the door. He wished that Mr. Hope-Davies, his man at Huntsman, from whom Ruby had ordered the suit, had given him a zippered fly rather than a buttoned fly to speed up the process, so badly did he have to urinate. He felt like his bladder would burst.

For Elias, already upset, Gus Bailey—who had written about his trial in *Park Avenue,* who had believed him to be guilty, and who had rerun his television show on the eight-year-old case shortly before his release from prison—seemed exactly the person he needed to attack after a day of social humiliations. His face twisted into anger, turning red. He gave out a loud, mocking laugh. "I hear that you're being sued for eleven million dollars," he sneered. "I hear that Kyle Cramden has got himself the meanest lawyer in the country, snake of snakes, the kind that tears people to shreds on the witness stand until they cry. They're going to get you. They're going to get you. They caught up with you at last." He moved closer to Gus, breathing hot, constipated breath on him as he pointed his finger into Gus's face and repeated, "They're going to get you. They're going to get you."

"Do you know what you look like right now, Elias?" asked Gus. "You look exactly like an ex-convict who crashed a high-society funeral reception on your first day out of prison. You're about to be kicked out of here, if you didn't know it already."

"You closet fag," said Elias, fury in his eyes and a touch of foam at the corners of his mouth.

All of a sudden, Elias, breathing heavily, put his hand over his heart again and fell back against the wall of urinals. He reached out to support himself, grabbing the flushing apparatus of the urinals on each side of him to keep from falling. His penis, which he had already taken out of his trousers, began to urinate all over him and the tiled floor of the men's room. Later that night, Gus wrote in his personal diary, "He must have pissed at least a quart." Elias looked beseechingly at Gus.

"What are you having, Elias? A heart attack or a stroke?" asked Gus.

Elias looked at him. His mouth was hanging open.

"To be perfectly honest with you, I'd like to just leave you here to die, but I can't do that. I'm too fond of your wife. Here, let me help you lie down on the floor, Elias, and then I'll go and get help," said Gus. "You pissed all over that six-thousand-dollar suit you're wearing. A man your age shouldn't work himself up into this kind of rage." He put his hands under Elias's armpits and lowered his head and shoulders slowly to the floor. He took a stack of face towels embroidered with the initial B for Butterfield from the sink and placed them under Elias's head as a pillow.

"Tell me one thing, Elias. What did you mean just now when you kept saying, 'They're going to get you'? Who's they?"

"You'll find out," whispered Elias.

Gus unfolded a towel and placed it over Elias's unbuttoned fly and soiled trousers. "Now, just lie still, Elias, and wait. I'll get your old friend Doddsie, who speaks so highly of you, about your famous fart, to call for an ambulance, and I'll find Ruby upstairs and bring her down here."

Gus told Emma what had happened. He got into the elevator and went up to the second floor.

"Doddsie, my name is Gus Bailey."

"I see your show on television, Mr. Bailey," replied Doddsie. "I read you in *Park Avenue*."

"I was just in the men's room downstairs and Elias Renthal has had what I think is a stroke. Emma is calling an ambulance. Have you seen Mrs. Renthal?"

Doddsie nodded with his head toward the Chatfields, who were still talking to Ruby, and Gus went over to them.

"Ruby, may I speak to you a moment, please? It's important."

"I'm not speaking to you, Gus Bailey," replied Ruby. "It was disgraceful of you to run that old episode of your series about Elias just before he got out of the facility in Nevada. You'd better not let Elias see you. He's furious with you." Once, before Elias had gone to prison, Gus and Ruby had been friendly. It sometimes saddened her that they could no longer be friends, since they had such an intense shared piece of their pasts, but what Gus had done to Elias and the jeopardy in which he had put their social standing felt unforgivable.

"None of that matters now, Ruby. Your husband just had a stroke in the men's room. There's such a thing as doing too much on your first day out of prison."

"Oh, my god. Is he all right?"

"I don't know. Emma called an ambulance. Doddsie is already down there. I'll take you down in the elevator."

"Oh, my god," said Ruby. "I knew we should have gone straight home after the reporters screamed at him coming out of the funeral. It was awful, awful. They screamed at him, 'Is it true you had to clean toilets?' He was so hurt."

A siren could be heard outside. Ruby started to cry. The word went through the crowd that Elias Renthal, who had just gotten out of prison, had had a stroke in the men's room on the first floor and urinated all over himself. People began lining the winding stairway to watch the drama. Lil Altemus pushed her way to the railing of the stairs. "Poor Adele," she said. "This is all people will remember about her funeral."

"Nobody goes in there until the medics have finished," said Doddsie, standing guard in front of the closed door of the men's room, blocking Ruby and Gus from entering.

"It's Mrs. Renthal," said Gus to Doddsie. "She has to go in."

"Hold it. Hold it," said Doddsie, in control. "They're coming out with the stretcher. Everybody stand back. These men need all the room they can get. Don't push in. Stand back. Mrs. Renthal, there will be room for you in the ambulance."

The medics had covered Elias's body with a rubber sheet. Elias opened his eyes for a second as he was being carried on a stretcher through the oval marble hall of the Butterfield to see the beautiful winding stairway packed tight with the friends of Adele Harcourt looking down on him, watching him, talking about him—"Ethan Trescher said he crashed"—as the medics made their way to a waiting ambulance with flashing red lights and a siren. He remembered the fart he had let out eight years earlier, the last time he had been in the club. He was wondering which of his two exits from the Butterfield was the more humiliating, as they were loading him on the gurney and sliding him into the ambulance. "I'm right here, Elias," said Ruby, a line that was quoted in all the New York newspapers the next morning.

IN THE ambulance on the way to New York–Presbyterian Hospital, Ruby sat alongside Elias's stretcher. She watched the frantic activity of the medics, knowing they were doing all they could to keep Elias alive. She felt helpless. The sable cuff on her brand-new Karl Lagerfeld suit from Chanel Couture was damp and smelled of urine. She realized she must have brushed up against Elias when they transferred him from the stretcher to the gurney. The sable smelled of asparagus. She wished Gert hadn't served asparagus the previous night for Elias's first dinner in their new house. She opened her twelve-thousand-dollar Hermès Birkin bag and took out a white lace handkerchief drenched in Karl Lagerfeld's newest perfume, which hadn't come out in the United States yet, which Baroness de Liagra had brought her from Paris. The card that had accompanied it said in French, "My tongue needs something to lick." Ruby held the handkerchief to her nose to keep from smelling her wet sable cuff. With her other hand she took out her cell phone and dialed her social secretary. "Oh, Jenny, yes, Adele's funeral was simply beautiful. Oh, you saw it on television? I'll tell Elias how well you said he looked."

She looked over at her husband. "Is he all right?" she asked one of the medics.

"Yes, ma'am, under the circumstances," answered the medic. Ruby went back to her cell phone. "Look, Jenny, there's a few things I wish you'd do right away. Mr. Renthal has had an indigestion attack, and we're taking him to the hospital. Phone the hospital right now, New York–Presbyterian, and tell them who he is, so the rooms will be ready when the ambulance gets there. Those check-in people never know who anybody is. Don't say anything about, you know, where he's been for the last seven years. Just say he is a distinguished financier, or something like that. He is going to need suite six hundred on the private tenth floor of the Harcourt Pavilion, the one Laurance Van Degan was in so long after his stroke. And tell them if they say they're all full that Mr. Renthal gave Adele Harcourt money in the millions for the Harcourt Pavilion. No, Jenny. It's not a bit serious, no, no. It's just all the excitement of being home again."

The two medics looked at each other over Elias's body but said nothing.

"Next, call Simon Cabot in London and ask him to call me on my cell phone. If the newspapers call, say Mrs. Renthal is at the hospital with her husband, and a statement will be forthcoming later in the day. It's urgent that you get Simon Cabot in London to call me on my cell. Tell Gert we won't be in for dinner as planned and tell her she's free to go to bingo night at St. Ignatius Loyola. Call Smythson's in London and tell them to cancel the order for the invitations to the party for the opening of the new house, and cancel that fancy calligrapher Simon Cabot hired to address the envelopes. Say there's been a postponement. Oh, yes, and call the manager for the Aquacade act at the Seraglio Hotel in Las Vegas and say that we have to cancel for the present time."

Watching her unconscious husband as the ambulance, sirens screaming, raced for New York–Presbyterian Hospital on One Hundred Sixty-eighth Street and Broadway, it occurred to Ruby that the indoor swimming pool she had copied from the indoor swimming pool at the Hearst Castle in California, and where she planned to give an Aquacade cabaret on the night of the party that would transform the Tavistock mansion into the Renthal mansion, might only be used for Elias's physical therapy, if he should live. The new trainer, Jaime, who had been the trainer for Konstantin Zacharias, right up until the night Konstantin was murdered at the villa in Biarritz, would guide Elias through his laps and kicks on his paralyzed left side. In her mind, she wondered if she would ever see her beautiful indoor swimming pool with hundreds and hundreds of gardenias floating in it, with synchronized swimmers and divers of great beauty performing to music, as she and Baroness de Liagra had planned in great detail over the previous months.

CHAPTER 21

IT WAS GENERALLY AGREED AMONG THE STAFF AT New York–Presbyterian Hospital that Mrs. Elias Renthal, or Ruby Renthal, or just plain Ruby, depending on how well you knew her, was a diligent and devoted wife during her daily hospital visits, reading the financial papers aloud to her husband, refusing to believe that he could not hear or understand her in his coma state, as the nurses kept telling her. "Of course he can hear me. Even in a coma, he wants to know the financial news. I know my Elias," she said over and over to the nurses. "Money's his favorite subject. That's why he and Konstantin Zacharias were so close."

The nurses and interns were utterly captivated by the glamour of Ruby, who dressed up for them each day and thrived on their compliments. Often she brought baskets of superb treats that Gert had made especially for them. She even promised that she would have Gert make her famous fig mousse for the staff, the way she used to make it for the late Adele Harcourt, after whom the private wing of the hospital where they all worked was named. "Tell Gert thanks," the nurses would tell Ruby, especially Tammi Jo, who always ate three helpings and said Gert's goodies were worth getting fat over. Word spread. For the first time in years, the Renthals were being discussed at lunch and dinner parties.

"Elias is still in a coma, but I hear that Ruby reads him the *Wall Street Journal* and the *Financial Times* every morning," said Addison Kent. His informant was an orderly at the Harcourt Pavilion, who had actually tasted Gert's fig mousse when Ruby's chauffeur, Jacques, carried it into the Harcourt Pavilion for Ruby to give to the nursing staff, the interns, and the orderlies. It was only a coincidence that Addison happened to be having what he called an affair-ette with the handsome young orderly who took Elias's temperature each day, tested his heartbeat, and gave him enemas.

It was inevitable that the story of Ruby's devotion would appear in Toby Tilden's gossip column in the *New York Post*. Addison called Simon Cabot in London, and Simon called Toby Tilden in New York, and Toby Tilden called a thrilled Addison Kent, who always read Toby Tilden's column the minute he awakened each morning. He saw the opportunity to make an important and useful alliance with Toby. Addison gave Toby bits of social information he heard at his lunch and dinner parties as the society walker for Perla Zacharias, and Toby wrote wonderful things in his column about Perla Zacharias's great generosity. Mrs. Zacharias enjoyed having her philanthropy publicized. Addison Kent missed the perks he had enjoyed when he had been the walker for Adele Harcourt, the most revered woman in New York. With Adele now gone, that position was wide open, and Addison dedicated himself to helping Perla Zacharias ascend to it, no matter what it took. He would ride her sable coattails all the way to the top.

CHAPTER 22

LIL ALTEMUS ALWAYS GOT A LITTLE MIFFED WHEN her stepmother, Dodo Van Degan, kept her waiting at the corner table in the back room of Swifty's for their monthly lunch, which neither of them enjoyed. She sipped her white wine as she looked around the room to see who was there. She waved to Ormolu Webb, who was having lunch with Dexter Grenville, the nephew of Billy Grenville, who had been shot to death by his wife, Ann. Lil always reminded Dexter that his grandmother Alice Grenville had been a great friend of her mother's and that they had had houses next to each other on Bellevue Avenue in Newport in the summers. "The Grenvilles were the real thing," Lil often said when their name came up in conversation, after Gus Bailey wrote the book that brought the almost forgotten murder up again.

"Hellohowareyou?" Lil said to the very rich Carlotta Zenda, who was at the next banquette, in the tone of voice she used to use when she had money and had to speak to what she called the "new people." It bothered her that people like Mrs. Zenda no longer yearned to be accepted by her. They had passed her by. Mrs. Zenda had become head of the board of the Metropolitan Opera, a position of social importance held by Lil's mother from the 1940s until the day she died. "It's the beginning of the end when these new people take over positions like that in New York," Lil had said on many occasions when referring to individuals such as Carlotta Zenda. Mrs. Zenda laughed when Lil's line was repeated to her. "She takes the Madison Avenue bus, Perla tells me," Mrs. Zenda replied.

"Hi, Lil. Sorry to be late," said Dodo, sitting down after Robert pulled out the table. "Octavio tells me you're already on your third glass of white wine. That's how my late alcoholic mother used to start her days. How do you like my new seventy-five-thousand-dollar face-lift?"

"Dodo, for god's sake, I hardly recognized you. You look completely different. And your hair! What in the world have you done to your hair?"

"Had it cut. Had it dyed. Had it highlighted. That's all," replied Dodo, who was pleased with her transformation.

"It's awfully blond," said Lil, looking at Dodo's hair and frowning.

"I don't give a rat's ass if you don't like it, Lil. Xavior likes it. That's all that matters to me," said Dodo.

"There is no need for vulgarity, Dodo," said Lil, in a haughty voice. "I didn't say I didn't like it. I said it was awfully blond. That's all."

"Awfully blond is the point, Lil, according to my lover."

"And your clothes! You used to look so dowdy, so old-maidish. I saw that suit you're wearing at Oscar de la Renta's fashion show and then at Bergdorf's. Too expensive for me, of course. I was shocked at how much it cost."

"That's the point too. Xavior picked it out, and I can afford it," said Dodo. "I'm a rich widow with a gay lover I simply adore and, more important, am adored by."

"Oh, Dodo, I mean really," said Lil, making a gesture of mock despair at the utter inappropriateness of Dodo's affair with a gay undertaker. "You're not thinking of marrying this Xavior person from Grant P. Trumbull Funeral Home, are you? Don't count on me to call that one in to Kit Jones to announce your engagement in her column."

"Of course I'm not going to marry Xavior. I simply adore living in sin. It's a much more permanent commitment."

"Oh, for god's sake, Dodo. People are still talking about you riding in the front seat of the hearse at Adele Harcourt's funeral, and you and Xavior shouldn't have been laughing. I was never so embarrassed in my whole life. Between you in the hearse and Elias Renthal having his stroke or heart attack or whatever it was in the men's room of the Butterfield, you ruined poor Adele's funeral."

"I'll have a gin martini straight up, three olives, Octavio," said Dodo.

"How in the world do you know that waiter's called Octavio?" asked Lil. "I come here every day for lunch, and I don't know his name is Octavio."

"You're not paying attention, because I call him by name every time we come here. Also, Xavior had quite a crush on him before he met me," said Dodo, hoping to make her stepdaughter apoplectic.

"Oh, look," said Lil, her attention diverted from Octavio. "There's Perla Zacharias joining Carlotta Zenda. Someone said the other night she was back in New York. She's giving money in every direction, people say. All the predictable social-climbing charities. The opera. The museum, the Whitney, MoMA, you name it, she gave to it, and all the board members are having her to dinner in return. And I can barely even speak about what is happening with the Manhattan Public Library. Darling Adele must be spinning in her grave. Oh, look. Now Addison Kent is joining the ladies. It's perfect. He's supposed to be the one who phones in all the positive publicity about Perla to Toby Tilden, or so Ormolu tells me."

"Xavior once had a little fling-ette with Addison Kent in the toilet of the funeral home at the time of Winkie's death," said Dodo. Lil hummed and shook her head and waved her arm in the air, as she always did when Dodo talked dirty to her, pretending not to hear. "He told me that Addison has given up his job in the jewelry department at Boothby's auction house and become the permanent walker of Perla Zacharias, taking her everywhere she is asked, even to the White House, where she sat next to the secretary of state. He takes Perla's thank-you notes to Brucie, the florist at the Rhinelander Hotel, to send with masses of orchid plants to her hostess of the night before."

"I'm riveted," said Lil.

"I can't believe I've told you some gossip you don't already know," said Dodo. "Are you going to snub Mrs. Zacharias, as usual?" asked Dodo.

"No. These days Mrs. Zacharias snubs *me*. Once I moved out of the Fifth Avenue apartment, she never had the slightest interest in getting to know me anymore. Money talks. Actually money *screams,* as Dolores De Longpre used to write."

IN HER relationship with Xavior, Dodo Van Degan was happy for the first time in her life. She loved to hear all the news of the town that he had heard from Jonsie at the wine shop on Madison Avenue and from Brucie, the florist at the Rhinelander Hotel. She often sat with Xavior at night in the Grant P. Trumbull Funeral Home when he was embalming a body. Afterward they would fool around a little. Just the previous night, Xavior had had his face between her legs and had said to her, "This is better than rimming."

Most of all, though, it thrilled her that she, a born mimic, could keep Xavior in hysterics as he went about his work with her accounts of her lunches with Lil Altemus. Lil and her daughter, Justine, had always just ignored Dodo. She was a family embarrassment. She had been a poor, distant relation of the Van Degans when her father had jumped overboard off the *Queen Elizabeth* in the middle of the Atlantic Ocean after an immoral incident with a seventeen-year-old Cockney deckhand in the engine room had scandalized the voyage. Dorothy Kilgallen, who happened to be on board for the maiden voyage, wrote a front-page story in the *Journal-American,* giving every detail of the perverted shipboard encounter, which caused enormous embarrassment to the Van Degan family. Dodo's mother, a hopeless drunk who once had been considered a beauty, had long lost her looks and spent more time at Silver Hill than she ever did with her forgotten daughter. Dodo grew up sleeping in maids' rooms of rich relatives, going to public school rather than Brearley, where her cousins all went. Now, in her new incarnation, she loved the feeling of making Xavior laugh. She felt honored when Xavior told her that his friends Jonsie and Bruele thought she was a camp. Dodo didn't even know what a camp was, but she liked the sound of it and took it as a compliment, as it was meant to be. Xavior was very good at needlepoint, and he made a needlepoint pillow for her birthday that said MY FAVORITE CAMP. No one had ever given her a gift that was made just for her before. She kept it propped up against the pillows on her side of the bed.

CHAPTER 23

PETER LOMBARDO, GUS'S SLANDER LAWYER, HAD been hard at work trying to prepare Gus for the upcoming deposition. He had just hired another, younger lawyer in the firm, Miranda Slater, whose parents Gus knew. She asked him the difficult sort of questions that Win Burch, the greatly feared lawyer for the former congressman Kyle Cramden, would probably ask him, using the mocking tone of voice that Burch was certain to use. He was known to bring people to tears during depositions. These theatrics were taking their toll on Gus, and Peter Lombardo could see it.

He and Gus had become close in the months of preparation, and Peter thought that Miranda Slater, the smartest and toughest of the younger lawyers in the firm, would be tougher on Gus than he would, or could. They had listened to a tape of the radio show on which Gus had said that he felt Kyle Cramden knew more about the disappearance of Diandra Lomax than he had ever let on, which was the basis of the slander suit that was so complicating his life. Just as difficult was the matter of going silent on the subject, which of course was required at present, and which Gus had a hard time doing. But he soldiered on—refusing to discuss the lawsuit or the upcoming deposition—for fear of being quoted.

On this day, however, Peter Lombardo was waiting for Gus when he arrived at his office and was without the newest addition of their legal team, Ms. Slater.

"Gus," Peter said uneasily, "something unexpected has come up. I had a call from Win Burch this morning."

Peter dispensed with the usual morning handshake. Gus took a deep breath.

"Oh, dear," he said. "I hate the sound of your troubled voice, Peter. What terrible thing has Win Burch wrought now?"

"I'm afraid this is going to upset you, Gus."

Peter walked into his office and offered a seat to Gus, which he readily took.

"Go on."

"Two men of foreign origin who claim they were trained in intelligence by the Mossad in Israel went to see Win Burch and Kyle Cramden. They claim to have done Perla Zacharias's investigation of Augustus Bailey, meaning you."

Gus sat up, startled, and gazed at Peter wide-eyed.

"Me? Perla Zacharias did an investigation of me? She's getting involved with the lawsuit?"

"The investigation began after you started writing about her, and it's apparently escalated since the book deal. She doesn't like you, Gus. She knows you know things. She's after you. People say she always gets even. She knows how upset you are about Kyle Cramden and Win Burch."

Gus replied, "I shouldn't be surprised, really. I always thought I was being followed, and I had my suspicions as to who was behind it. Did I tell you about the time at Claridge's in London when I went into my room and there was a man standing there?"

Peter rested his hand on his chin. He couldn't help but notice how weathered Gus seemed. The light in his eyes had faded, replaced by a new, uncertain appearance.

"Gus," he inserted calmly, "if you were being followed, you certainly didn't tell me. That much I would've remembered."

Gus leaned forward, placing his hands on the edge of Peter's desk.

"I was scared, Peter. My heart was beating a mile a minute. There was this big tall heavy guy with a mustache in a gray flannel suit. Cool as a cucumber. Not a bit unnerved by my unexpected arrival. 'I was checking your minibar, Mr. Bailey,' he said. So likely. Third World men with aprons to the floor check the minibars at Claridge's, and they don't know the names of the guests whose minibars they are checking. I was afraid of him."

"It sounds like you interrupted whatever it was he was there to do."

Gus nodded.

"I opened the door. I said I never use the minibar. He left."

"Jesus, Gus."

"How did he get a key to get into my room at one of the most expensive hotels in the world? What was he looking for, or what was he planting?"

Peter sighed, crossing his arms over his chest. Gus went on to explain how a year later he saw the same man in New York at an auction at Boothby's of Perla Zacharias's Fabergé eggs. Gus spoke frantically, explaining how the man recognized him and then vanished quickly into another room. Gus was convinced he must have been one of Perla's guards.

"He gave me the creeps," Gus remarked, almost in a whisper.

Peter smiled, reaching out his hands.

"Oh, come on, Gus. Really? The same guy? Are you sure? Don't you think you're just overexhausted with this whole ordeal?"

Gus crossed his legs and folded his arms.

"Don't placate me, Peter. It was the same guy. I told you

about the doorman in my building who told me a man in a green Nissan was following me every time I left the building?"

"Gus, that could simply be a crazy fan. You're getting carried away."

Gus closed his eyes for a moment and cleared his throat. While he knew he sounded crazy, it was all true. The guy had been there, and Gus wasn't about to dismiss it as a mere fluke. *Things like this just happen to me,* he thought. *They always have and always will.*

Gus studied the look on Peter's face and immediately realized he didn't want to know whatever news his lawyer had to impart. There was a tremendously awkward sort of expression taking hold as Peter opened his mouth to speak.

"Gus, these two men Perla hired—well, they've told Win Burch a very distressing story about you. I'm embarrassed to have to repeat it to you."

Gus felt a lump forming in his throat.

"What?"

"They said some documents have come into their possession that allege you molested a young boy when you were staying at the Hôtel du Palais. Supposedly there is a maid who says she walked in on you."

Gus, stunned, stared at Peter. "But that's not true," he said quickly. "No such thing happened. No such thing has ever happened. That's based on an old rumor that someone tried to start about me when he didn't like how he was depicted in one of my books. It never got off the ground because it was so absurd. That's exactly the kind of ruinous story that Perla Zacharias would spread, and she's got enough money and power to make people pay attention this time around."

Gus could feel the adrenaline rushing through his body. His fingers began to tremble.

"I know it's not true," Peter replied immediately.

"It's not," Gus repeated.

"Listen, Gus—I think Win Burch knows it's not true, but he's going to bring it up in the deposition, which is being video-taped and will be available to the media."

"Dear God," said Gus, covering his face with his hands. "This is the sort of story you can never live down."

Collecting himself, Gus sat upright. His defeated expression was replaced with a new one of determination. He recrossed his legs and crossed his arms smartly.

With each thought Gus grew angrier.

"Call the manager of the Hôtel du Palais. His name is Valentino Piazzi. He used to be at the Ritz in Paris. He knows me. Ask Valentino if a maid made a report on this incident to the manager of the hotel at the time. Or has she just suddenly re-membered this?"

Peter waved down Gus's directives.

"It's a form of extortion," he said calmly. "They think you'll settle quickly rather than go through the deposition, knowing that the story will be out."

Then Peter paused for a moment, leaning back in his leather chair.

"Gus, there's other gossip about you. Gossip that, unlike this preposterous story, might be closer to the truth. You must know that."

Gus sighed, looking down at the striped tie that he'd bought for himself at the Turnbull & Asser shop just a few days earlier.

"I do, yes. It's very old gossip, however."

The room grew silent but for the distant sound of cars honk-ing on the streets below.

"Probably true, whatever you've heard," Gus added as casu-ally as he could.

"Heard?" Peter inquired.

"Oh you know, that I'm deep within the closet."

Peter shifted uneasily in his chair and nodded.

"Well, maybe I am . . . in the closet. So what? What you haven't heard is that I've been celibate for almost twenty years. Such a relief, celibacy. That should read well in Toby Tilden's column after Win Burch plants it."

"Gus, you didn't have to tell me all this," said Peter.

"Yes, I did. Actually, I feel quite relieved having said it. I'm beyond eighty, you know. Mustn't have any more secrets. Can't die with a secret, you know. I'm nervous about the kids, even though they're middle-aged men now. Not that they don't already know. I just never talk about it. It's been a lifelong problem."

Gus got up and walked to the window of the small conference room where they were meeting. He looked down at the street twenty-seven floors below. Peter could see that he took a handkerchief from his pocket and wiped his eyes. All his life Gus had dreaded leveling with his children on that topic.

"You have no idea how wonderful my sons have been," he said, tearing up. "If I still drank, I'd order a martini right now. Straight up with a twist. And I'd light up a joint at the same time."

"Gus, I've always heard great things about your sons. And your sexuality should have nothing to do with this extortion plot. Please don't lose sleep over it. Do you want to postpone this rehearsal for the deposition?" asked Peter.

Gus turned around and managed a smile.

"No, let's get back to work. There's no way I'm going to be blackmailed into a settlement."

"I thought you always wanted to settle from the beginning."

"I did, but not this way," said Gus. "I've gotten tough in my old age, Peter."

"I like to see you pissed off," said Peter. "It adds color to your face."

CHAPTER 24

THAT NIGHT GUS ARRIVED HOME FROM PETER Lombardo's office and pulled his laptop from the other side of his bed to write in his diary before he went to sleep.

It's really very strange that Perla Zacharias should turn up as she has, in yet another area of my life, in conjunction with the lawsuit for slander that was brought against me by former congressman Kyle Cramden. So odd that her investigators should give false information about me to the man who is suing me.

One of the things that stands out most in my mind about Perla is how she emerged triumphantly from the courthouse after the American nurse, Floyd McArthur, was found guilty of setting the fire that caused the deaths of Perla's fourth husband, Konstantin Zacharias, and one of his eight nurses, Flora Perez, who perished with him from smoke inhalation. Like the superb actress that she is, Perla stopped briefly for the photographers, as Simon Cabot had instructed her. Her face was solemn. She deflected the questions of the reporters with a sad smile and shake of her head, as if the *tragedy was too painful to discuss, indicating that she would not be taking any questions. When she turned to signal her secretary to alert her chauffeur to pull up the SUV, her eyes met mine for an instant. That was when I became a participant in the story, not just a reporter. I was standing in the crowd of reporters staring at her. For a brief moment her eyes hardened.* She hates me, *I thought.* It was I who made her famous. Famous is what she has always wanted to be. Actually, I suppose I made her infamous.

GUS TELEPHONED the real estate tycoon Maisie Verdurin, who was having another of her famous dinner parties for sixty, where nearly every guest was a person of accomplishment in the world of media and money in New York.

"Maisie, it's Gus." Years earlier, way back in the fifties when they were all young, before she had become a full-fledged real estate agent, Maisie had found Gus and his late former wife, Peach, their first apartment in New York after their marriage. Years later, after Gus moved back to New York following his Hollywood career, he became a regular at Maisie's dinner parties.

"You're not calling to back out on me again, are you, Gus? I'm going to be furious with you." said Maisie. "Last time I had you seated next to Baroness de Liagra from Paris, and you backed out at ten minutes of eight, as I remember."

"No, Maisie, I'm not backing out. I'm coming. I promise. Best conversation in town is at your tables. But I need a favor from you," said Gus.

"What?"

"Who are you seating me next to? "

"I'm just doing the place cards now. I can't give you the baroness again. She's in Paris."

"I hear she wears a monocle," said Gus. "Very Violet Trefusis."

"Who's Violet Trefusis?"

"A famous lesbian of her day."

"Let's not have that conversation," said Maisie, and they both laughed.

Suddenly Gus's voice turned serious. "Listen, Maisie. Is Lil Altemus coming?"

"I always have Lil," said Maisie. "She classes up the joint."

"Will you seat me next to Lil and put Addison Kent on the other side of her and somebody's wife with no glamour or chitchat next to him, so that Addison will ignore her and overhear a story that I'm going to tell Lil about Perla Zacharias?" asked Gus.

"May I ask what this is all about?" asked Maisie, her curiosity piqued. If she was going to rearrange her table for him, she felt it was only right that Gus Bailey tell her exactly what he was up to.

"Lil's getting a little hard of hearing, so I can raise my voice. I want Addison to repeat the story to Perla. It's very important to me that Perla hears, and Addison will probably go directly into the bathroom and call Perla on his cell phone."

"As the hostess of the evening, am I allowed to know what the story is all about?" asked Maisie.

"It has to do with some letters in my possession that Perla wrote in English in her own handwriting to her mysterious third husband that no one talks about," said Gus. "One letter in particular could be very embarrassing."

"I'll go along with that. I found Perla a buyer for her villa right on the Bay of Biscay in Biarritz, which she put up for sale after the trial. I got her seven hundred million. At the time, it was more than had ever been paid for a house in that area," said Maisie. "Richest man in Russia."

"What happened?"

"She didn't want to pay me my commission. She thought the honor of selling her villa would bring me a lot of real estate publicity. All that money and she's trying to cheat me out of my commission. I screwed it up for her. I told my Russian billionaire buyer that it was a bad-luck house, that everyone who had ever owned it had come to a bad end, which wasn't altogether untrue. I sold him another house, just as big, in Cap Ferrat. Yes, of course I'll seat you next to Lil, who's getting deaf, and seat Addison Kent next to Lil. It'll liven up the party. Now I have to figure out whose wife has no glamour or chitchat for the other side of Addison. Oh, Mrs. Luby. Sylvia Luby. She'd be perfect."

"See you at eight," said Gus.

"OH, GUS, I'm so happy that you're seated next to me," said Lil. She was wearing her Van Degan pearls that she could not bear to sell, even though she needed the money so badly. "Maisie is so good at seating her tables. It's nice to have an old friend like you." She whispered into his ear, "I'm wearing a new hearing aid for the first time, and I don't want anyone to know. What scandalous thing are you writing about now?"

"I'm in possession of photocopies of sixteen love letters Perla wrote in English in her own handwriting to that third husband of hers, the mystery husband no one knows anything about, the one she paid to marry her as a ruse to get Konstantin Zacharias to pursue her again after his brothers talked him out of marrying her the first time."

"Be careful to my left," said Lil, pointing her head in Addison's direction. "Biggest mouth in town and Perla's walker."

"The actual letters are in a safe-deposit box in New York, which only I and one other person have access to. I didn't seek out the letters or pay for them. I never met the third husband. Some very revealing things come out in a few of them."

"Like what?

"Like what her baby brother—her half brother that she doesn't want anyone to know about, by the way—told the counselor at the drug rehab center in Johannesburg she put him in about the mysterious death of her second husband, from whom she inherited two hundred and thirty million of her first fortune. That is certainly going in my book. You know they ruled it a suicide, but he was shot—twice in the heart. This is just another thing I need to investigate."

"Gus, you do lead such an interesting life. Secret letters. Being followed. And that man in the gray flannel suit in your room at Claridge's whom you told me about over dinner some months back."

"I keep thinking of that guy too. Wondering what he was doing in my room," said Gus. "Maybe he was after my laptop, or maybe he was planting some drugs to get me in some kind of media trouble."

"Didn't you tell me you saw that same man at the auction of Perla Zacharias's Fabergé eggs at Boothby's?"

"Yes. I believe he's in her employ. I've become quite fearful of him."

Addison, leaning in close to Lil to listen to her conversation with Gus about Perla's letters, accidentally knocked over his glass of red wine.

"Addison, for god's sake!" exclaimed Lil, her hands thrown up in disgust. "You spilled your red wine all over my dress. Why are you leaning in so close to me?"

"Oh, Lil, I am sorry," said Addison. "Just leave your dress in a shopping bag with your doorman and I will pick it up in the morning. I know exactly the right cleaners for red wine. You'll never be able to tell."

"This dress is practically falling apart, it's so old," said Lil, dabbing futilely at the stain with her napkin. "It's from Bill Blass's last collection. I offered it to the Costume Institute at the Met, but Anna turned it down, and now it's ruined."

Addison shook his head in a feigned display of sympathy and then, after a few respectful beats, he shot out of his chair, nearly knocking it over in the process, and ran to find a private spot from which he could call the third richest woman in the world and update her about these disturbing developments.

CHAPTER 25

Ruby Renthal sat in a corner of Elias's hospital room on the VIP floor of the Adele Harcourt Pavilion reading the latest issue of *Park Avenue* magazine, with Gus Bailey's article on Adele Harcourt's funeral, while Elias, still in a comatose state, slept on. From the beginning of his coma, she had talked to him and read to him from the *Wall Street Journal* and the *Financial Times*. "Of course he can hear me," she said over and over to the nurses, when they expressed their doubt that Elias could hear anything she was saying. *If it's about money, he can hear it,* she thought, as always, but no longer said aloud. Only Tammi Jo, her favorite nurse, agreed with Ruby that Elias could hear and understand, even though he was in a coma. Tammi Jo, fat and funny, always managed to work it into the conversation that she had gone to nursing school with Floyd McArthur, the male nurse in prison in Biarritz for killing Konstantin Zacharias. "Oh, I knew Floyd McArthur," said Tammi Jo, after reading Gus Bailey's article on the trial in Biarritz. "Strange guy, but kind of a healer in a way. He had this magical touch with sick babies. No way did he kill Konstantin Zacharias." Ruby loved that news and couldn't wait to tell it to Elias after he came out of the coma. Tammi Jo was the only one Ruby told that the best dry cleaner on the Upper East Side of New York couldn't get the asparagus and urine smell out of the sable cuffs on her brand-new eleven-thousand-dollar Karl Lagerfeld suit that she had only worn once, at Adele Harcourt's funeral on the day of her husband's stroke. Baroness de Liagra was going to take it back to Paris so that Lagerfeld could replace the sable on the cuffs. Tammi Jo was spellbound by stories of Ruby's kind of life. She didn't even mind when Ruby complained that she felt it necessary to carry her packages in plain shopping bags, as some of the women in society were doing these days so as not to flaunt their wealth too much while the country was sobered by a recession: "What's the point of having it if you don't get to flaunt it? I'm helping the economy by buying ridiculously expensive things!" Tammi Jo knew a good gig when she saw one. She wanted to leave the Adele Harcourt Pavilion and go to live in the big mansion on East Seventy-eighth Street during Elias's long convalescence ahead and eat Gert's gourmet dinners and fig mousse in the servants' dining room, along with Jenny, Ruby's secretary; Blondell, her maid, who had previously worked for Adele Harcourt; Jacques, her chauffeur; and George, her butler, who had been Adele Harcourt's butler.

Ruby called over to Elias whenever she read something she thought he would be interested in. "You won't believe this, Elias. It's a good thing you're still out of it, I suppose. Gus Bailey writes in his diary in *Park Avenue* about Adele Harcourt's funeral. He quotes 'New York aristocrat' Lillian Van Degan Altemus saying, 'That ex-convict ruined poor darling Adele's funeral, after she gave her fortune to the city of New York.' That's so typical of Lil, isn't it? She's broke, you know. She takes the Madison Avenue bus these days. Her stepmother got all the Van Degan money. The stepmother, who's twenty-five years younger than Lil, lives with a gayette who works in a funeral parlor. Oh, how the mighty have fallen. Elias and I know a thing or two about the mighty falling."

"Go on reading Gus Bailey's article to Mr. Renthal," said Tammi Jo. "That should wake him up."

Ruby glanced over at Elias.

"'All of the great names of New York society gathered on the stairway of the Butterfield Club to watch the financier Elias Renthal be taken out on a gurney.' I wonder how Gus knew how much your suit from Huntsman on Savile Row cost. He writes that you urinated all over your brand-new six-thousand-dollar suit when you had the stroke in the men's room of the Butter-field. He writes that he just happened to be in the men's room at the same time." She read on to herself with a surprised look on her face. "Hey, Elias. I never knew you pointed your finger in Gus's face and kept saying, 'They're going to get you. They're going to get you.' No wonder you had a stroke! I didn't know Gus put towels under your head when he went to find me. I didn't know he covered your privates, so you wouldn't be em-barrassed when they photographed you. I know you don't like Gus Bailey, but he never once wrote that we crashed Adele Harcourt's funeral reception. He said there was a mix-up on the list."

There was a knock on the door and an orderly carried in an enormous orchid plant. There was no space large enough to put it down. Tammi Jo, who always had a solution, knew of a metal medical table near the ladies' room down the hall and directed the orderly where to find it before someone else took it. Ruby knew even before she opened the card who had sent the orchid plant from Brucie's flower shop in the rear of the Rhinelander Hotel. She even knew it cost a thousand dollars.

"Elias, I wish you could get a look at the size of this orchid plant that Perla Zacharias has just sent you. It's like something they'd have at a memorial service at St. Ignatius Loyola."

Ruby opened the blue card with Perla's monogram in the blue envelope and read it aloud to Elias: "'Elias, dear old friend of my darling Konstantin, I pray for you daily and know that you will be coming out of the coma soon and will be back wheeling and dealing and running things. When you are well enough to talk on the telephone, please call me. I need you to introduce me to someone. It is terribly important to me. With love, Perla.' What the hell is that all about, Elias?"

Rereading the card in an attempt to determine Perla's meaning, Ruby failed to see Elias's body stirring in bed. First a finger, then a hand, then the slight shift of his body. After a few minutes Elias spoke, in a weak, quiet voice.

"How long have I been out?"

Ruby looked up, surprised, and ran to his side. "Elias, Elias, my darling."

Elias squinted, blinking slowly.

"Am I still alive?" he asked.

"Yes, yes, my darling. You are alive! You're out of the coma. You came through it. I knew. I knew. I'll call the nurse, the doctor, everyone. Let me call the desk." Ruby dialed excitedly, "Tammi Jo, come, come quickly. My husband is out of the coma. Oh, Elias, I'm so happy."

Tammi Jo was crying over the phone she was so happy for the lovely Mrs. Renthal.

"WHAT'S THE date today?" asked Elias in a hoarse voice, after he'd been awake for about an hour.

"Tell me the date," repeated Elias, when no one answered.

"Here's the *New York Times*. It's March twelfth. You've been in the coma for three weeks. Why?"

"This is the night they're honoring Max Luby in Brooklyn," said Elias.

"Oh, don't worry. I backed out of that one right after the Chatfields asked us to the shoot at Deeds Castle on the same date as Max Luby's party," said Ruby.

"Listen to me," said Elias. "You have to go to Brooklyn tonight, and you have to get all dressed up in one of those new gowns your muff diver friend ordered for you at the couture shows in Paris."

"I'm so happy you retained your dignity during your coma," said Ruby.

"And you're going to knock them dead at the church hall."

"I don't get it, Elias," said Ruby. "You've been out cold for three weeks. I thought you were dead half the time, except for your farts, which I grew to rely on to know you were still alive, but you came through all of that, and the first thing you can think to say is about Max fucking Luby with the thousand-dollar toupee and the light blue gabardine suits?"

"You gotta go, babe," said Elias.

"But Max Luby doesn't like me, and I don't like Max Luby," said Ruby.

"He's my best friend, and he flew out to see me every weekend when I was at the facility in Nevada, and he took care of my money for me," said Elias. "Now that I can't trade anymore in the stock market, that's going to be Max's job in my new life. Max is going to be in charge of my money. I need him. We're going to have to ask them to dinner and go to their house to dinner. Please do this for me."

She and her husband stared at each other. "I am so happy to see you awake, Elias."

THE ROOM was filled with doctors, nurses, and orderlies. Ruby took out her cell phone and stepped out to call her secretary, Jenny. "Oh, Jenny. Mr. Renthal has come out of the coma. Isn't it marvelous? Thank you, Jenny. I'll tell Elias when this mob of medical people lets me get nearer to the bed. Now, there's a change of plans for the evening. I have to go to a testimonial dinner tonight in Brooklyn for a business associate of my husband's. He insists I go, and I can't exactly say no-I-won't-go to a husband who's just come out of a three-week coma, can I? First, call the home of Max Luby in Brooklyn. The phone number's in the contacts on the computer. Ask for *Mrs.* Luby. Her name is Sylvia, but you call her Mrs. Luby. Big fat lady. Shops at Loehmann's. Get the picture? She's never liked me. She tells everyone that I never used to invite her when we were giving parties in the old days. Say that Mr. Renthal has come out of his coma and that Mrs. Renthal will be attending the dinner tonight in Brooklyn. I tore up the invitation when it came and threw it out, so you'll have to get all the details and addresses. Time, place, that sort of thing. Make sure the chauffeur has a copy and knows exactly where he's going. I don't want to be driving up and down streets in Brooklyn, looking for the right church hall. Then track down Frieda, my manicurist, and tell her she *must* be at my house in an hour. If she has to cancel one of her other customers, tell her I'll pay for that too, and extras. I hear her son's in trouble again, dealing dope, so she could probably use the money, legal bills being what they are. And call Bernardo. Tell him it's an emergency and could he please please please come to my house at six to do my hair. I'll be wearing the new yellow satin gown from Karl Lagerfeld that Baroness de Liagra brought back from Paris. Ask Blondell to check it to see if it's wrinkled from the flight over and to be extra super careful if she has to iron it."

Back in the room, Ruby gathered up her things and moved toward Elias's bed. "Excuse me, everybody. Let me get near my husband for an instant. Elias, my darling, I'm going to have to leave to get ready for Max Luby's testimonial."

"You're going to Max's testimonial?" asked Elias, delighted.

"It's my welcome-back-from-the-coma present for you," said Ruby.

"Thanks, babe." They smiled at each other.

She leaned in to kiss him good-bye. In a voice heard only by Elias, she said, "Tell me one thing before I go."

"What?"

"Who does Perla Zacharias want to meet through you?" She knew Perla was one of the first people her husband had called after regaining consciousness, his curiosity piqued after reading her card.

"Lord Biedermeier, my former publisher."

"About what?" asked Ruby.

"About your friend Gus Bailey, I suppose. She didn't like the way Gus wrote about her in *Park Avenue,* and she was right. And now she's worried about his book. She saw in the *Post*'s profile of me that I had a book under contract with Biedermeier before I went to the facility and she asked me to introduce them."

"My husband needs a shave," said Ruby to Tammi Jo as she was going out the door. "What's that nice orderly's name? The good-looking one with the shaved head? Oh, yes, Sidney. Ask Sidney to shave him first thing in the morning. I'll call his barber, Toshi, to come up tomorrow afternoon to cut his hair here."

Ruby took the elevator down from the tenth floor of the Adele Harcourt Pavilion. She was on her cell phone with Jenny, starting to make a list of the things she had to do. When the elevator stopped on the third floor, Gus Bailey stepped in. Each was surprised to see the other.

"Well, I certainly know where you're coming from," said Gus. "How is Elias? Is he still in the coma?"

"No, the most marvelous thing just happened. He has just within the last couple of hours come out of the coma. What are you doing here?"

"My annual checkup," Gus said, shifting uncomfortably. This was not lost on Ruby, who had always been quite perceptive. It had served her well as she and Elias had made their climb to the top. She let Gus's tentativeness slide for a moment and changed the subject.

"I just read your piece on Adele Harcourt's funeral in the new issue of *Park Avenue,* or on the return from prison of Elias Renthal, depending on how you look at it," said Ruby.

"One of the embarrassing things about writing about people you have dinner with is that inevitably you'll run into the person at a party or in an elevator," said Gus.

"I'm not unhappy with the story, Gus. It happened. You saw it. That's what you do for a living. And you were nice not to say that Elias and I crashed Adele Harcourt's reception, which we did. It sounds so trashy to crush a high-society funeral reception on your first day out of prison. But, as you probably remember, I used to be pretty trashy before I married Elias."

Gus laughed. The elevator doors opened and the unlikely duo moved through the lobby to the sidewalk.

"You look nice when you laugh, Gus. You ought to do it more often. Tell me something. Did you just lie to me in the elevator about getting a checkup? Did the doctor with the office on the third floor just give you some bad news?"

Gus was silent for a moment before answering flatly, "Yes, he did, as a matter of fact. What in the world prompted you to ask me that? Does it show?"

"I felt it. You have a different look in your eyes. You seem different. Haunted, almost. It must be very serious. You just found out that you have cancer, didn't you?" said Ruby.

"I didn't know you had such a spooky side, Ruby," said Gus. "I haven't had time to think about it yet. When I'm ready to talk about it, I'll give you a call. First I have to get used to having it again."

"What's he going to do?"

"Dire things, I suppose. No chemo for me, by the way."

"What did he say?"

"I don't know."

"What do you mean you don't know?"

"I tune out when he talks to me and nod my head as if I'm listening."

"I care, Gus," said Ruby, reaching out and grabbing his hand.

"I know you do," he replied, giving her hand a squeeze back. "Sorry it didn't work out for us to stay friends."

"The least I can do is give you a ride back to your apartment."

"Okay," said Gus. "I saw that dark green Mercedes-Benz limousine at Adele Harcourt's funeral. Yeah, I'd like a ride in that."

"Do you still live in that divine little penthouse I once saw in *Architectural Digest*?"

"I've been there for years," said Gus.

"What are you doing tonight, Gus?"

"Not much. Why?"

"How would you feel about getting into black tie and taking me to a testimonial dinner in Brooklyn for Max Luby, my husband's money manager, that Elias asked me to go to practically the very instant he came out of the coma?"

"That is my idea of a really rotten invitation," said Gus.

Ruby laughed. "Are you turning me down?"

"Of course I'm turning you down. You should call Addison Kent. That's the sort of thing he likes to do."

"I bet you didn't know that Max Luby handles Perla Zacharias's money too," said Ruby, dangling Gus's favorite subject in front of him like a carrot on a stick.

"I didn't know that, but it's not enough of an enticement to get me to go to his testimonial dinner in Brooklyn," said Gus.

"I just thought it might take your mind off things," said Ruby. "Well, here's something else that might interest you. Perla just sent a thousand-dollar orchid plant to Elias."

"And Addison Kent, Perla's walker, probably delivered the note on the blue stationery that accompanied the orchid to Brucie, the florist at the Rhinelander," said Gus. "The music goes round and round, as they used to say in my day. Here's where I get off." He sighed wearily.

"You should ask me up one day to see your terrace," she said as he got out of the car.

Gus turned back to her. "Come forsythia season, I'll call."

Reaching out to him as he started to walk away, Ruby called to Gus.

"Listen, Gus, I don't know what I'm talking about, but we used to be friends, and God knows we have a very deep connection. I think that thousand-dollar orchid plant to Elias from Perla has something to do with you," said Ruby. "Be careful."

"What's that mean?"

"I don't know. Just be careful. You've pissed off some very important people, Gus." said Ruby.

WHILE RUBY was having her nails done by Frieda, and her hair done by Bernardo, and was being helped by her maid Blondell into her yellow satin dress that Karl Lagerfeld had made especially for her at the behest of Baroness de Liagra, she was talking on the telephone to the baroness herself in Paris on a three-way hookup with Simon Cabot in London. Each was urging her to take advantage of the dreaded testimonial dinner by going to the microphone and thanking Max for his years of duty to her husband.

"But I can't stand the guy," said Ruby.

"Well, tonight you love him," said Simon. "And don't forget that for a second."

"This is what I've been telling you about," said the baroness. "Think of it as a rehearsal for what you're going to be. Use what happened to you. Don't hide it."

"This is a perfect way for you to start becoming the new Ruby Renthal," said Simon. "Tell them that Max visited your husband every weekend at the facility in Las Vegas," he suggested.

"Tell them about the clank of the prison door," said the baroness.

"Don't tell about Elias cleaning the toilets," said Simon.

ELIAS HAD assured Ruby that she was to be seated at the head table, but Ruby soon realized that she had been demoted to a lesser table by Sylvia Luby, who never could stand her. It was the sort of slight that Ruby understood and smiled at. Sylvia was fuming at the head table as she watched Ruby, whom she had expected would complain about her seating, in deep conversation with her dinner partner, a charming Brooklyn resident named Joe Carey whom Ruby, an expert conversationalist, soon discovered was a friend of Gus Bailey's.

"So you know Gus Bailey," said Ruby. "Small world."

"We had a Zacharias connection," said Joe.

"I've heard the name," said Ruby. They both laughed. "Actually, I just saw Gus this afternoon. I ran into him at the hospital. He'd just been to his doctor. I think he's sick."

"I was afraid of that the last time I saw him. He didn't look well."

Ruby and Joe talked about Gus for a while, how they each met him and their favorite Gus Bailey stories. They were both surprised at how easily they got along.

"You're a nice guy, Joe Carey," said Ruby.

"And you're a beautiful woman," replied Joe. His gaze lingered on her face for a moment, searching for an opening.

"And a married one," said Ruby. "Hey, I'm on. I forgot to tell you I was going to speak." She rose from her seat.

Like Ruby, Sylvia Luby was dressed in yellow, but from Loehmann's in Brooklyn, not Karl Lagerfeld for Chanel Couture in Paris. Sylvia's dress was a large size with long sleeves and a thick white belt that called attention to her substantial waistline. It had been her turn to speak about her husband of almost fifty years when Ruby Renthal unexpectedly rose from her table—"dazzling, simply dazzling," as Max said to Elias the next day at the Adele Harcourt Pavilion. She walked up to the microphone at the head table and introduced herself to the sold-out hall of people she had never seen before and probably would never see again, except for her dinner partner, Joe Carey.

No one had to ask the audience to quiet down. She walked like a movie star going up to collect her Golden Globe. She loved the feeling that came over her as every eye stared at her.

"My name is Ruby Renthal," she began. She spoke in the throaty voice she had learned all those years ago when she had been riding high and was good friends with Loelia Manchester Minardos, from whom she learned all about class.

"My husband is Elias Renthal. He was recently released from the federal facility in Las Vegas, Nevada, where he served seven years, following a grossly inappropriate charge. During that painful time, his great friend and financial partner Max Luby, with whom he has been friends since they were young men in Cleveland, flew out every weekend to visit my husband at the facility. Max knew the terrible sound of the facility door clanking shut behind him, and still he went every weekend, leaving poor Sylvia so he could meet with his old friend. Oh, thank you, darling Sylvia. My husband said it was something he would never forget. The first thing he thought of when he came out of his coma this very afternoon was Max Luby. His first words were, 'This is the day that Max is going to be honored.' Thank you, dear, darling Max. You have always had the place of honor in our hearts." At that moment she believed the lie she had just told. She knew that he had kept tabs on her when Elias was in prison and had reported to Elias about her. She turned to Max and kissed him on both cheeks. Then she turned back to the audience. "Thank you very much for allowing me to speak."

Everyone in the room rose, except the people in wheelchairs, and gave her a standing ovation. She loved the feeling of the applause. Max, who liked her as little as she liked him, was astonished by her star power. He had never realized how beautiful Ruby was until he saw her in the glow of her success. As the crowd cheered, Max took Ruby over to say hello to Sylvia.

"Oh, Sylvia, how pretty you look," said Ruby, leaning forward to kiss her, but Sylvia did not respond, despite the flashing bulbs of cameras the guests had brought going off in their faces. "And we've both picked yellow. I love your belt. You must come and see the new house on East Seventy-eighth Street. I'll send the car over to pick you up one afternoon and we'll have tea and catch up."

By the time Sylvia Luby got to the microphone to tell about her almost-fifty-year marriage to Max Luby, a speech she had rehearsed over and over in front of the bathroom mirror, the caterers had begun to serve the prime rib main course on thick white plates that clattered when they hit the table, and no one was listening to poor Sylvia, who knew she'd lost her audience, except for Max, who had heard her speech several times before and laughed in the right places. Everybody was talking about Ruby Renthal, who had already left for Manhattan in her green Mercedes limousine, with her chauffeur, Jacques, at the wheel.

CHAPTER 26

A DDISON KENT SERVED HIS PURPOSE AT MAISIE
Verdurin's dinner party a few weeks earlier, just as
Gus and Lil and Maisie had planned. After giving
Sylvia Luby a fake compliment on her yellow evening dress
from Loehmann's with the belt around her ample waist, he ignored the poor woman completely and never said another word
to her, as he was far more interested in listening to the conversation of Lil Altemus and Gus Bailey to his left. He leaned in
toward Lil to listen to Gus tell her about the copies of the sixteen letters Perla Zacharias once had written to the man who was
to become her third husband. He got a lot of information before
he clumsily spilled his wine all over Lil Altemus.

PERLA KNEW it was true. The letters had been written by Perla
to a gigolo she briefly had been married to during an earlier
phase of her life. She remembered writing the letters in her own
hand. She had placed her much younger brother, Rocco, from
the last of her father's five marriages, into an alcohol and drug
rehab center in Johannesburg. She could remember writing her
lover that her brother had told his drug counselor at the rehab a
very different version of the death of the second of her four

husbands than hers. Perla was a smart woman. She didn't need Simon Cabot to tell her that it would not do at all to have a story like that in circulation at a time when she was finally starting to be invited to the top houses in New York, London, and Paris because of her enormous and much-publicized philanthropy. She had learned from Konstantin when to attack and, more important, when to back off in a situation. She didn't give a fuck about Kyle Cramden, and if this ruined his case, so be it. She had other cards to play. It would be okay to let Gus think he had won this round. It would be better and more devastating to get him later, when he started to feel secure, breathing a sigh of relief that this lawsuit was over. That's when she would strike. As long as she had the money to stop it, *Infamous Lady,* the book that he'd been telling people around town was the thing he lived for these days, was never going to happen. She wanted to squash that asshole like a bug.

First off, she ordered her two investigators who had passed along the story of child molestation in Biarritz to former congressman Kyle Cramden and his lawyer Win Burch to desist from repeating that story. The maid at the Hôtel du Palais in Biarritz had not walked in on Gus molesting a young boy. No such molestation had taken place. It was based on an old rumor that one of Gus's enemies tried to start many years ago when he did not like the way he was portrayed in one of Gus's novels. After some resistance on Gus's part, mainly just an attempt to make her sweat a bit, a settlement had been arrived at between Peter Lombardo and Win Burch at two o'clock in the morning on the night before the deposition. Christine Saunders had been right about Peter, he shot enough holes in the congressman's case to ensure that Gus would never have to face the dreaded Mr. Burch on the stand. The deposition did not take place. The settlement, although less by far than the millions the congressman had sued for, was still very large for someone who lived on a salary, as Gus did.

CHAPTER 27

WHEN LORD BIEDERMEIER'S SECRETARY, VERONA, buzzed him to say that Elias Renthal was on the phone, he was somewhat surprised, but he hoped this meant that the former convict was ready to start writing his memoir again.

"This is Lord Biedermeier speaking," he said.

"Biedermeier, this is Elias Renthal."

"Mr. Renthal. I'm so happy to know that you are out of your coma that I have been reading about," said Lord Biedermeier, who had a great curiosity as to what this call was about.

"I'm out of the coma but still in the hospital. You will think this a curious invitation. I know what a busy schedule you have, but I wonder if you could come up to the Adele Harcourt Pavilion tomorrow to have tea or a glass of wine with me. There is a person who is most anxious to meet you. And I am not at liberty to reveal the name."

"Yes, I can come," said Lord Biedermeier, without even checking his calendar. Elias had had a book under contract with his company since before he was incarcerated. Now would be the perfect time to get that memoir going again, with the entire city abuzz about Elias Renthal and his beautiful wife, Ruby.

"Tenth floor of the Adele Harcourt Pavilion at New York–Presbyterian," said Elias. "It's the VIP floor. Suite six hundred."

Ruby, rushing, made a quick hospital stop to check on Elias's progress before her hair appointment at Bernardo's and her lunch engagement at Swifty's with Baroness de Liagra, who had just flown in from Paris. She handed Tammi Jo a box of cookies that Gert had baked that morning.

"Gingersnaps," said Ruby.

"Oh, I love gingersnaps. I'll probably eat the whole box. There's no one like Gert when it comes to cookies. No, I'm only kidding, Mrs. Renthal. I'll take it to the nurses' station. They'll be thrilled."

"How is Mr. Renthal?"

"He's much better today," said Tammi Jo.

"Do you think so? Good," replied Ruby.

"He's just like his old self, not that I ever knew his old self, but what I imagine his old self must have been, full of vim and vigor. He had a very healthy BM."

"Actually, I don't need *that* full a report," replied Ruby, her nose wrinkled in a show of distaste. "Just that he's doing well is enough information for me. Have you changed your hair, Tammi Jo? You look different."

"Thank you for noticing, Mrs. Renthal," said Tammi Jo, as she put both hands to her coiffure. "This is my Audrey Hepburn look."

"Oh," replied Ruby.

"Visitors today. Lord Biedermeier, who Mr. Renthal says is his publisher," said Tammi Jo. "I Googled him and found that he's Gus Bailey's publisher also."

"Lord Biedermeier is coming to meet my husband? He didn't tell me that."

"Yes, and someone else too, but I don't know who the someone else is. I'll bet it's someone very fabulous, if he needs to keep them a secret."

"Oh," said Ruby. She knew who the mystery guest would be. Someone who spent an inordinate amount of money on beautiful orchid plants.

"RIGHT THIS way, Lord Biedermeier," Tammi Jo said, relishing the opportunity to call someone by a European title, as it felt very chic to her, like something Audrey Hepburn would do. "I'm Mr. Renthal's nurse. I'll take you to his room.

"I love the books you publish, especially Gus Bailey's. The first thing I read in every issue of *Park Avenue* is Gus Bailey's diary. Could you give Gus Bailey a message for me, Lord Biedermeier? I know he's writing a novel based on Perla Zacharias and, well, I went to nursing school with the male nurse who's doing time in the Biarritz prison for the death of Konstantin Zacharias. I could tell him a thing or two. We used to think of Floyd as a healer. Oh, here we are."

She opened the door and said to Elias, "You have a visitor, Mr. Renthal. Lord Biedermeier."

Biedermeier walked through the sitting room and through the open bedroom door and up to the bed where Elias was propped up with pillows. He had on his new Turnbull & Asser blue silk pajamas, which Tammi Jo later told her mother cost six hundred ninety dollars. The price tag was still on, and there were four pairs, in different colors, all at the same price. Tammi Jo was transfixed by the extravagance of the Renthals.

"What a pleasure this is," said Lord Biedermeier.

"I've been in a coma," said Elias.

"Yes, it has been well publicized. There's no one like Simon Cabot," said the publisher, establishing himself at the beginning of the meeting as an insider.

"I never saw this suite before," said Lord Biedermeier. "Pretty fancy."

"People like the Van Degans and the Rockefellers always use this suite during their illnesses," said Elias, who, even after prison, felt it necessary to establish his importance.

Tammi Jo couldn't resist making her contribution to the lore of Suite 600 in Harcourt Pavilion. "Do you remember Antonia von Rautbord? The society lady who was in a coma for so many years? Such a sad story. She was in this suite until they moved her to a rest home. She used to have her hair and nails done, even in the coma."

Neither Lord Biedermeier nor Elias was interested in Tammi Jo's contribution, and neither responded. Tammi Jo poured Pellegrino water with lemon slices into lovely antique glasses engraved with the initial R that Jacques, the chauffeur, had brought over from the new house on East Seventy-eighth Street, now that Elias was having visitors. The glasses with the engraved R had been purchased at a Rothschild auction in Geneva by Baroness de Liagra as a housewarming present for Ruby Renthal. Tammi Jo placed a small table next to Lord Biedermeier's chair and put down the glasses of Pellegrino water and passed two silver trays of Gert's tea sandwiches, which Ruby called society sandwiches. The two men did not speak during those moments, waiting for Tammi Jo to leave. "Would you prefer India or China tea?" said Tammi Jo in a throaty voice, imitating Ruby.

"Oh, no, no, Tammi Jo. Everything is lovely. Thank you so much. Now, Lord Biedermeier and I would like to be alone. Would you close the door behind you? Thank you, Tammi Jo."

"So why am I here?" asked Lord Biedermeier. "Are you ready to start working on your memoir again, adding the story of the seven years in prison and your stroke?"

"Facility, not prison," said Elias.

"Prison sounds better. It's a great story, Elias. One of the richest men in the world on his knees cleaning toilets. It just doesn't get any better than that."

He stopped when he saw the look that began to appear on Elias's face. He spoke quickly again to explain himself. "I meant that from a theatrical point of view, or a storyteller's point of view."

"I didn't ask you here to tell you my story. We can discuss my book later," said Elias.

"Have you actually written it?" asked Biedermeier.

"With a little help from a hired hand who will receive no credit," answered Elias. "I'll just need to update it to include recent events."

"I'll bet we could get *Park Avenue* to run an excerpt. I'm sure my friend Stokes Bishop would agree to it. It would be great publicity. 'The Renthals Retake New York,' something like that. We'll get Annie Leibovitz, poor dear with all her troubles, to photograph your beautiful wife, Ruby, and put her on the cover. We'll do a big party at the Four Seasons, and everyone who's anyone in the city of New York will come."

"We'll see," said Elias. He knew that a big party at the Four Seasons in his honor was a good idea, part of a well-thought-out plan created by Simon Cabot to get them back into the life they had enjoyed before their fall. "That's another conversation entirely. For lunch, not a hospital bed. I asked you up here to meet somebody who wants to meet you. She and I share a great dislike for one of your authors."

Elias pressed a button, and the door opened. Standing there in front of Tammi Jo was a small but very noticeable woman who gave off an aura of money and power. She was wearing a sable coat. She had an attitude of superiority about her that very, very rich people sometimes acquire, which has nothing to do with class or background, merely with money. Her face had been stretched too tight by far in surgery. Her closest friends, who were her hangers-on, said among themselves that they almost didn't recognize her after her latest operation. She bore a resemblance to the much younger Ormolu Webb, whose plastic surgeon she had recently used.

Perla turned to speak to Addison Kent, who had escorted her to the Adele Harcourt Pavilion, as he now escorted her to all her lunches and dinners and appointments since he had unofficially become her walker. "You wait here, Addison. There is something that Elias and I need to discuss. I'm sure this lovely nurse will keep you company," she said, pointing to Tammi Jo but not looking at her. Tammi Jo didn't think it was the right time to tell Perla Zacharias that she had gone to nursing school with the man who was in prison for causing the fire that had killed her husband.

"Mrs. Zacharias," announced Tammi Jo, as if she were Doddsie at the Butterfield Club. Tammi Jo was thrilled to be with such people. She followed as Perla walked into the room, to pour another glass of Pellegrino water with a slice of lemon. Tammi Jo thought Perla had style, the way she let her sable coat float off her shoulders onto a chair. Tammi Jo picked it up, hugged it, and hung it on a hanger in a closet, unable to take her eyes off the famous Mrs. Zacharias, who people said was richer than the Queen of England. Perla had been professionally made up, and her hair had been smartly cut in the latest fashion by Bernardo, the fashionable hairdresser of choice these days, although it barely masked the horrible disfigurement from her face-lift. She approached Elias in his bed and kissed him on both cheeks. Later, Elias told Ruby he had hardly recognized her with the new face.

"I have prayed for you every day, darling Elias," she said.

"That's some orchid plant you sent, lady. The rumor on the floor here among the nurses and interns and even Ruby is that it cost a thousand bucks," said Elias.

"You're worth it, Elias, and, as the world knows, I can afford it," she said.

Biedermeier immediately recognized the very rich woman whom his author Gus Bailey had made into an internationally recognized name. "Lord Biedermeier. I would like you to meet a lady you have heard a great deal about. This is Mrs. Konstantin Zacharias. She is the widow of the greatest financial genius of his time, who was tragically asphyxiated in a fire started by an unstable male nurse who is currently doing ten years in the Biarritz prison."

"I know the story well. I read about it in *Park Avenue*," said Biedermeier. He didn't mention that one of his bestselling authors was writing a novel based on the subject. "Yes, I recognized you, Mrs. Zacharias. Helmut Newton took those wonderful pictures of you inside the courtroom in Biarritz at the time of the male nurse's murder trial." That night he said to his dinner partner, with admiration, "She just looks rich, even with all the plastic surgery."

"Your author Mr. Bailey's novel based on the murder and the murder trial is what I am here to discuss," she replied, like a CEO calling a meeting to order. Tammi Jo pushed two chairs closer to Elias. "Would you close the door behind you?" said Perla to Tammi Jo, as if she were speaking to a servant. "And take some Pellegrino and ice and lemon to Mr. Kent in the other room." When Tammi Jo opened the door with the glass of Pellegrino in her hand, Addison nearly fell over because he was listening at the other side, his ear pressed to the door.

"They're talking about Gus Bailey," whispered Tammi Jo.

CHAPTER 28

GUS WAS NERVOUS AS HE SAT IN THE OFFICE OF his publisher, Lord Biedermeier. His book editor, Beatrice Parsons, was on vacation and unable to attend the meeting, which made him feel even more uncomfortable and vulnerable. He wished he had found another agent after his own retired, but after so many years of writing books for Biedermeier he had a good relationship with his publisher and he had thought he could handle his affairs himself. He had never imagined he would be in such a troubling predicament.

"I wanted to discuss *Infamous Lady* with you, Gus," said Biedermeier. "I'm concerned about the topic. Everyone knows the book is about the circumstances surrounding Zacharias's murder, and I just wonder if people aren't going to be sick of it by the time the book comes out. You've been on it too long and covered it exhaustively for *Park Avenue*. People are losing interest in the Zachariases. There's been a trial. There's been a verdict. The nurse was found guilty and is serving his sentence in the Biarritz prison. The story is over."

Gus's worst nightmare was happening. He simply couldn't believe Biedermeier was actually playing this game; that Perla had gotten to him, too. He slumped forward and could barely hear what his publisher was saying to him. He had been hoping this nonsense was behind him after he settled his lawsuit and showed Perla Zacharias that he would not be bullied. Compared to this, Win Burch felt small-time. He had poured so much of himself into this novel; so much of him was caught up in its writing. It was what he went home to at night, and if he lost the book he'd lose everything. Gus felt weary and sick. And the news from his doctor had not been good. How could he start over now? He feared he didn't have the time.

"But, we have a contract and I've written so much already and I've been promised the first interview with the male nurse, Floyd McArthur, who's in prison. I've gotten to know his family and his lawyer, and they want me to do the interview. He has never spoken to anyone in the media, but he agreed to talk to me. There is enormous interest in his story. Aren't you interested in that? I'll have so many things like this to reveal in the book that I wasn't able to talk about in the magazine," Gus pleaded. He thought he felt tears pricking at his eyes. He knew if the publisher did not support the book, even if he contractually had to publish it, it was dead in the water before it was even in bookstores.

Biedermeier hesitated. Then he made an elaborate gesture of dismissal. "I really think we should brainstorm other topics for you," he replied.

The two men looked at each other. Biedermeier had won the moment. "What about this Madoff fellow?" he said, in a more pleasant tone of voice. "That is a topic people are interested in, and it's ongoing. Perhaps you can find some people to interview who lost their fortunes. I think we can even pay for you to fly down to North Carolina to check out his new accommodations, so to speak."

Gus was quiet for a moment; there was a hint of darkness in his expression.

"I'm not going to North Carolina," said Gus, straightening with resolve. "I'm going to Biarritz to meet with the nurse. I don't want to miss that hearing."

"I told you I'm not interested in the Zacharias story," said Biedermeier, a "boss" tone overpowering his usually charming British accent. Stern as he sounded, Gus noted his publisher would not meet his eyes.

"Then I'll go on my own," said Gus. "I can use it on my television series."

"I thought you were broke," said Biedermeier. "You've told that to half the town." He had heard a rumor that Gus had had to put his house in the country up for sale to pay his legal bills.

"I am, but I have a backer who's as interested in this story as I am. Same person who bought and brought me the sixteen letters that Perla wrote to the mysterious third husband. The very information that got Perla to stop helping Kyle Cramden and Win Burch crush me in that awful lawsuit."

"Who?" asked Lord Biedermeier.

"It's a secret backer," replied Gus, letting him know he wasn't revealing the identity. "By the way," said Gus, "I had an interesting conversation with Ruby Renthal."

"Really," Biedermeier said, again not meeting Gus's eyes and nervously rearranging the manuscripts on his desk while Gus spoke.

"Yes. I heard from Ruby that you went to visit the billionaire ex-convict and the frequent widow was a surprise guest. Perla Zacharias herself. You're traveling in the big-money circles these days."

Gus continued, "I don't suppose your surprise rendezvous with the third richest woman in the world at Elias Renthal's hospital bedside had anything to do with your sudden change of heart about the topic of my novel."

CHAPTER 29

DODO VAN DEGAN WAS LATE FOR LUNCH AGAIN at Swifty's, as was her habit when the obligatory monthly lunches with Lil Altemus took place. Actually, she had started not to mind the lunches and no longer did imitations of Lil for Xavior. Dodo had arranged with Robert that no bill ever be presented at Swifty's, so that there would be no fuss between them as to which one would pay for lunch that month. For her part, although she never would have admitted it, especially to Dodo, Lil had begun to enjoy hearing Dodo's mortuary stories, from her nights of sitting with Xavior while he was embalming a famous person.

"Did Xavior embalm that actor in *Batman* who overdosed on prescription drugs?" asked Lil.

"No. That was his day off, and he missed it. He was so disappointed," answered Dodo.

"How did Xavior get into the business of undertaking?" asked Lil one day.

"Oh, it's such a sweet story," said Dodo, who loved to talk about Xavior. "When he was thirteen years old, he waited five hours in line outside the Grant P. Trumbull Funeral Home to see Judy Garland, who had overdosed, in her casket. Xavior said she was wearing her red shoes from *The Wizard of Oz*. He said at that moment he knew that he wanted to be an undertaker when he grew up. Don't you think that's a sweet story, Lil?"

"Look, there's Ruby Renthal and Baroness de Liagra, sitting at the corner table. They've become great friends, I hear from Maisie Verdurin," said Lil, arching her eyebrows and humming.

"I have an idea for you, Lil. I think you should go to work," said Dodo.

"Go to work? What in the world are you talking about? What could I do? I'm over seventy years old," said Lil.

"You're seventy-six, Lil, not seventy. Remember, I'm family. But you're hale and hardy, I'll say that for you. I was talking to Maisie Verdurin about you last night at Linda Stein's wake at Grant P. Trumbull's. She said you'd be a great real estate woman and you could come work for her."

"Me? Maisie said that? How ridiculous!" said Lil.

"She said you knew all the rich widows who are selling off the big apartments to all the nouveaus and looking for little ones in the right buildings. She said the Murdochs bought the old Rockefeller apartment for forty million dollars, and the space hadn't been touched for years and needed everything done to it. Think what your commission would have been on that. She said you had a built-in clientele. She said with the Altemus name and the Van Degan connection, all the old grand dames would go to you because you're one of them who did exactly that. You're tough. You're snobby. You can be imperious, and you have good pearls that I once dropped in your pea soup. You'd be perfect."

"Would I have to go to real estate school?"asked Lil as the idea began to take hold on her.

"Yes, but Maisie can help you out with that."

"It's hard for me to imagine myself having to go to an office every morning at nine o'clock and having an hour for lunch. Do you suppose that's what it will be like?"

"I suppose, at least until you sell your first twenty-million-dollar apartment," said Dodo. "After that, you can take your clients to Swifty's for lunch and stay as long as you want."

"Do you know something, Dodo? I *would* be great doing that, finding the right apartment for the old dowagers like me, making sure they get top dollar for the apartment they are selling. I've always loved to argue with the head of the board of the building. I know how to put them in their place," said Lil. "Shall I call Maisie, or should you? Oh, Dodo, I can't thank you enough for making that suggestion. My heart is beating so fast with excitement."

GUS WAS ON IBERIA AIRLINES ON HIS WAY TO Barcelona to change planes and fly to San Sebastián, where he would be met by a car and driven on to Biarritz twenty miles away for the one-day trial of Floyd McArthur, the male nurse who had been found guilty of setting the fire that had asphyxiated Konstantin Zacharias. Longing for his wife and children, McArthur had stupidly made an escape from the old Biarritz prison without a euro in his pocket and had quickly been apprehended at the Spanish border and returned to his dank and lonely cell. Now he was to face punishment for the attempted escape.

Gus always traveled first-class on his assignments in foreign destinations. A wise literary agent called Mona Berg had installed that clause in his contract when he had first begun to work at *Park Avenue* nearly twenty-five years earlier. His secret benefactor, whose name he refused to divulge to anyone, was a generous and passionate soul who felt that if Gus were going to the court hearing in Biarritz, he should travel in the same manner in which *Park Avenue* magazine would have sent him.

The benefactor, who had private reasons for despising Perla Zacharias, was Joe Carey, the man Gus had met at Le Cirque the night before his granddaughter's birthday and later had met with several times at a remote restaurant where neither would be recognized. Joe Carey had been a great friend of the murdered Konstantin Zacharias, although he had not been invited to Konstantin's elaborate funeral in Biarritz, where the Infanta of Spain and the Duke and Duchess of Chatfield had been members of the International Set of mourners. He knew his exclusion had been Perla's doing. Joe Carey, who lived in Brooklyn and was worth six hundred million dollars, thought it was important for Gus to be seen in the Biarritz courtroom, if only to show that Perla had not been able to keep him out, as she had bragged she had at a London party, so when Lord Biedermeier refused to pay for Gus's trip to the one-day trial, Joe Carey had offered to foot the bill. In addition to first-class travel, Joe also had seen to it that Gus stayed at the Hôtel du Palais in Biarritz, where the notables had stayed during the trials.

Perla, who played the role of grieving widow very well, wished to have McArthur's ten-year sentence extended, for five more years, if possible. Simon Cabot had advised her not to attend the one-day trial. He said it would make her look vindictive and unsympathetic to the public.

In a box at the opera, Perla had told Addison, on whom she was relying more and more, that Simon Cabot had told her she should not be seen in the courtroom in Biarritz. She had whispered into Addison's ear, during Renée Fleming's aria, that he should fly to Biarritz and attend the trial in her place, reporting everything to her. If asked, he was to say that she was still too aggrieved to attend.

GUS HAD settled into his seat comfortably. From his carry-on bag, he took out a sleeping pill for later and a novel that everyone was talking about called *Empress Bianca* by Lady Colin

Campbell, about another famous lady caught up in a scandal. He was looking at the menu for dinner when a late-boarding passenger came to sit in the aisle seat next to his window seat. A Louis Vuitton carry-on bag was tossed on the seat and a second, larger Louis Vuitton bag was being placed in the compartment above. It was then that Gus Bailey looked directly into the face of Addison Kent, a man he had taken an instant dislike to the first time he met him, at Lil Altemus's Easter luncheon party at her old apartment on Fifth Avenue when Addison was the walker for Adele Harcourt. Now he was well known as the walker for Perla Zacharias. He felt that his position as walker and confidant to the very rich widow had brought him stature in international society, in whose outskirts Perla moved.

Gus realized instantly that they were both headed for the same courtroom in Biarritz. He had heard from his friend Simon Cabot in London that he had advised Perla not to attend the trial.

Addison Kent was equally distressed to find himself next to the man Perla considered an enemy for the eight and a half hours of the upcoming flight. He looked around the first-class cabin to see if there was another seat. There wasn't. He had the last first-class seat. He sensed that Gus disliked him.

"Hello, Gus. I hope it's all right if I call you Gus. We seem to know a lot of the same people. We met for the first time at Lil Altemus's Easter lunch. I was accompanying Adele Harcourt that day."

"Yes, I remember," said Gus. "And now you 'accompany' Perla Zacharias, who is sending you to Biarritz to cover things for her. I imagine we are heading for the same destination."

Addison appeared flustered. What caused Addison's distress was that he had heard from Perla that she had succeeded in getting Gus's book about Konstantin's death pulled, and that Gus was being censored at *Park Avenue* as well. Addison said to the flight attendant, "May I use the men's room before we take off?"

"If you rush," said the flight attendant.

Addison zipped open his Louis Vuitton bag, the same bag he had used to take Winkie Williams's casket clothes to Francis Xavior Branigan at the Grant P. Trumbull Funeral Home the night before Winkie's cremation. He shuffled through it and took out his cell phone. He raced to the men's room and dialed Simon Cabot in London.

"I thought you said that Perla said that Gus Bailey is off the story. Wasn't this all settled in Elias Renthal's hospital room? Well, he's on the same plane I'm on. In fact, I'm sitting right next to him. What do I say to him if he starts to talk to me?"

"Take a couple of pills and go straight to sleep," said Simon.

"SEÑOR, WOULD you please move your carry-on to beneath the seat in front of you?" requested a different flight attendant.

"It's not mine," said Gus. "The guy's in the bathroom. Here, I'll do it for him."

Gus lifted the Louis Vuitton bag and, as he was zipping it up, something inside caught his eye. He put his hand in and took out the gold cigarette case with the lyrics of "The Extra Man" engraved inside that Cole Porter had given to Winkie Williams. He put it back, zipped the bag, and placed the bag under the seat in front of Addison's.

Addison sat down and prepared himself for sleep so that he would not have to talk to Gus. He adjusted his seat so that it stretched out into almost a bed. He threw the blanket over himself, put on the eye mask provided by the flight attendant to keep out the light, and turned away from Gus.

"Whom did you make your report to that I'm on board to attend the escape-from-prison trial in Biarritz?" asked Gus, who was writing the experience as it was happening in the green leather notebook that he always carried. "Did you call Perla? Or Simon Cabot? Simon's an old friend of mine."

Addison's body stirred, but he pretended to be asleep and did not reply. He knew Gus was the kind of reporter who could easily identify his real background, rather than the refined one Winkie Williams had created for him, and he didn't want that to happen.

"Did I ever tell you I ran into Winkie outside the Grant P. Trumbull Funeral Home the day before he committed suicide? Winkie offered me a cigarette that day on East Eighty-first Street and Madison Avenue. I remember it so well. He had a beautiful gold cigarette case that Cole Porter had given him that he told me he was leaving to the Costume Institute at the Met. It went missing after Winkie's suicide. Lil is on the board of the Institute. She thinks a cleaning woman stole it, but that's not my theory. Your klepto reputation precedes you."

Addison, terrified, continued to pretend to sleep.

CHAPTER 31

PERLA'S FAMOUS FRENCH LAWYER, PIERRE LA Rouche, had been shocked to see Gus enter the courtroom, after having been assured that Perla had had both the book and magazine articles he wrote about her stopped. Gus had written during the criminal trial that La Rouche was "an elegant fellow with a mean streak, who chain-smoked in an affected manner with a tortoiseshell cigarette holder." La Rouche didn't like Gus, and Gus didn't like La Rouche, who he felt had been unnecessarily cruel to Floyd McArthur when the bewildered nurse had been on the stand.

During breaks in the proceedings, the guard watch was much less rigid than it had been during the earlier criminal trial. Floyd McArthur, the American male nurse, was doing ten years. On several occasions during the long day, Gus had been able to engage McArthur in conversation in the prisoner holding room, where they put the shackled nurse during the breaks. During the criminal trial, he had been guarded every moment as if he were a terrorist.

Gus, who had been sympathetic to the nurse in the criminal trial, talked quickly and in a low voice. He told McArthur that there was a rumor in circulation that he was taking the fall for the deaths of Konstantin Zacharias and one of his eight nurses who perished with him, and that he would be receiving a sizeable stipend at a future time. "I am so sick of hearing that story," said McArthur in an exasperated tone of voice. "Certainly you don't think I would give up seeing Wanda and the kids for some money down the road." He went on a rant about the horrors of prison life in Biarritz. "There's rats in the cells and the toilet overflows all the time and there's often shit on the floor."

Gus didn't want to waste precious time on that sort of information. "Tell me about Konstantin that last night before the fire," Gus said.

Floyd said he had admired Konstantin Zacharias. They had often taken afternoon walks together through the old city, where Konstantin enjoyed hearing about Floyd's wife, Wanda, and the children. Konstantin regretted that he had never had children of his own to pass on his fortune and banks to. Despite Konstantin's vast wealth and his reputation for toughness in financial negotiations, McArthur said the banker was always kind and thoughtful to all the nurses, guards, and servants, which he couldn't say about "the lady of the house." He was cautious in denouncing her, but his dislike was apparent. Floyd said that Konstantin's long-time doctors, especially Dr. Sedgwick, whom Konstantin had known and trusted for years and who had often stayed for long visits at the villa, had been changed. The new doctors, not one of whom Konstantin had felt close to, had kept him overmedicated. He had become paranoid. McArthur said Konstantin thought his enemies in the Russian mafia, whom he greatly feared, were hiding behind the curtains in his dressing room, which he had to pass through on his way to his bathroom. He said none of his friends were allowed in to see him. He said he missed his brothers. He said there were screaming fights about changing the will, cutting out Konstantin's brothers and sisters.

"Listen, Mr. Bailey," said Floyd.

"What do you mean Mr. Bailey, for god's sake. The name is Gus."

"Call Wanda when you get back to the States, Gus. Send her my love and love to the kids." There were more things Gus wanted to know, but a guard entered and was furious to see Gus in the holding room. He ordered him to leave, or he would have him thrown out of the courtroom for the afternoon session.

"I'll call Wanda and say I saw you, Floyd, and I'll send your love to the kids," said Gus as the angry guard hurried him out of the holding room. Gus didn't have the heart to tell Floyd that Wanda was planning to divorce him, to take back her maiden name, and to ask for full custody of the kids.

THE SEASON had ended in Biarritz, and the bar at the Hôtel du Palais, usually filled to capacity with an international fun-loving clientele, was dark and virtually empty when Gus walked in to meet a Spanish reporter friend, who had not yet arrived. He was reading his notes from the conversation he had been able to sneak in with Floyd McArthur during a break in the proceedings. When he looked up, he saw a man at another table staring at him. It was the man in the gray flannel suit who had been in his room at Claridge's and at the auction of Perla Zacharias's Fabergé eggs that hadn't been destroyed in the fire at the villa. There was no question in Gus's mind that he was being followed by this mysterious man. He had thought it had ended with the lawsuit, but now that he had thrown down the gauntlet and defied Perla's attempts to kill his book and kept on writing, publisher be damned, he realized that when she found out, he could be in even greater danger than before. The fear came back, stronger than ever.

GUS WAS in a pensive mood when he flew back to New York the next afternoon on Iberia Airlines from Barcelona. He was relieved that Addison Kent was not on board. Addison had flown on to Paris from San Sebastián to attend a lunch party given in a "glorious apartment" in the Hôtel Lambert in honor of Perla Zacharias, a lunch party that Addison simply could not miss. It was not until a week later that the baron's butler noticed that a pale blue Fabergé egg that had been part of the center-piece was missing. A maid was fired.

CHAPTER 32

WITHIN TWO WEEKS OF RECEIVING HER NEW York real estate license, Lil Altemus, lunching at Swifty's with Maisie Verdurin, for whom she now worked, was receiving congratulations on all sides for having found a buyer for the sixteen-room apartment at One Sutton Place South, one of the most prestigious buildings in the city, belonging to her first cousin, Minnie Willoughby. "Minnie's mother and my mother were sisters," explained Lil to each person who stopped by her table. "Poor darling Minnie, she practically hasn't left her bedroom for two years, except for medical visits, and all those beautiful rooms were just sitting there empty. Quite honestly, I think the maids are stealing things from her, and she doesn't even notice, as she never leaves her room. Granny's Lowestoft tureen that Minnie always had in the center of her dining room table just simply is not there. I said to her, 'Minnie, I don't think it's safe for you here.' At first she said, 'Never, never, never,' she would never sell, she'd lived there for over thirty years, but when I said I thought I could get her twenty million dollars, she began to listen, ill as she is. Then you found that pushy hedge-fund couple, Maisie, not our kind but perfectly all right as far as those money-money-money people go, and I know practically everyone on the board of the building, which helped a great deal, and everything fell into place. Isn't it exciting? I haven't felt so happy in a long time. Maisie, let's have a glass of champagne."

"But where will cousin Minnie go to live? In one of those assisted-living places where you take your own furniture?" asked Maisie.

"Not at all. Believe it or not, I've grown rather fond of my little apartment on East Sixty-sixth Street. I'm having it all done over. I've gotten rid of those red damask draperies from the Fifth Avenue apartment that looked all wrong from the beginning and hired a charming young man named Markham Roberts, he's the latest hottest thing, to brighten it up, and it's really quite cozy. There's an apartment in my building that's coming on the market, and Minnie's going to move there. Do you remember my old cook, Gert, whom Ruby Renthal stole from me? Gert has an Irish niece named Lil after me, and we're going to change her name to Bridey—we can't have two Lils on the same premises—and she's going to move into the little maid's room there and take care of Minnie. Now I must run. I have an appointment with old Marjorie Watson at River House about letting me sell her place." Lil looked in both directions and then mouthed but did not speak the word *Alzheimer's*.

CHAPTER 33

THE TALK AROUND TOWN AT LUNCH AT SWIFTY'S and Michael's and '21' was about Elias and Ruby Renthal's coming-out party at the Four Seasons that everyone of importance in New York was receiving invitations to. There had been talk that Stokes Bishop would host the party, but Simon Cabot and Baroness de Liagra had prevailed and the party was being hosted by Elias and Ruby, as their own return to New York after his seven years in prison. The name Ruby Renthal was in the air.

Simon Cabot, the international public relations figure best known for making the unpopular Camilla Parker-Bowles, mistress of His Royal Highness Prince Charles, acceptable to the British public following the tragic death of Princess Diana, issued the following release to Kit Jones, Toby Tilden, Christine Saunders, and others of equal stature in the New York media:

> Ruby Renthal, the beautiful, gallant, and loyal wife of billionaire financier Elias Renthal, will be on the cover of the October issue of *Park Avenue* magazine, dressed by Oscar de la Renta and photographed by Annie Leibovitz in front of the Renthals' gardenia-filled indoor swimming pool at their

magnificent New York mansion, with aquatic ladies swimming and kicking in unison, in the manner of Esther Williams and Busby Berkeley in the great days of MGM.

There was, of course, no mention of the vast artistic contribution of Baroness de Liagra in choreographing the Aquacade especially for Ruby.

Ruby Renthal, Ruby Renthal, Ruby Renthal. Everyone in New York was beginning to talk about Ruby Renthal.

EAST FIFTY-SECOND Street between Park Avenue and Lexington Avenue was jam-packed with chauffeur-driven limousines dropping off the three hundred guests at the awninged entrance of the Four Seasons, the city's most prestigious restaurant for the rich, famous, and powerful. Horns honked. Police whistles blew. On the sidewalk, smartly uniformed doormen opened the doors of the limousines and another opened the door of the restaurant, saying to the regulars, "Good evening, Dr. Kissinger"; "Good evening, Mayor Bloomberg"; "Good evening, Mrs. Rockefeller"; "Good evening, Ms. Vanderbilt." Paparazzi, flashing their cameras, pushed through the hundreds of spectators, who cheered and screamed for their favorites as they emerged from their limousines. It was controlled pandemonium. "Oh, my god, there's Faye Converse, the old-time movie star," cried out Lillian Hoolihan, Gert Hoolihan's niece, who had changed her name to Bridey when she went to work for Minnie Willoughby. "She's still beautiful at seventy-six," said Bridey. She wrote down Faye Converse's name below Mick Jagger's on the list of the famous people she'd seen that she was planning to read to the other maids at bingo night at the Sodality of Mary. Gert and Tammi Jo, who had been hired to be Elias Renthal's private nurse, had

high positions in the Renthal household and had been allowed by Ruby to enter the restaurant and watch the arriving
guests from the bottom of the stairway leading up to the party
room.

Upstairs in the restaurant, it was Brucie's finest hour. Ruby
had taken a liking to Brucie during the several years she had
lived at the Rhinelander Hotel when Elias was doing time in the
facility in Las Vegas and, in return, Brucie had become her most
ardent admirer. His pal Jonsie, from the wine shop, said that
Brucie worshiped Ruby. So it was no surprise that Ruby had insisted to Elias that Brucie do the flowers and decorations for the
party at the Four Seasons. It was the biggest job of his career,
and he rose to the occasion. The centerpieces, the fifteen-inch
red candles, and the goody bags bearing gifts for the departing
guests at the end of the party all fell under Brucie's supervision
He had created a new scented candle named for Ruby Renthal as
one of the gifts.

AN EMERGENCY call from Johannesburg about her drug-
addicted half brother, Rocco, who had this time urinated on the
dance floor of the Tits and Ass Club while smoking a joint and
had landed in jail for the second time in a month, had delayed
Perla Zacharias considerably, much to the dismay of Bernardo,
who was waiting to do her hair and makeup before he went to
do the same for Ormolu Webb. Addison Kent was frantic, and in
order to save time, Perla suggested that he wait outside the Four
Seasons and be there when she finally arrived, as she did not
wish to walk up the stairs to the party unescorted any more than
Addison wanted to walk up the stairs alone, as he had not been
invited directly, merely as an escort for Mrs. Zacharias. Addison
had the taxi drop him at the corner of Fifty-second Street and
Park Avenue and walked the half block east to the entrance of

the Four Seasons through the nearly impenetrable crowd of fans and paparazzi. "Excuse me. Excuse me," he kept saying in the tone of voice he had learned to use when speaking to what he considered to be lesser people. "Coming through, please. I'm a guest at the party. Coming through, please," he said several times, inadvertently bumping into Bridey Hoolihan and knocking her Instamatic camera out of her hand just as she was about to snap Caroline Kennedy, her favorite Irish American, emerging from her car. "Fuck you, asshole," screamed Bridey at Addison as she leaned down to pick up the smashed camera from the sidewalk. In her brief time living in New York, Bridey had learned a new language that was quite different from how she'd spoken at Our Lady of Sorrows in Roscommon, Ireland. Addison, unabashed, ignored her and pushed on, finally breaking through the crowd to the entrance of the Four Seasons. "Has Mrs. Konstantin Zacharias arrived yet?" he said to the doorman in the same uppity voice. The doorman took an instant dislike to Addison. "Don't know the lady, and you can't wait here," he said.

"No, no, you don't understand. Mrs. Zacharias is a very important international woman and a close personal friend of Elias Renthal and she specifically told me to meet her at the door."

"Then move over there out of the way. You're holding things up here," said the doorman, waving him away, totally unimpressed with Addison's self-importance. "Good evening, Mrs. Schlossberg," the doorman said to Caroline Kennedy as he bowed his head in respect and opened the door. The doormen knew the riff from the raff.

Addison, stung deeply at being spoken to in such a manner by a doorman, retreated into a corner of the entrance, so rattled that he needed a smoke. Unconsciously, he patted his jacket down until he found his gold cigarette case. At the very same moment, Lil Altemus was exiting the limousine of her stepmother, Dodo Van Degan, with Dodo and Dodo's lover, a very excited Xavior Branigan, who had never been to such a party before. As Lil climbed the steps, her eye caught the gold cigarette case that Winkie Williams had promised to leave to the Costume Institute at the Metropolitan Museum. She stormed forward and grabbed the cigarette case out of Addison Kent's hand as Bill Cunningham, the star society photographer from the *New York Times,* who knew an aristocrat when he saw one, took Lil's picture over and over.

"I'll take that, thank you very much," she said in her most patrician outraged voice. "That poor maid, Immaculata or whatever her name was. I accused *her* of stealing Winkie's cigarette case and told all my friends not to hire her, and all the time it was *you*! I knew you were a phony from the first time you walked into my house with Adele Harcourt at my Farewell to Fifth Avenue lunch party. What about this emerald ring?" she said, holding up the ring on her finger to Addison's face and shaking her finger. "Did you steal this too?"

"No, no, honest to God," cried Addison, close to tears.

"I can only imagine what your great friend Perla Zacharias will do to you when she hears about this, which she will! You shouldn't be allowed into this party. I'm going to have a word with Elias Renthal about you!"

"Come along, Lil," said Dodo. "You're holding up the line, and the photographers are taking pictures of you. Xavior, take Lil's arm. We're going in."

"Well, the tables have turned," said Xavior, who had once tricked with Addison Kent in a men's room at the Grant P. Trumbull Funeral Home and then been snubbed by him. He took Lil's arm, as if he were a family member, and rendered a look to Addison that clearly said, "You're toast, Miss Kent."

"I never liked him, never, from the first day I met him," continued Lil as she entered the restaurant.

Addison, devastated, began to cry at his public shame.

"Out! Move, fella! Officer," said the doorman.

"No, no, I'm going. Will you please tell Mrs. Zacharias," he said in a pleading voice.

"I'm not telling Mrs. Zacco nothing! Officer! Officer!"

Addison, frightened now, backed off into the crowd. He ran wildly to the corner of Lexington Avenue, sobbing all the way. He didn't know where to run. He had recognized Bill Cunningham from the *Times*. He knew there would be pictures. For the first time in his life, he thought of his mother, who, after the failure of her cheese soufflé at Tootie Scott-Miller's lunch party, had jumped to her death out the window of the Tavistock mansion, which was now the home of Elias and Ruby Renthal, whose party he had not been allowed to enter.

NO ONE ever said about Perla Zacharias that she was not a very clever, perhaps even brilliant, woman. No one knew Perla better than Perla knew herself. In the privacy of her room, she talked to herself in the mirror and was totally, brutally honest with herself. In her social quest, she still had high ambitions, despite several setbacks that had been written about in *Park Avenue* magazine in articles by Augustus Bailey, whom she loathed. Nonetheless, her desire to assume the philanthropic mantle of Adele Harcourt had never abated. Adele had been dead for more than a year now, and no one had stepped forward to take her place. Perla knew that no one must ever realize the extent of her vile vicious temper, or she would never attain the high position in New York that she felt she was ready to assume. Her half brother, Rocco, for whom she felt dislike and who she often wished had never been born, was one who knew the cruelty of her temper, but he had long since tuned out his sister, who kept him back in Johannesburg, never to visit or ever see her grand houses in New York, London, and Paris. Rocco could do imitations of her rage that kept the servants in hysterics, and he delighted in embarrassing her memory in Johannesburg, by doing things like urinating on the dance floor of the Tits and Ass Club, the lowest dive in Johannesburg, while smoking a joint. The rage she felt at her brother, and at others such as Gus Bailey, often lingered for long periods. Some had witnessed her anger, but they were her servants, her guards, people too insignificant for her to concern herself with.

As late as she was for Elias and Ruby Renthal's party, she did not wish there to be any leftover anger fermenting within her, so she asked her chief of staff, Willard, dressed as always in gray flannel, to ask her driver, Mohab, in livery copied from the livery of the staff of the Prince of Wales at Clarence House, with whom she dined on charity nights, to drive slowly around the park before pulling up in front of the Four Seasons. Arriving, she rolled down the darkened window of her Rolls-Royce, "I am scheduled to meet Mr. Addison Kent here outside the Four Seasons. Will you tell him that Mrs. Zacharias has arrived."

"Mr. Addison Kent couldn't wait any longer, Mrs. Zacharias," said the doorman.

"I beg your pardon?" said Perla,

"He wasn't having a very good time waiting, so he took off," said the doorman.

"Took off? What do you mean he took off?"

"Took off. He ran down the street," replied the doorman.

"You'd better have a word with that one," said Perla to Willard.

"What are the orders, Mrs. Zacharias?" asked Willard. "I know you don't want to walk into the party without an escort."

"How would you like to walk me in, Willard? Just take me to the top of the stairs. I don't want you to go through the line with me. I don't want to have to introduce you to anybody. Just get me to the top of the stairs and then you can leave."

"What are you going to do if you bump into Gus Bailey?"

IN THE splendid bedroom of the house on East Seventy-eighth Street, Elias and Ruby Renthal emerged from their separate dressing rooms to look at each other in their party finery. But Elias stalled the proceedings with an urgent need to use the facilities.

"Elias, we can't be late. This party is about us, and you're holding us up," called out Ruby.

Nothing hurried Elias. When he finally came out of the bathroom he pointed to the bathroom door. "Don't anybody go in there until next Tuesday."

"No cheap talk today, darling."

"Honey, I never saw you as beautiful as you look right now," said Elias.

"Well, thank you, sweetheart. That really touches me. I had Bernardo. I had Frieda. I had about ten people working on me, all at the same time. How do you like the dress? Oscar was here up until about twenty minutes ago, sewing me into it. It's called Ruby Renthal Red. I changed the seating a few times. Darling, there's no way you can put Sylvia Luby next to the Duke of Chatsworth. You know we're being taped for the *Today* show, don't you? Matt Lauer's going to do the interview. Oh, listen, by the way, Elias. I think we ought to have a drink, just the two of us. To open a split of champagne. Like this," she said as she opened the small bottle and poured the champagne. "Listen, Elias, I want to tell you something, straight from your wife's lips. *Thank you,* Elias. *Thank you.* I'm proud of us. We went through some rough spots, and we came through them. We did it. We've turned out the town. I love you, Elias."

Just then Ruby's secretary, Jenny, entered the room. "The car's ready in front and it will take you and Mr. Renthal to the service entrance of the Four Seasons. We have a room for you with a dressing table, Mrs. Renthal. Bernardo will be there for the evening, in case you need any help with makeup and hair."

"OH, HONEY, you look fantastic; you're beyond," said Brucie to Ruby when she entered the Pool Room with Elias to begin greeting their guests.

"Oh, Brucie, look how beautifully you have transformed this room," cried Ruby. "Look, Elias. I've never seen anything like it. Oh, listen, the music is starting. Come on, Elias, we have work to do. We should be standing at the top of the stairs."

GUS WAS perfectly content to watch the party rather than participate in it. He knew all the stories of all the people. The dancing had started. Yehudit Tavicoli, wearing new emeralds, was dancing with Joe Carey, who she let everyone know was the richest man in Brooklyn. "Hey, Gus," called out Elias Renthal. "Come over here and have your picture taken with me." Gus, startled, let himself be hugged by Elias as he waved to the photographers at the same time. "This is a first, Elias," said Gus. "Did Ruby put you up to having our pictures taken?" Elias had something he wanted to say to Gus, before he lost the moment. "Why don't you lay off on Perla? The story's over. The killer is in jail."

"You're right, she probably didn't do it. I have no concrete evidence that says she did. But something odd happened there and I'm just so intrigued by all the unanswered questions. The trial seemed so rigged. They knew before it started that the male nurse was going to be found guilty and would be sentenced to ten years. Why did the police keep the firemen out? Why were the locks all being changed? Why weren't the surveillance cameras working? Maybe it won't add up to anything, but there's so much I want to know."

"You could get yourself in trouble, Gus. Do you ever think about that?"

"I do," Gus replied.

"Have you seen Ruby?" asked Elias.

"From afar. She's a beauty, Elias."

"She'd like to hear that."

"I intend to tell her."

"I don't suppose you and I will ever be friends, Gus, but I'm happy that you hold Ruby in high esteem."

Elias eased back into the crowd. Gus stood at the top of the stairs just in front of the room where the dancing was taking place. The Pool Room looked wonderful. He always marveled at the elegant simplicity of Mies van der Rohe's proportions and Philip Johnson's design. This year the Four Seasons was celebrating its fiftieth anniversary, and Gus had been a regular there for half that time. At first the chain-metal curtains on the windows had made him dizzy; now he found them soothing.

How many times had he waved to Philip Johnson sitting at his corner table in the Grill Room? How many lunches, dinners, and parties had he attended here? He remembered the day when Anna Wintour had been confronted by a lady in black from PETA, who had tossed a dead raccoon at her table, knocking over her double espresso. Was it two years ago that he saw former president Bill Clinton and Vernon Jordan munching on cotton candy in the middle booth? And then there was the fire in the Brasserie kitchen that caused both the Grill Room and the Pool Room to be engulfed in smoke, forcing the power lunchers to flee into the street.

Gus looked down now, checking the crowd. The room was almost full; the guests were talking and laughing while the friendly young waitstaff moved effortlessly among them. There was Lil Altemus talking to Maisie Verdurin, both in the same business now. Lil, liberated from God's Waiting Room on her way to Real Estate Heaven. He glimpsed Kit Jones, who seemed to be listening intently to something Dodo Van Degan was whispering. He wondered what tidbit Kit was getting for her column. Simon Cabot and Baroness de Liagra were toasting each other while the irrepressible Julian Niccolini hovered with a bottle of champagne.

Quite a scene, Gus thought. Here were the rich, those who were about to become richer and those who were hanging on by their thumbs. These were the people he had spent a lifetime listening to and writing about, who never seemed to tire of telling him their secrets. He was always amazed by their willingness to talk at cocktail parties, lunches, and dinners—even during random encounters on the street. He had long ago decided that listening was an art, and he had mastered it. But what was surprising was how quickly his subjects returned to his willing ear after their secrets were revealed in the pages of *Park Avenue* magazine, or in his novels. Even O.J. Simpson had given him a big smile when he had covered Simpson's most recent trial. And Phil Spector had been incredibly friendly when they had stood side by side in the men's room of the courthouse in Los Angeles. Gus was about to leave his elevated perch and make his way down to the crowd when he saw Stokes Bishop walking toward him. Stokes stopped to speak with Alex von Bidder, one of the owners of the restaurant. Alex had always seen that Gus got a great table and a great meal. But right now, Gus had something important to say to Stokes.

"You're the most popular man at the party, Gus. Everyone wants to talk to you," said Stokes.

"I've got something to straighten out with you, Stokes. I've had a bit of an epiphany. I was pretty pissed, and blabbed too much, which is one of my more unattractive traits. I realize that we all have someone to answer to, and you have Hy Vietor, the billionaire who is answerable to no one and who didn't go along with your plan to help me out. It's over. It's erased. It's all gone."

"Well, I'm glad. I'm sorry we had a falling-out. You're great, Gus. You're a superstar. Enjoy it. Say, I hear you have a big birthday coming up. Do you want help with a party?" asked Stokes.

"I had started to plan one myself, but the party's off, Stokes. I'm pretty sick. I just returned from a quick trip to the Dominican Republic, where I had a stem cell treatment, and now I'm going off to a clinic in Bavaria. I'd rather pursue those options than the chemo I'm being offered here. I have high hopes."

"Why don't you write up the clinic experience for the magazine? Like Thomas Mann and *The Magic Mountain*. It could be an interesting piece."

GUS BAILEY was in the Grill Room before the official dinner started, perusing the place cards to see if there were any interesting seating arrangements so he could know where to look to see the most compelling dramas of the evening. He blanched when he got to his own seat; it turned out he didn't need to look much farther than to his right, because there, sitting in front of the place setting next to his, was a card on which *Mrs. Konstantin Zacharias* was written in the most elegant calligraphy.

Gus didn't have much time to react before he saw the infamous lady herself heading directly toward him. She was somewhat distracted by something having to do with her foot, so she didn't see him until she was almost directly in front of him. At that point she had nowhere to go.

He saw the blotches appearing on her cheeks and the hand holding her evening bag start to tremble. Gus cut her off before she could start in. "Listen, Perla, I know this has been coming for a long time and we both have a lot of things to say to each other, but I'm not going to make a scene on Ruby Renthal's big night. I suggest we step out of the dining room and over near the stairs and get this over with."

The calm Perla had achieved when her driver had taken her on the detour through the park evaporated at the sight of Gus Bailey. She wanted to cut him dead and walk away, but he was right, she did have a lot of things to say to him. The two moved out of the dining area together at a clipped pace.

"So, Mr. Bailey, the last time we spoke you were writing a novel. Tell me, how is that coming along? It should be just about finished, no?" Perla said through clenched teeth, a grotesque smile spreading across her face.

Gus would not allow this horrible woman to get to him. He could tell she was revving herself up to lace into him. He had long since decided that he would finish this book no matter what and do what he had to do to get it published, Biedermeier or no Biedermeier. Perla's money and influence would have to stop somewhere.

She continued, "It's amazing how *pathetic* people like you are, Gus. You just go around telling your stories and thinking you're someone of consequence. But what you don't realize is, people who have the resources I do don't lose. I'm shocked you haven't arrived at this realization before, but I'm more than happy to teach you this lesson in any and every way I can. In fact, I relish the opportunity to show you of how little consequence you are."

He stared at her defiantly, letting her feel uncomfortable in the loaded silence that spread between them before he replied, "Darling, without people like me you would have nothing to fill your precious library. You know it's books that line the shelves there, correct? It's not just another place to throw a cocktail party?

"You can make your large donation and have your name plastered across the front of the building, but I'm the reason they'll come—to take out the books with *my* name plastered across the *cover*. And that's just the way it is in Manhattan society, isn't it, my dear? I don't have to buy my way in."

Gus didn't know what was going to happen. He could literally see the anger rise through Perla's body until it reached the top of her stretched forehead. Her fists were clenched and her lips were clamped shut, as if she were holding back a scream. For a moment, he felt fear.

Then, in a sudden move, she turned and ran down the stairs. Halfway down she stumbled. Her Mickie Minardos shoe lay in the middle of the staircase, its heel broken. Perla Zacharias turned and looked at her shoe and then up at Gus like a disfigured Cinderella.

Perla had to get out of there before she completely lost her composure. She plucked up her broken shoe and slowly hobbled out of the Four Seasons, one shoe on, one off. The last Gus heard and saw of Perla Zacharias that night, she was on her cell phone yelling at her driver to bring the car around, *immediately*.

AFTER PERLA'S abrupt departure, Gus sat down and enjoyed a lovely dinner. For the first time in years he felt light and at peace. He had survived Win Burch. He had survived Perla Zacharias. He knew she wasn't gone forever—people who were as rich as she was always found a way back in—but her success in society was neither here nor there to Gus anymore. Not tonight, anyway. He'd had his moment of triumph over her and, more important, he was going to write his book and no one could stop him, no matter how much money they had. And the cancer, well, he would think about that another day.

⊙〰〰〰⊙

"GUS, FINALLY a hug," said Ruby. "We can skip the compliments on how great I look. I've already had a thousand of them." They both laughed.

"Did you see that Elias and I had our picture taken together laughing like we were best friends?" asked Gus.

"That was Simon Cabot's idea," said Ruby.

"Of course it was."

"Gus, for somebody as sick as you are, you look great," said Ruby.

"The magic of stem cells."

"You're always in the avant-garde, Gus. Why does some inner voice keep telling me that you're moving out of my life? And now you're leaving. I felt it the minute you walked in that you were off somewhere."

"I am. Tomorrow. I had to come to see you in your finest hour, Ruby. You pulled it off. You're the new queen of New York."

"LIL," SAID Gus to Lil Altemus when he passed her on the stairway, where Gus was getting ready to leave. "Have you heard that I grabbed Winkie Williams's gold cigarette case out of Addison Kent's hands outside the front door?" she asked him. "Oh, what a scene we had."

"It's the talk of the party. I hope the *Times* refers to you as a real estate tycoon rather than as a socialite. I hear you got the exclusive on Adele Harcourt's apartment."

"I practically grew up in that apartment," said Lil. "I hear you're off."

"Yes."

"Oh, Gus, I don't want you to go. Have your treatment here. Have your big birthday party. Maybe we could arrange for it to be in Adele's apartment. Perhaps we could persuade your new friend Ruby Renthal to let Gert make the fig mousse! What a party that would be! Just like old times!"

Gus smiled and kissed Lil on the cheek. "It would be great, Lil, but it is not to be. Good-bye. I'll e-mail, now that you're a big executive."

Gus ran down the stairs, opened the door, and went out into the night.

ABOUT THE AUTHOR

Dominick Dunne was the author of five bestselling novels, two collections of essays, and *The Way We Lived Then*, a memoir with photographs. He had been a special correspondent for *Vanity Fair* for twenty-five years, and the host of the television series *Dominick Dunne's Power, Privilege, and Justice*. He passed away in 2009 after completing *Too Much Money*.

DISCARD